MW00484661

THE DOPEMAN'S BODYGUARD 2

NO LONGER PROPERTY OF
DENVER PUBLIC LIBRARY

Tranay Adams

Lock Down Publications and Ca$h
Presents
The Dopeman's Bodyguard 2
A Novel by *Tranay Adams*

Tranay Adams

Lock Down Publications
Po Box 944
Stockbridge, Ga 30281

Visit our website @
www.lockdownpublications.com

Copyright 2020 The Dopeman's Bodyguard

All rights reserved. No part of this book may be reproduced in any form or by electronic or mechanical means, including information storage and retrieval systems without permission in writing from the publisher, except by a reviewer who may quote brief passages in review.
First Edition July 2020
Printed in the United States of America

This is a work of fiction. Names, characters, places, and incidents either are products of the author's imagination or are used fictitiously. Any similarity to actual events or locales or persons, living or dead, is entirely coincidental.

Lock Down Publications
Like our page on Facebook: Lock Down Publications @
www.facebook.com/lockdownpublications.ldp
Cover design and layout by: **Dynasty Cover Me**
Book interior design by: **Shawn Walker**
Edited by: **Kiera Northington**

Stay Connected with Us!

Text **LOCKDOWN** to 22828 to stay up-to-date with new releases, sneak peaks, contests and more...

Thank you.

Submission Guideline.

Submit the first three chapters of your completed manuscript to ldpsubmissions@gmail.com, subject line: Your book's title. The manuscript must be in a .doc file and sent as an attachment. Document should be in Times New Roman, double spaced and in size 12 font. Also, provide your synopsis and full contact information. If sending multiple submissions, they must each be in a separate email.

Have a story but no way to send it electronically? You can still submit to LDP/Ca$h Presents. Send in the first three chapters, written or typed, of your completed manuscript to:

LDP: Submissions Dept
Po Box 944
Stockbridge, Ga 30281

DO NOT send original manuscript. Must be a duplicate.

Provide your synopsis and a cover letter containing your full contact information.

Thanks for considering LDP and Ca$h Presents.

Let Me Holla at Chu!

It took me exactly nine months to complete this piece. It wasn't because I had writer's block. It was because I fell out of love with writing. I didn't have that spark in me any more. And truthfully, I don't know if I will ever fully get it back. Thankfully, I was able to gain some of my passion back to finish this series, though. I love y'all, so I couldn't leave you hanging without giving you the conclusion to this series and FEAR MY GANGSTA 4. Anyway, enough of my rambling. Enjoy!

Tranay

Tranay Adams

Chapter 1

Whitney stood at the stove over a Pyrex pot, whipping cocaine into crack. Occasionally, she'd pour a little baking soda inside the glass pot and continue her mixing, looking down at the murky water inside. While she was busy doing this, Tyrell had busied himself with unloading the kilos and placing them onto the kitchen table. Once he was done, he broke the boxes down and laid them on top of each other in the corner of the kitchen. Having done this, Tyrell leaned up against the counter and watched Whitney work her magic. One of the reasons Tyrell decided to make Whitney his girl was because she was good at whipping up work. The bitch could turn two bricks into four—like a magic trick, or some shit. Whitney had learned her trade from her father, who used to be the chef for a famous ghetto D-boy. Her father and the czar made a lot of money together, but when he found out that her old man was having an affair with his wife, Whitney's mother, the dope boy killed them both, and himself.

"What chu got going over here?" Tyrell asked curiously, a smile etched across his lips. He was so happy about the haul they'd made off with. He knew that with his drugs and Whitney's recipe for whipping coke, he was going to become a very rich man. He was sure of it.

"Come and see," a smiling Whitney told him, and motioned him over with her latex-gloved hand. Once he came over, she pointed down inside of the pot for him to take a look inside it—which he did. "What chu think?" she asked with a smirk, looking back and forth between him and the pot.

"Looks good. You definitely know what chu doing. Yo' old man taught chu well." Tyrell smiled and pulled her close, kissing her in the mouth. He then smacked her on the ass and walked over to the kitchen table where he'd placed all of the bricks. He picked one up and looked it over, admiring it. He then picked up another brick and studied it. He smiled hard, real hard. The lick he'd just hit was one that every hustler had dreamed of. With what he had in

9

his possession, he was going to get back up on his feet and be Top Dawg.

"Yeahhhh, that's right. A nigga 'bouta be the man that he's supposed to be, Tyrell thought as he scowled and smiled wickedly. He cast his mind back to the moment he and Whitney got a hold of the truckload of coke.

It was pitch-dark, and the night was deathly quiet. A Toyota pick-up sneakily backed its way up the driveway of Shavon's house and stopped once it got five feet away from the garage door. Tyrell and Whitney jumped out wearing sunglasses and black bandanas over the lower half of their face. The first thing Tyrell did was, lower the flat-bed's door and walk over to the garage door, kneeling at its padlock. Seeing that the lock was secured by a sturdy copper padlock, he whipped out his .44 magnum revolver. He then pulled off his bandana and folded it up, placing it over the padlock. Using the butt of his revolver, he struck the padlock twice before it broke free. Afterwards, he removed the padlock and tossed it over into the grass. Once he tied the bandana back over the lower half of his face, he stood upright and lifted the garage door as quietly as he could. Once he did this, he pulled out a small flashlight from his back pocket and clicked it on. He gave Whitney the signal to watch his back, as he headed inside the garage over to the tarp, where he believed the boxes were hidden beneath. Lifting the tarp, he revealed all of the boxes that contained the kilos of coke inside them. The crafty bastard couldn't help smiling from behind his bandana, seeing that his prize was right before his eyes.

Tyrell looked over his shoulder and motioned for Whitney to come over. Once she was at his side, he told her what he wanted her to do. He told her, "It's all here. All one-hundred boxes of the shit. Let's load these bitchez up, fast. I'm not tryna get caught and get into a shoot-out with niggaz."

"Okay." She conceded and started loading the boxes into the flat-bed of the truck. Tyrell clicked the beam of his flashlight off and started helping her load them shits up, too.

***

"Who the hell are you people? And what the fuck are you doing in my house?" An elderly voice came from the doorway, startling Tyrell and Whitney. They whipped their heads to the doorway, and found Ms. Pearl standing there with a baseball bat held at her shoulder, ready to knock someone's head off their shoulders. Ms. Pearl was a seventy-eight-year-old lady with a caramel complexion and long snow-white hair. She had discoloration in her right pupil, which she was blind in. She looked like she weighed about one hundred and twenty-five-pounds.

"Oh, shit!" Tyrell said, and then turned to Whitney. "I thought chu said she was asleep."

"She was asleep. But now her ass is up!" Whitney told him, before turning the fire off from under the Pyrex pot. Actually, Ms. Pearl had Alzheimers, and Whitney was her caretaker. The old lady had been doing okay lately, but right now she was having one of her episodes.

"Grandma, it's me, Whitney! And this is my man, Tyrell!" Whitney pointed to Tyrell.

"Whitney?" A confused expression crossed Ms. Pearl's face. "Chile, who the fuck is Whitney?"

"Your granddaughter! Your daughter Deanna's child!"

Ms. Pearl's eyebrows slanted, and her forehead crinkled, top lip curling upward. "Youza goddamn lie, I don't have any chillren!"

Swoooop! Swoooop! Swoooop!

Ms. Pearl swung her baseball bat with all the might her tiny frame could muster. Tyrell ducked, dodged, and jumped back from the attempted assault. When Ms. Pearl came back at him again, he caught the baseball bat with his right hand. She tried to pull the baseball bat back, but Tyrell was stronger than her. Ms. Pearl clenched her jaws and kicked Tyrell in his balls. Tyrell's face twisted in pain, and veins bulged over his face and neck. He fell to the floor, holding his balls while still clutching the baseball bat.

11

Ms. Pearl took off running toward the living room. Tyrell threw the baseball bat aside and scrambled to his feet, feeling like both of his balls where lodged into his stomach.

"Get her, baby! I'ma give her a sedative to knock her out!" Whitney told Tyrell. She took a chair from the kitchen table and placed it before the stove, climbing it. She opened the double doors of the cabinet, and rifled through it until she found the small bottle and syringe she was looking for. She jumped down onto the linoleum and pulled the orange cap from off the syringe. She spat the cap on the floor and stabbed the needle into the head of the small bottle, drawing its contents inside the syringe. While she was doing this, she heard a lot of screaming and racket coming from the living room, where Tyrell and Ms. Pearl were scuffling. When Whitney looked up, she saw Tyrell falling to the carpeted floor with her grandmother in a bear-hug. There was a toppled lamp, an upside down table, a shattered vase, and La-Z-Boy chair lying around them.

"Heelllllp, hellllp me! Pleeeease!" Ms. Pearl hollered louder and louder, struggling to break Tyrell's hold on her. He tried to place his hand over her mouth to shut her up, but she bit the shit out of him.

"Aaaaaaah! Fuck!" Tyrell took a quick glance at his palm, and saw the blood oozing out of his hand. He then hugged Ms. Pearl tighter, still feeling the pain in his throbbing nut sack. "Baby, hurry up! Fuck taking you so long?"

"I'm coming, baby. Hold on!" Whitney called out to him, as she sat the bottled sedative down on the kitchen counter. She bit down on the syringe and scurried toward the living room, pulling her belt free of her jeans. Whitney ran inside the living room, and slid across the carpeted floor, stopping beside her man and grandmother.

As Ms. Pearl continued to holler over and over again for help, Whitney outstretched her arm. She rolled up the sleeve of her house coat and fastened her belt around her frail, wrinkled arm. She then smacked her grandmother's arm until a discolored vein bulged. Whitney licked her thumb and rubbed it on the vein, leaving a wet spot behind. Next, she eased the needle into Ms. Pearl's arm, and drew the plunger back, which caused her burgundy blood to invade the fluid inside. Whitney looked back and forth between the syringe and her grandmother's face, as she slowly pushed the sedative into her bloodline. Slowly, Ms. Pearl's eyes rolled to the back of her head, and her cries for help grew quieter and quieter. Before Whitney and Tyrell knew it, the old lady was fast asleep, snoring.

Whitney and Tyrell lay flat on their backs on the floor, staring up at the ceiling, breathing heavily. They'd gotten quite the workout from restraining Ms. Pearl and injecting her with the sleeping medication. Once Tyrell caught his breath, he got up on his feet and went inside the kitchen. With his left hand, he turned on the faucet, and cool water poured out. He held his wounded palm under the cold, flowing liquid, and rinsed the blood away. Next, Tyrell grabbed a clean dish rag and tied it around his injured hand.

"Baby, help me get her up and back inside her bedroom," Whitney said as she grabbed a snoring Ms. Pearl under her arms. She was hunched down, and waiting for Tyrell. Tyrell hurried back inside the living room and grabbed hold of Ms. Pearl's legs. One of her house slippers fell off as they carried her toward the steps, but they ignored it and kept moving along.

Once Whitney and Tyrell laid Ms. Pearl down in her bed, they pressed a chair underneath her doorknob, so she couldn't get out. They then headed back inside the kitchen, where Whitney finished cooking the crack and let it cool off; succumbing to its hardened form, which looked like stale pizza dough. Afterward, she went about the task of cutting off a few ten-dollar pieces from what she had cooked up. Whitney pulled out her crack pipe and packed it with rocks. She then fired it up. Her eyelids shut as a jovial expression spread across her face. Tyrell looked at her with a crooked grin on his face.

"Is it good, baby?" Tyrell asked, as he leaned forward in his chair, in anticipation of what her answer would be. His eyes were fixed on her.

13

"Oh, it's good, baby, real good," Whitney assured him, before firing up the crack pipe again. She blew smoke out of her nostrils and mouth before handing the lighter and the crack pipe to him. Holding his cell phone to his ear with his shoulder, Tyrell took the crack pipe and the lighter. As he listened to the telephone ring, he smoked some of the crack. Instantly, he started gagging and coughing with his fist to his mouth. He smiled at Whitney and gave her the thumbs up, letting her know that her whip-game was stupid.

"What's up, Fat Daddy?" Tyrell smiled, showcasing some of his rotten and missing teeth. "Guess whose back in business, big dawg?" He stuck his tongue slightly out of the corner of his mouth as he nodded, in response to what his cousin said at the other end of the line. "That's right. Nigga, you're family, you know, I'ma show yo' ass some love."

Chapter 2

Jerrica, the woman that ran off with Baby Boy's car, darted back and forth across the bedroom, grabbing clothing and underwear. She'd tossed everything inside the two opened suitcases, and then ran around grabbing more to toss inside the suitcases. Once she was done, she smacked the suitcases closed, leaving some of the clothing hanging out of them. She then slipped on her jacket, grabbed her car keys and the two suitcases. Jerrica flipped off the light switch and headed into the living room. She took one last look at her apartment, and took a breath, hating to leave her place, but realizing she really didn't have any choice in the matter. Jerrica found out that the niggaz (which included her brother) that kidnapped Baby Boy were found shot dead inside their van. With them pushing up daises, little mama was sure that Baby Boy was sending his goons after her. She was sure they would find her too, especially with her still holding on to Baby Boy's car and shit. Jerrica had tried to slang that bitch, but niggaz didn't want to buy it from her, for they knew whose car it was, and how much trouble it would bring should they be caught with it.

Jerrica flipped off the light switch, and closed the front door on her way out. She made her way down the staircase, struggling with the suitcases, and nearly falling. It took her a while, but she finally managed to make it to the elevator. She pressed the down button, and boarded the elevator, punching the button for the garage. Jerrica's nose scrunched up, and she pinched it close, looking around the elevator and spotting urine in the corner. Once again, some low-life mothafucka had taken the liberty to piss inside the elevator. It was shit like this that made her glad she was moving out of the hood, and moving in with her father's family out in New Haven, Connecticut.

The elevator doors opened, and Jerrica made her way across the garage floor, heading for her car, which was parked beside Baby Boy's vehicle. Jerrica sat the suitcases down at the rear of her whip, and opened the trunk. She placed her suitcases inside the trunk and slammed it shut, before making her way around to the driver side door. Jerrica opened the driver's door, and jumped in behind the wheel, sticking her key inside the ignition. As soon as she did, Latrell, who was wearing a bandana over the lower half of his face, slipped a length of rope over her head with his gloved hands. With a grunt, he pulled the rope tight around her neck, causing her to make an "Ugh," sound. Jerrica's eyes bulged, and her mouth hung open, veins swelling on her forehead, as she struggled to slip her fingers under the rope to loosen its stranglehold.

"I've got myself a fighter, huh?" Latrell said with beads of sweat oozing out of his pores, and running down his face. He pulled back on the rope some more, tightening its strain harder on Jerrica's throat. Blood clots formed in her eyes, and she thrashed around wildly inside her car, kicking off one of her shoes in the process. She gagged and gagged, trying to get free, and when that didn't work, she started honking the horn of her car as loud as she could, hoping that someone would come to her rescue. It wasn't long before she started moving less and less, finding her life force slipping from her body. Seeing that she was slowly beginning to die, Latrell pulled back savagely on the rope, which eventually caused him to snap her neck, right before he officially suffocated her. Jerrica took her last breath, and went rigid inside her whip.

"Goddamn." Latrell laid his head back, breathing heavily, sweat sliding down his forehead. Using the end of the black bandana he was wearing, he dabbed his wet face dry. Suddenly, his cellular rang and he pulled it out, seeing that it was Baby Boy calling him. He pressed the small green telephone on his cell phone, and pressed it to his ear.

"You take care of that business we discussed earlier?" Baby Boy asked him.

Latrell looked up at Jerrica's dead eyes through the rearview mirror, and confirmed the kill to his boss. "Yeah. I just finished taking care of that for you."

"Good. I've got one more thang I want chu to handle for me tonight. It's out there where you live at in Hawthorne. You'll meet Diabolic and a couple of the other guys there."

"What exactly is it you want me to do?"

"I'm not finna talk on this phone and end up on an indictment. Diabolic will explain everything to you once you get there. Now, do you have an ink pen so I can give you the address?"

"Nah, I keep everything up top," Latrell referred to his memory, "Just gemme the address."

Baby Boy gave him a very familiar address, and disconnected the call before he could respond. "That's my crib. What the hell are they going to my place for? Unless—the shipment." Latrell wasn't sure, but he believed that Mank and Korey had something to do with Baby Boy's shipment getting hit. This was because he remembered Shavon saying something about the youngstaz putting something up inside the garage she'd forgotten to inquire about. Latrell figured it had to be the shipment of coke. He wasn't sure, but if he was a betting man, then he'd bet his life on it. With that thought in his mind, Latrell hopped out of Jerrica's car and left her dead body behind, inside it. He fled to his whip, which he started up, and raced back to his house, hoping he'd reach his family before something tragic happened.

Vrooom!

Latrell flew up the block in his whip, nearing a yellow traffic light he knew he most likely wouldn't make. He didn't give a fuck though. He was going to clear the intersection, before the light turned red. He was determined to reach his family before it was too late. With that in mind, Latrell mashed the gas pedal, speeding up his vehicle. The traffic light turned red as he approached the intersection. An old Mexican man wearing a big straw hat, sandals, and walking with a cane, started across the street. He hadn't made it halfway across the street before Latrell's speeding car stole his attention, its headlights shining two big orbs on him.

The old Mexican man looked in Latrell's direction, and his eyes widened fearfully. He took off, running as fast as he could, which caused his hat to fly off his head. Feeling a speeding Latrell closing the distance on him, he dove from out of the path of his car, which narrowly missed him. The old Mexican man landed hard on his stomach in the middle of the street, wincing. Slowly, he turned over on his back and looked in the direction of Latrell's car, which disappeared into the night. The old Mexican man dipped his hand inside his shirt and pulled out a gold crucifix, which he kissed, and thanked God for sparing his life.

Latrell took his right hand from off the steering wheel, and pulled out his cell phone. He looked back and forth between the windshield and the screen of his cellular, searching his contacts for Shavon's cell phone number. He turned the volume on his stereo down and placed his cell on *speaker*. He listened to its ringing impatiently, praying Shavon would answer.

"Come on, come on, come on, pick up, pick up, pick up!" Latrell urged Shavon, like she could actually hear him. "Hello? Baby?" he said into the device, thinking someone had picked up his call. He listened closely, and discovered that the answering service had picked up. "Goddamn it! Fuck!" He pounded the steering wheel with the fist he clutched his cellular in. He then hit up Shavon again and again, and got the same response. Seeing he needed to make a right turn coming up, Latrell sat his cell in his lap and made a sharp right turn. He was going so god damn fast that his tires screeched at the corner, and his whip nearly flipped over. As soon as the car came back down on all four tires, Latrell picked his cell phone back up from his lap, and continued to hit up Shavon, hopeful that she'd answer his calls.

Diabolic pulled a black Chevrolet Astro van up outside of Shavon's house and murdered its engine. He looked back and forth between the house and the black leather gloves he pulled over his hands, flexing his fingers inside them. He then pulled his ski-mask from between the seat, pulled it down over his face, and adjusted the eye holes of it. Next, he pulled out his handgun, with the silencer on its tip, and cocked that bitch back. Afterward, he looked to his goons, who were strapped up with them thangz, with silencers on them as well.

"Y'all niggaz ready?" Diabolic asked them. They were both rocking black ski-masks and dressed in black from head-to-toe, like he was.

"I don't know about this big ass nigga," Trevante referred to their comrade playing the backseat, "but I stay ready," he said from the front passenger seat, where he checked the magazine of his blower, and smacked it back in. He then cocked his shit. Trevante was a brown-skinned youth with 360 waves on his head. He was handsome, with a muscular physique. Homie looked like he belonged more on someone's runway, as a model, than running among a pack of cold-blooded killaz. But here he was, getting down and dirty with niggaz of his ilk.

"What about chu, big dawg?" Diabolic looked to the back, at the other goon.

"Nigga, I stay ready, but whatta 'bout that nigga Latrell?" Huge replied with a deep baritone voice. He was a muscle-bound dude, built like a brick shit-house. He had an almond hue, a goatee, and rocked his hair in short twisties.

"That nigga gets here when he gets here. Y'all niggaz come on." Diabolic hopped out of the van, and he and his goons rushed Shavon's house, where they saw a silhouette move past the window. They were hurriedly moving across the lawn toward Shavon's house. Just then, a car was speeding down the street. Latrell was behind the wheels of the car. His brows furrowed up when he saw three black shadows running hastily through Shavon's yard. Latrell tossed the cell phone into the passenger seat and floored the gas pedal, flying down the block, en route to his crib.

***

Mank sat on the couch with the PS4 controller in his hand, waiting for Korey to return, as he took pulls from a blunt, smoke wafting around him. Before him, on the coffee table, were bags from Taco Bell, balled up wrappers, a box of Swisher Sweets, and two different sizes of pill bottles of weed. He was getting blown while Korey was eating and playing the game. Their session was paused because Korey had to take a shit.

Mank heard the toilet flush, then the water running, and air freshener being sprayed. He looked down the hallway to see Korey emerge from the bathroom adjusting his jeans on his waistline, and advancing in his direction. "Nigga, hurry up so I can finish whooping yo' black ass!"

"Man, that Taco Bell fucked my stomach up!" Korey said as he entered the living room, rubbing on his stomach. He plopped down on the couch and took a sip from the straw that was inside his Taco Bell cup.

"I told you 'bout eating that bullshit. Here, nigga," Mank blew out smoke from his nose and mouth, as he passed Korey the smoldering blunt that was pinched between his finger and thumb. Mank's eyelids were low, and his eyes were pink and glassy. It was obvious the young nigga was high as fuck.

Korey took a couple of pulls from the blunt. He allowed the bleezy to hang from his lip, narrowing his eyelids into slits, as smoke rose into the air from it. He un-paused the game, and he and Mank got back to playing. They could hear Shavon's cell phone going off, but they'd be damned if they stopped their session again. They were zoned out. Besides money and pussy, playing video games was their life.

Shavon was busy inside the kitchen, sweeping the floor and singing Ella Mai's "Trippin'". Once she'd gathered all of the trash into a pile, she leaned over with the dust pan, and swept the pile into it. She'd stood upright, and her forehead wrinkled, hearing ringing. Her eyebrow rose, and her ear pricked up. Shavon leaned forward and listened closely. She heard her cellular ringing again. Quickly, she dumped the trash inside the garbage can in the corner of the kitchen, put the broom and the dust pan up, and hurried out of the kitchen.

"I know you two big head niggaz heard my goddamn phone ringing!" Shavon smacked the shit out the back of Korey's head, as she walked past him in the living room. She then headed toward the hallway.

"Ow, fuck is yo' problem?" Korey frowned up, but he didn't dare turn his head from the television screen. Mank was whipping

20

his ass like he was a runaway slave, and he was trying to catch up to him.

Ba-booom!

The front door swung open from a powerful force, and a masked up Diabolic, Trevante, and Huge ran in, brandishing handguns with silencers on their barrels. Diabolic looked up and saw Shavon running toward the hallway. He kept his eyes on her, but leaned his head toward Trevante.

"Go get that bitch!" Diabolic ordered Trevante. Instantly, Trevante ran after Shavon, as she hauled ass down the hallway and slammed her bedroom door shut. He kicked on the door, where the lock was located, three good times, before that bitch went flying open.

Mank and Korey tried to grab their guns, which were located on the coffee table. But when Diabolic and Huge pointed their guns at them, they threw their hands up in the air.

"I wisha mothafucka would!" Diabolic threatened through gritted teeth.

Right then, everyone's attention was grabbed when they heard Shavon in the hallway punching, kicking and screaming at Trevante, as he struggled to gain control of her. She cocked back and fired on his ass, whipping his head around. He frowned up and spat blood on the carpeted floor. He then slowly turned around to Shavon and kicked her in the stomach. Her eyes bulged, and she doubled over, holding herself. Trevante followed up by backhanding her with the hand he held his gun in. She fell to the floor, on her side, holding herself and blinking her eyelids in pain. Her eyes were glassy with hurt.

"Mothafucka, I'll kill you!" A scowling Mank jumped to his feet, ready to defend his big sister's honor. Huge clocked him in the back of his skull with the butt of his gun, which dropped him down to one knee, wincing. Mank touched the back of his head, and looked to his finger tips: they were bloody. At this time, Diabolic was shutting and locking the door behind them. When he turned around, Huge was pulling Mank up to his feet, and patting him down in search of more weapons. Once he realized that the young nigga wasn't packing anything else, he stood upright and held him by the back of his shirt.

Trevante escorted Shavon back inside the living room, with his arm wrapped around her throat, and his gun held at her temple. She was bleeding at the corner of her mouth, and there were tears in her eyes from the pain she'd felt, having the wind knocked out of her from Trevante's vicious kick in her stomach.

"You," Diabolic pointed at Korey with his gun. Korey looked at him with raised eyebrows, and pointed his thumb at his chest, like, *me*? "Yeah, you; kick that coffee table over!" Diabolic commanded. He didn't want the opposition to have guns within their reach. Korey kicked the coffee table over, and sent the Taco Bell bags, balled up wrappers, guns, and everything else spilling to the floor, "Alright, front and center." Diabolic motioned him over and pointed to the space before him with his blower. Korey approached Diabolic. Diabolic roughly spun his back to him and patted him down thoroughly to make sure he didn't have any other weapons on him. He didn't. "That bitch clean, my nigga?" Diabolic asked Trevante of Shavon. Earlier he'd seen him pat her down for weapons inside of the hallway.

Trevante nodded and said, "Yeah, she's clean."

"Yo', man, what the fuck is this all about?" Korey inquired, with his head turned sideways, addressing Diabolic. It was obvious to him that Diabolic was the H.N.I.C, from the way he was taking charge. So he was the mothafucka he should be addressing.

"Dope, young boy! And lots of it!" Diabolic barked. "One-hunnit kilos to be exact!"

After hearing Diabolic mentioning the bricks, Mank and Korey's hearts dropped into their stomachs. They didn't think that hijacking the birds would come back to haunt them. They truly believed that they were going to be able to get the shipment off, and go on with their lives, spending the gwap however they wanted to. But somehow, the homie who the shipment rightfully belongs to had caught up with them, and it was time to pay the piper. "So, where is the product? And don't gemme that shit about you not knowing what the fuck I'm talking about 'cause I done did my homework, nigga."

"My nigga, on everything I love, I don't know what the fuck you talking about," Korey swore up and down, lying through his teeth. His heart was beating like an African drum, and his palms were beginning to sweat. He found it hard to put up a front, with the lives of him and his loved ones in danger, but he had to do his best to convince Diabolic that he was telling the truth.

"Okay, I see now you think I'm talking outta my ass here, so maybe after I have my young nigga pop lil' mama standing there," he pointed at Shavon with his gun while he held the back of Korey's shirt with the other, "you'll see I'm not playing witcho monkey-ass."

"Bro, I don't wanna know what chu talking about. I ain't never laid my hand on so much as a Tylenol, let alone some coke!" Korey said, lying his ass off. Diabolic narrowed his eyelids into slits. He couldn't believe that Korey was really testing his gangsta.

"Alright," Diabolic told him. He then looked up at Trevante. "Pop that bitch like a zit!"

With the order given, Trevante lowered Shavon to the floor, and placed his gun to the back of her dome piece. She instantly bowed her head, and put her hands together, quietly reciting a prayer. A wide-eyed Mank looked at Trevante as he moved to make good on Diabolic's threat. His heart thudded and he looked to Korey, mouth hanging open. He felt like shit had gone too far, and Korey needed to just tell them where the bricks were.

Korey was about to give Diabolic the location of the birds, but Mank spoke over him.

"The garage!" Mank blurted. "The bricks are inside of the garage." He then looked to Korey and mouthed: "I'm sorry, man." Korey nodded. He wasn't upset with Mank. He was about to tell them where the weight was anyway.

"Okay. To the garage we go," Diabolic announced, and headed for the kitchen, where the backdoor was located. Huge fell in line behind him, bringing Mank along with him. Trevante pulled Shavon up to her feet roughly, and escorted her toward the kitchen.

I knew it! I knew the boys were hiding something inside of that goddamn garage, Shavon thought, with Trevante shoving her across the threshold of the kitchen. She balled her face up angrily, and bit down on her bottom lip, clenching her fists. She had to check herself, to keep from firing on Trevante's ass. Shavon knew that *that* would be a bad move, seeing as how he was strapped, and she wasn't.

Chapter 3

Once everyone had gotten outside, Diabolic ordered Mank to open the garage door. Mank's stomach twisted into knots when he saw that the padlock on the garage door had been broken. It was then that he knew in his heart that the bricks were gone. But still he hoped that he was fooling himself, praying in his heart that the bricks were exactly where they'd placed them.

Please, God, let these birds be inside of this garage, please, Mank thought, with his head bowed and his eyelids shut, removing the broken padlock from the garage. He sat the padlock aside and opened the garage. Once he flipped on the light switch, the light shone on everything inside. The bricks were gone!

Mank's eyes bugged and his mouthed formed an O. His heart thudded out of control, and sweat began to slide down the back of his neck. Diabolic and Trevante exchanged glances, with Trevante shrugging. They looked back to Mank who was rifling through the garage, looking through boxes and looking behind shit. When he realized that the dope was gone, he pressed his hands to the side of his head and looked around frantically. He knew that he and his loved ones' asses were in the fire now.

"What the fuck is the hold up?" Diabolic called out to Mank. Mank dropped his arm at his side and turned around. He walked out of the garage, standing a few feet away from Diabolic, and within reaching distance of Huge.

A fearful Mank wiped his sweaty palms on his shirt, and swallowed the lump of terror in his throat. He wiped the bubbles of sweat from his forehead with the back of his hand. He then addressed Diabolic. "It's—it's not here. It's gone."

"What the fuck you mean it's not here? You just told me it was inside of the fucking garage!" Diabolic spat heatedly. He wanted to blow Mank's head off his shoulders, but he didn't want to risk him dying within the whereabouts of the keys.

Mank looked over his shoulder at the garage, and turned back around to Diabolic. "I know. And it was. No bullshit! Somebody broke inside of our garage and stole the whole lot!" He looked down at the broken padlock on the ground, and picked it up, showing it to him. "Look, here's proof!" Diabolic stared at the broken padlock for a second, and then he looked to Huge. He gave the enormous man a nod. Swiftly, Huge struck Mank in his stomach with the butt of his gun, which doubled him over. He then followed up, whacking him upside the head for the second time with the butt of his gun. Mank fell to the ground, face scrunched up in pain.

"Fuck it! Waste 'em all!" Diabolic commanded.

"Noooooo!" Shavon called out to Mank, seeing Huge about to blow his brains out.

"Stop!" Latrell's voice resonated from Diabolic's back. Everyone looked over their shoulders and Latrell jumped down onto the ground, holding his gun at his side.

"'Bout fucking time, nigga," Trevante said to Latrell. He was supposed to have been there a while ago.

"I can't let y'all kill 'em, they're my family," Latrell said.

Diabolic's face balled up with hostility, and he gritted. "You mean you were in on this shit?" He took his gun from the back of Korey's skull, and pointed it at Latrell.

"Nah, bruh, I don't know anything about all of this, I swear to God Almighty," Latrell said with sincerity in his eyes. Right then, Diabolic didn't know why, but he believed him.

"Drop the gun, and kick it over into the grass!" Diabolic ordered him. Once Latrell followed his instructions, he held up his hands in the air, waiting to find out what his fate would be. "Let's say I believe you. What do you expect for me to do now? Huh?"

"Look, call up yo' brother, and tell 'em we'll get his shit back. How many did you say were missing again?" Latrell asked.

"One-hunnit birds," Diabolic answered.

Upon hearing how many bricks they'd have to get up, Latrell's eyebrows raised. He didn't know how the hell he was going to come up with that much weight, but he had to. The lives of his family depended on it.

"Alright, one hunnit keys—tell yo' bro to give us some time, and we'll get 'em his shipment back. He's got my word. I'll make it happen." Determination dripped from Latrell's eyes. He could do anything he put his mind to, no matter what it was. Homie was a go-getter.

Diabolic switched hands with his silenced handgun, and hung his arm around Korey's neck. He reached inside of his pocket and pulled out his burn-out cell phone, hitting up Baby Boy. The kingpin answered after three rings. Diabolic told him where they were, and gave him the rundown. Latrell, Shavon, Mank and Korey looked worried as Diabolic chopped it up with Baby Boy. They could tell by the concentrated expression on Diabolic's face that he was listening intently to whatever Baby Boy was telling him.

"Yeah, he's right here," Diabolic answered his brother, looking up at Latrell. "Alright. Will do. Peace." He disconnected the call and slid the cell phone back into his pocket.

"Okay, here is the deal, y'all gon' get us our shit back, all one-hunnit bricks of it. If you don't, then this mothafucka gon' get popped!" He switched hands with his gun and shoved Korey forward. Next, he grabbed Mank by the front of his shirt, pulling him into him. Right then, Trevante released Shavon and lowered his gun at his side.

"Wait a minute, what are you saying?" Shavon looked at him with great concern, wondering what he planned on doing with her younger brother.

"I'm saying that we'll be holding onto this lil' young-ass until you come up with that product. You don't come up with it, then start making funeral arrangements. Y'all asses gotta week, that's seven days."

Shavon walked up on Diabolic, saying, "Wait a minute, you can't just take my brother. We'll make sure you get your work back, but—"

Whack!

Diabolic back-handed Shavon with the hand he held his gun in, dropping her instantly. She fell to the ground, holding her stinging and bruised cheek, wincing. A scowling Latrell tried to run up on Diabolic, but he turned his gun on him, stopping him dead in his tracks.

Diabolic smiled wickedly and said, "Smart man, very smart man." He swept his handgun before Korey whose eyes got as big as saucers, and his mouth dropped open.

Choot!

The bullet ripped through the air and entered Korey's chest, dotting his shirt with blood. His eyes rolled to the back of his head, and he fell to the ground, slow and languidly..

"Nooooooo!" Mank called out, outstretching his hand toward his best friend.

"Nooooooo!" Shavon called out, extending her hand from where she was lying on the ground.

"Nooooooo!" Latrell called out as well, hating to have seen Korey get gunned down.

Once Korey hit the ground, Latrell and Shavon scrambled over to him. Shavon rested his head in her lap and held one of his hands. The boy stared up at her blankly, as he wheezed and breathed in rasps, a hole in his chest, oozing blood. Tears welled up in Shavon's eyes and streamed down her face.

"That's for taking our shit in the first place, lil' young, dumb mothafuckaz!" Diabolic spat on the ground and mad-dogged Korey as he bled out. He then turned to his niggaz and said, "Y'all niggaz, come on." He shoved Mank toward Huge. Huge tucked his gun into the small of his back and hoisted Mank over his shoulder, while Mank was kicking and screaming.

"Lemme go, man! Lemme the fuck go!" Mank struggled to get away, but he couldn't break Huge's grip.

"Stay cool, Mank, stay cool! We're gonna get the dope up and come get chu, G. I promise you! You hear me, Mank? I promise you!" Latrell called after him as Huge carried him along, with Diabolic and Trevante bringing up the rear.

"Babe, help me get 'em in the car, we've gotta get 'em to the hospital!" Shavon called out to Latrell, with tears sliding down her cheeks, slicking her face wet.

Latrell found his blower in the grass, and tucked it at the small of his back. He scooped Korey up into his arms, and ran out of the backyard toward his car, with Shavon on his heels.

***

"Step on it—goddamn it, he's dying!" Shavon called out from the backseat, in hysterics, tears spilling down her cheeks uncontrollably. She was sitting with Korey's head propped up in her lap, holding his crimson hand, looking down into his eyes as they were rolled to their whites. The young man's chest rose and fell, as he wheezed with every breath that he took, causing more and more blood to run out of the hole inside of his chest. Nearly his entire shirt was stained red. It looked like he'd been splashed with a pitcher of cherry Kool-Aid.

"Hold on, baby boy, just hold on! We're gonna get chu there, Korey. You hear me, baby? We're gonna get chu there. Just don't die, please, don't die." She took the time to wipe her sweaty face with the back of her hand, and left a bloody streak behind.

Beep, beep, beep, beeeeep!

Latrell honked the horn like a mad man as he sped through traffic, dipping in and out of lanes, narrowly avoiding hitting other drivers and pedestrians. He gripped the steering wheel tightly, and clenched his jaws, occasionally glancing up at the rearview mirror into the backseat, at Shavon's face. He couldn't help praying that Korey stayed with them. He had mad love for the young nigga. He was family, and he looked at him like he was his younger brother.

Come on, Korey, man. You can't leave us, G. You've gotta hang in there. You're stronger than this, Latrell thought to himself as he flew past a light that had just turned red. He hung a few corners until he found himself on another main street, scarce with vehicles. He floored the gas pedal, whipping past houses, real fast, making the lines in the street look like blurs. Before he knew it, to the right, he found the emergency sign for the hospital, and a slight smirk formed on his lips. He wiped the sweat that dripped from the corner of his brow, with the back of his hand, and glanced up into the rearview mirror, talking to Shavon. "We're here—it's coming up, get ready to get out!"

Urrrrrrk!

Latrell brought his car to a hurried stop outside the emergency ward, and hopped out. He ran around to the opposite side of his whip, and pulled the door open. Shavon hopped out and he reached inside, scooping Korey into his arms. The young man's bloody arms and legs dangled as he was carried to the double electric doors of the emergency unit, like he was a soldier that had been seriously wounded on the battle field. He was nearly dead weight, so Latrell was occasionally stopping to catch his grip on him while running. He looked back and forth between Korey and the emergency ward, seeing the youngsta's pale, sweaty face and rolled back eyes.

"Come on, Korey! Hang in there, G! We're in the home stretch, baby boy!" Latrell told him, while running, bouncing up and down. He crossed the threshold of the emergency unit, with a disheveled and bloodstained Shavon on his heels. Her hair was a mess, and panic was written all over her face. "I need a doctor, somebody, get me a goddamn doctor, please!"

Korey continued to wheeze and bleed, blood trickling on the floor as Latrell ran through the emergency room with him, garnering the attention of everyone inside the facilities. The nurse stationed behind the desk buzzed for help, and the double doors of the back room automatically flew open. The hospital staff spilled open, rolling a gurney and an IV pole. Latrell ran over to the gurney and placed Korey down upon it.

"What happened?" one of the doctors asked Latrell.

"He—uh—he—um—he got shot in a drive-by!" Latrell answered as he and Shavon looked at the hospital staff attending to Korey. The doctor asked a little more info about Korey, as he and the rest of the staff turned the gurney around, running it towards the double doors of the back room.

Boom!

The double doors of the emergency ward flew open. The hospital staff rushed Korey along on a gurney, tearing open his shirt and exposing the black bleeding hole in his chest. His eyes were low, and his pupils moved around aimlessly. He tried to say something, but ended up coughing up blood.

"Hold on, baby boy, hold on!" a teary eyed Shavon told Korey, running alongside the gurney, clutching his bloody hand. Latrell was right beside her. Tears spilled down her cheeks in buckets, seeing Korey lying there and bleeding out. In her mind, images of Korey and Mank kept morphing back and forth. Her mind played tricks on her. She squeezed her eyelids shut, and more tears spilled. She sniffled and wiped her dripping eyes with the back of her hand. "You've gotta fight, Korey, fight! Fight for yo' life with all that you have, don't give up! You hear me, Korey? Don't give up!"

"Tyrell—Tyrell stole the dope. He—he saw us storing it—," Korey blinked his eyelids, as tears slid out of the corners of his eyes, and he swallowed the spit in his throat. "He saw us storing it inside of the garage. He's—he's got it."

A surprised expression spread across Shavon's face. She couldn't believe what she'd heard. She knew that she had to get in contact with Tyrell, and fast, if she was ever going to get her brother Mank back.

"Ma'am, I'm going to need you to let him go. We'll take care of him from here," one of the doctors told Shavon. She was worried about Korey dying on her.

Korey stared up at the ceiling with tearful eyes, and blood on his bottom lip. He watched a movie of his life play out before his eyes in bright, vivid colors. He saw all of the good and bad times he shared with his family, Shavon, Latrell, and Mank. He tried to reach out and touch the images, but he was far too weak to lift his arm, so he just lay there, watching his movie.

"I'm sorry, ma'am, but you've gotta go. We've gotta do our job," the doctor that had spoken to Shavon earlier said, prying her hand free from Korey's hand. Slowly, Shavon's palm and fingers released Korey's hand. Right then, another doctor looped an oxygen mask over Korey's nose and mouth. Inside of the mask fogged with each weak breath that Korey took, his lungs expanding and shrinking. One of the hospital's staff went on to cut open Korey's shirt. When they pulled it open, they revealed the hole in his chest, which was bleeding profusely.

Standing where she was, inside the hallway, Shavon hugged Latrell and buried her tear-soaked face into his chest. Latrell looked down the hallway as he comforted his woman, rubbing her back, and watching Korey and the hospital staff grow smaller and smaller as they flew down the corridor.

"Stay strong, lil' bro," Latrell said as a lone tear descended down his right cheek, from his glassy pink eye.

Chapter 4

Huge threw Mank over his broad shoulders and carried him inside the house, with Mank kicking and struggling to get away. No matter how hard the young nigga fought, he couldn't break the bonds that restrained his wrists, or shake the black pillowcase hanging over his head.

"On my dead granny, rest in peace, my nigga! You take this shit off my wrists, and I'ma get in yo' big ass. I'ma break you off something real proper, like, you feel me?" Mank swore as he continued to kick his legs wildly and jerk from left to right. He was being carried down in the basement by Huge, with Diabolic and Trevante following behind. The light from upstairs shone on the foursome as they descended the staircase. Diabolic and Trevante hung around the bottom of the steps while Huge carried Mank over to the center of the basement, and pulled the drawstring, restoring light to the spacious dwelling.

Huge stood Mank up on the ground. He then reached behind his back and pulled out a big ass Rambo knife, the light in the ceiling reflecting off the blade of the knife. He snatched the black pillowcase from Mank's head and tossed it aside. When the young nigga saw that big ass knife, his eyes got as big as baseballs. Fear gripped his heart, but it quickly vanished when Huge used the blade to slice off the zip-cuffs that bound his wrists. Next, Huge removed his ski-mask and pulled off his shirt, throwing it aside. Now, you could see this mothafucka was buff with the shirt on, but without it, he looked even bigger. His body was tatted up, and boasted his gang affiliation. Trevante and Diabolic stood in the background watching everything go down. Huge pulled his gun from out of the front of his jeans and passed it to Trevante, without taking his eyes off Mank.

"You said you gon' beat my ass, right? Well, I'd like to see yo' ass try, lil' nigga!" a scowling Huge told Mank, standing there in all of his glory. His figure cast a shadow that towered over the shorter man.

"I'd like to see that, too," Trevante said, after lighting up a half smoked blunt and passing it to Diabolic, who had his ski-mask rolled halfway up his face. He took a few puffs of the fat ass blunt and blew out a big cloud of smoke.

"David versus Goliath, I can't wait to see this shit," Diabolic said. "I'll tell you what, kid, just to make it interesting, if you whip Huge's ass, I'll let chu walk tonight," he told Mank.

"I smell bullshit!" a scowling Mank responded.

"My right hand to God," Diabolic swore as he lifted his hand, palm showing.

"You've gotta bet," Mank said, as he pulled his T-shirt over his head and tossed it aside. He had some size to him. He had muscular arms, pecs, and rock-hard abs. A small trail of hairs led from his navel down into his jeans.

"It's yo' funeral, youngsta," Huge said as bent his neck from left to right and wagged his fingers, as he jumped up and down. He then cracked the knuckles on both of his massive hands. After Mank followed suit, they started shadow boxing, making the noises professional fighters make in the ring. Chins tucked, fists up, they circled one another, homed in on each other's movements. Suddenly, Mank jabbed Huge with his right and connected again with his left. Huge swung at him, but he ducked. The young nigga gave him three to the body and an uppercut, which threw his head backward. The blow busted his mouth and sent blood up into the air. The blood came back down and splattered on the floor. Huge staggered backward a little, but caught himself. He smiled fiendishly at Mank, exposing his bloody teeth. He swallowed the blood that collected inside of his grill. He then wiped the blood that dripped from his bottom lip, with the back of his fist.

"Come on, big man! Come on!" Mank motioned him over with both of his hands as he stood in a fighting stance. Huge ran at him and swung as hard as he could at his head. Mank ducked him again. Following up, he punched him in his side and his kidney, which made him howl in pain. He then cracked him in his mouth, busting and bloodying his grill. Huge righted himself and threw his fists back up. Mank moved in on him, setting him up with a jab. Huge blocked the jabs and the body shots he followed up with. He tried to kick Mank in his leg, but the young nigga swatted his foot down. The big man leaned in with a punch to Mank's jaw, which whipped him around in a one-hundred-eighty degree turn. Huge being the bigger, stronger man, his punches were three times as powerful as Mank's.

"Hahahahahahaha!" Huge laughed maniacally as he watched a dazed and confused Mank swinging wildly, with his back to him. Huge whistled for his attention. When he turned around, he rocked his jaw, which dropped him down to his hands and knees. The young nigga spat blood on the floor. Slimy ropes of blood hung from his bottom lip. When Mank looked at Huge, he saw two of him, through blurry eyes. Huge charged at him and kicked him in the head, treating his skull like a football. Mank spun around in midair before slamming back down on his back. "I give it to you, youngsta, you've got heart! But unfortunately for you, that ain't enough to box with *the god!*" Huge placed a knee on each of Mank's arms, pinning him down to the floor. He then went to work on him, raining blows on his face, and sending blood flying. More and more dots of blood appeared on the floor, with each punch that landed. The beating was so brutal that Trevante and Diabolic cringed and turned their heads. They couldn't bear to watch the barbaric actions of Huge any longer.

Huge stopped pummeling Mank and looked down at his handiwork. The youngsta's face looked like bloody hamburger meat. There was a knot the size of a golf ball on his forehead, and a smaller knot was beside it. One of his eyes was swollen shut, his nose was twice its size, his top lip was as big as a hotlink, and half of his top row of teeth was missing. Mank moaned and groaned in pain, as he lay with his arms and legs stretched out.

Huge got off Mank and picked up the youngsta's shirt. He used the shirt to wipe the blood off his busted knuckles, before discarding it. He then grabbed Mank by his ankle and dragged him across the floor. Huge picked up a shackle that was bolted to the wall, and tugged on its chain, testing its strength. The chain was firmly attached to the wall, so he went ahead and clamped the shackle around Mank's ankle. Afterward, he picked up his shirt and ski-mask. He tucked the ski-mask into his back pocket and slipped his shirt over his head. Trevante handed him his gun back and he tucked it in the front of his jeans. The three men looked over at Mank as he lay defeated. Diabolic tapped Huge and they headed up the staircase. Trevante flipped off the light switch and followed them up the staircase.

"I'm hungry as a hostage," Diabolic said. "Huge, you feel like whipping up some of yo' famous chili?"

"I've got chu faded, just lemme wash up," Huge replied.

"Hell yeah, man, that shit be bomb ass fuck with some Jasmine rice and cornbread," Trevante chimed in.

Mank was left on the basement floor, wheezing with every breath he took. He had a feeling he had a couple of fractured ribs. This was confirmed when he rolled over onto his side, and jolts of pain shot up his ribcage.

"Aaaaah, fuck!" Mank frowned up as he held his side, while lying on the floor. He used his tongue to feel around inside of his mouth. His face balled up as he poked at a loose, broken tooth at the back of his mouth. He was sure it was loose enough to pull out, so he yanked it free and looked at it. The broken tooth was coated in blood. Mank threw it aside and spat blood on the floor. Ropes of slimy blood hung from his bottom lip and chin, threatening to fall to the floor. Mank looked to the left, over his shoulder, and saw the lights from the lamp post shining through the basement window. He laid his head down on the cold, hard cement floor. As he wheezed and winced, he stared at the light shining through the window. Suddenly, he saw Korey lying in a hospital bed with his eyelids shut, hooked up to different medical machinery, with tubes in his nostrils to help him breathe. "You can't—you can't let these bitch-ass niggaz beat chu, Korey. You've gotta fight—you've gotta fight like I just did, except you've gotta win. You hear me? You've gotta win."

Mank continued to stare at the image of his best friend. He was in pain and exhausted, so his eyelids felt extremely heavy.

Before he knew it, his eyelids were shut, and he'd drifted off to sleep.

***

Shavon and Latrell sat in the waiting room, wrapped in each other's arms. They sat there, looking exhausted and worried, with Korey's blood on their necks and clothes. It had been hours, and they still hadn't gotten word from the doctor as regards Korey's condition. They feared the worse, but were hoping for the best.

Shavon called Tyrell back to back, but he didn't answer, so she left him several messages. Within her heart she knew he wasn't going to answer. There wasn't a doubt in her mind that he knew exactly what she was calling about. She had to push him to the back of her mind for now, because at the moment Korey's well-being was most important to her. Latrell and Shavon had drifted off to sleep. Latrell was slouched in his seat, with his head tilted back. His eyelids were shut, his mouth was open, and he was snoring loudly.

Dr. Clarkson entered the waiting room, wearing a surgical cap over his head, a mask, which was around his neck, and scrubs. He stopped before Latrell and Shavon, casting a glance at them, and then back at the document on his clipboard. "Are you guys the family of Korey Tyson?" he inquired. Instantly, Shavon's eyelids peeled open, and she shook Latrell awake. He peeled his glassy, pink eyes open and wiped the drool that dripped from the corner of his mouth, with the side of his hand. When his eyes landed on the doctor, he and Shavon sat up and straightened out their shirts, giving him their undivided attention.

"Uh, yes, we're the family of Korey Tyson," Shavon answered.

"Hi, I'm Doctor Clarkson." He shook hands with both of them, and they told him their names. Shavon asked about Korey. He gave her a full report. "He's in a coma right now. It's up to him if he recovers from this. He's young, and from what I can see, he's healthy. So, I don't see why he shouldn't come out of this.

Unfortunately, if he does wake up, due to the damage that the bullet we removed caused, he'll be paralyzed from the waist down for the rest of his life." Upon hearing this, Shavon bowed her head, and massaged the bridge of her nose. Latrell threw his arm around her shoulders, and rubbed her arm soothingly. He told her that everything was going to be all right, and kissed her on the side of her head. He then looked back up at the doctor. Dr. Clarkson had very sorrowful eyes. Besides losing a patient on the operation table, this was the second worse part of his job, telling the patient's loved ones bad news. "I'm terribly sorry."

"Thanks, doctor." Latrell shook his hand. Dr. Clarkson waved goodbye and headed for the door. He stopped and turned around, once a teary-eyed Shavon called him back.

Her cheeks slickly wet with tears, Shavon told the doctor, "I want to be notified the moment he comes out of that coma, you hear me? The moment my lil' brother wakes up. You have someone call me." Dr. Clarkson nodded and continued out of the door to conduct other business. Once he was gone, Shavon walked over to Latrell who was staring out of the large window of the waiting room, which gave all of the visitors a view of the city. Shavon could see her and Latrell's reflection in the window, as she approached him; he appeared to be in deep thought. "What're we gonna do now? We've gotta get up those keys, or they're gonna kill Mank."

Latrell cupped Shavon's face and looked into her eyes. "I'll tell you what we're gonna do. We're gon' strap up and get on our ski-mask shit. We're gonna hit every dope boy, kingpin, and nigga we know that's holding weight, so we can collect these keys and get lil' bro back. You ready to make these streets feel our pain?" Shavon wiped her wet cheeks and sniffled. The sad expression that was on her face was now replaced with a scowl of determination. She was officially in beast-mode, and ready to do whatever she had to do to get Mank back. She nodded *yes* to Latrell's question. "Good," Latrell said. Still cupping her face, he kissed her forehead, and then her lips.

***

Two nights later

Baby Boy was ducked off inside his study, with his shoes propped up on his desk, smoking a fat ass cigar, and blowing smoke rings up into the air. The thought of King Rich came across his mind as he fondled the small urn, containing his father's ashes, which hung from the gold necklace around his neck. He stared ahead at nothing, as he continued to take puffs of his cigar, continuing his fondling of the small urn, recalling a point in time that changed his life forever.

"Pop, you're really sounding like Muhammad Ali, not wanting to go to war!" Baby Boy hollered out to King Rich while they were inside his study. "All of the soldiers we done lost over the beef with this nigga! Us squashing our differences gon' make us look weak. On top of that, the hittaz we lost gon' turnover in their fucking graves!"

King Rich was about to take a sip of his drink, but he turned to address Baby Boy. "I made sure the families of the soldiers we've lost are well taken care of. It doesn't make any sense to keep going at it with Montray and nem when we're moving on to greener pastures. If he wants them lil' punk-ass street corners, then let 'em have 'em. The move we're about to make will have us making major drops in surrounding cities. We'll be supplying the niggaz that's supplying the streets."

Baby Boy tilted his head to the side and stared at his father for a moment, narrowing his eyelids into slits. It was like he was trying to see if he was the same person that he'd grown up worshipping and admiring. "I thought I'd never see the day that you'd put money over principles, old man." King Rich had just taken a sip of his drink. When Baby Boy said this, he whipped his head around to him. "It hurts my heart to admit it, but I've gotta say it," King Rich placed his glass down on the desk top, and could feel the disrespect following behind his son's previous statement, "you acting like a real bitch-ass nigga, right now!"

King Rich balled his face up angrily, and with a grunt, he gave Baby Boy a backhanded slap. The assault came so swift that Baby Boy didn't even see him raise his hand. Before he knew it, he was falling to the floor with a busted mouth, wincing. Diabolic had just entered the doorway of the study, to see his brother colliding with the carpeted floor. Baby Boy shook off the daze he was left with from the attack. His eyebrows sloped downward, and his nostrils flared heatedly. He pounced up from the floor and charged toward his father. But before he could reach him, Diabolic snatched him up. The little nigga fought against his restraint, but he couldn't break his hold.

"Get off me, man! Get the fuck up off me!" Baby Boy shouted as he continued to try to break free of Diabolic's hold.

"That's our father, man!" Diabolic told him, as he strengthened his hold on him.

"I don't give a rat's ass! Don't no-fucking-body put their goddamn hands on me and get away with it. This old-ass nigga got me fucked up!" Baby Boy mad-dogged Diabolic, looking him up and down. He then looked to King Rich. He was sitting on top of his desk sipping his drink with a Glock dangling between his legs. Baby Boy frowned up, looking at him like he was crazy. He was expecting them to throw hands. He never thought the day would come when he'd see his father threatening to shoot him. "You plan on shooting me, old man? Huh?"

"I've raised you boys from pups to dogs," King Rich responded as he stared ahead. He didn't even bother to look in Baby Boy's direction. "I've housed you, clothed you, fed you, and gave you everything you could imagine coming up. As your father, I'd lie down right now and die for you, if need be. But what I won't do is duke it out witchu, like you're some common thug in the goddamn street. Nah, to hell with that! I told myself the night your mother, God rest her soul, pushed you out of her womb, and into this world, that should the day ever come when either of you dared to raise your hand to me, I'd shoot chu dead. Right where you stand." King Rich took a sip from his glass, as tears slowly accumulated in his eyes and rolled down his cheeks. He then sat

his glass down beside him and looked to Baby Boy. He he cocked the slide on his gun, which was a warning to his youngest son, "Nigga, run up on me if you want to."

Baby Boy stood there, wrapped up in Diabolic's arms for a moment, examining his father's eyes. He could tell from the look written on his face that he wasn't bluffing. He would murder him in cold-blood, right there in his study, if he forced his hand. Baby Boy shoved Diabolic off of him and ran out of his father's study. He tripped and fell, running down the hallway, but quickly got back upon his feet.

Baby Boy ran out of his father's mansion and hurried down the steps. He hopped into the driver's seat of his drop-top black 2020 Mercedes-Benz AMG GT, with two toned black and ox-blood leather colored seats. He fired that bad boy up, and its headlights popped on. He then sped around the cobblestone driveway, toward the enormous double gates. The gates opened, and he zipped through them. The cool air was blowing against him, which disturbed his frizzy hair, and made his tie flap behind him.

Baby Boy glanced down and saw the dots of blood on his white suit. He stole a look in the rearview mirror and saw blood threatening to drip from his busted bottom lip. "Ol' punk-ass, old-ass nigga, gon' put his mothafucking dick beatas on me? On me? Nigga, you got me all the way fucked up!" Baby Boy switched hands on the steering wheel and whipped his handkerchief out, using it to dab the blood from his wound. Each time he touched his bleeding lip, he winced from the stinging pain. Once he felt like he'd cleaned up the blood, he settled back down in his seat and gave the streets his undivided attention.

It was dark out, and the moon shone on the windshield of his Benz. He whipped his car through traffic, dipping in and out of lanes. He pulled his cell phone from inside his suit, and hit up a notorious killa that had filled several contracts for him in the past. He made arrangements to meet up with him, and confirmed the dough he needed upfront. "Alright, I'll see you then," he disconnected the call, and stuck the phone back inside his suit. Before he realized it, he was arriving at his crib. He punched in the code to enter through the enormous gates, behind which his baby mansion sat. A moment later, the gates opened and he drove inside.

Baby Boy hurried down the steps of his crib, switching hands with the black leather pouch filled with the first half of the blue faces he had earmarked to pay the assassin off with. Baby Boy tossed the pouch into the passenger seat and jumped inside his car. Firing it up, he zipped off of the grounds of his estate en route to see The Agent of Death.

Baby Boy pulled up inside the parking lot of the Snooty Fox Motor Inn, killed his engine, and hopped out of his car, pouch in hand. He made his way across the parking lot, bypassing a black motorcycle he knew belonged to the killa. He tore his eyes off the motorcycle, and continued toward the room the killa was staying in. Baby Boy rapped on the door. He then took a cautious look over his shoulders, to see if anyone was watching him, but there wasn't an eye on him. When he turned back around to the door, he cleared his throat, with his fist to his mouth. Right then, he heard the door lock coming undone, and then the door was pulled open. Baby Boy found himself standing before a tall, white man, with a muscular build. The man was ruggedly handsome, and resembled Hugh Jackman, except he had blonde hair. The man, who went by the name, Worth, was wearing a black T-shirt, black jeans and boots. Down at his side, he held a black .9mm handgun, with a silencer on the tip of its barrel. His lips were greasy, and his jaw was swollen with food.

Worth sucked what looked like tomato sauce from his fingers. He then stepped aside and allowed Baby Boy inside his room. Once Baby Boy crossed the threshold, he took a look around the dwelling. There was a small table and chair against the window, a dresser, which the television was placed on, a nightstand and a full-sized bed. The comforter that draped the bed was green, with flowers on it. A black Kevlar bulletproof vest lay on top of it. A black leather duster hung off the back of the chair by the window. On top of the small table, there was a black motorcycle helmet, a

Pizza Hut pizza box, a two-liter Pepsi, a cup of the same soda, and a stack of napkins.

Worth shut the door behind Baby Boy, and locked it behind him. He tucked his gun at the small of his back. He grabbed a few napkins, and wiped his greasy mouth and hands. He chewed down his food, and used the cup of soda to wash it down.

"Care for a slice of pizza?" Worth held his hand out toward the pizza box.

"No, thank you." Baby Boy declined his offer.

Worth turned his head to the side and said, "You sure? It's a meat-lover."

"Nah, I'll pass. I'm full. I ate earlier." Baby Boy placed his hand on his stomach.

"Okay. Well, have a seat, so we can get down to business." Worth pulled up his jeans and sat down on the chair, with the small table beside him. Baby Boy passed him the pouch and sat down on the bed. He watched him thumb through the many blue faces inside the pouch, before zipping it up and tossing it upon the table top. He then took the picture that Baby Boy had taken out of his suit and passed to him. Instantly, Worth recalled the very familiar face in the photograph. It was King Rich. He knew that the old head was one of the major players in the underworld. He had big dawg status, money, power and sophistication. Worth also knew that King Rich was Baby Boy's father. He'd fulfilled several contracts for the OG over his career; during some of those interactions he'd ran into Baby Boy quite a few times.

Worth never asked questions when it concerned the person he was about to take out. He figured it wasn't any of his business. But judging from the blood on Baby Boy's suit, he assumed he'd gotten into a fight with his father and wanted him wiped off of the map. Well, that—and the fact that he wanted to be the head honcho of his organization.

Baby Boy gave Worth a few places he could catch King Rich slipping. Then, he gave him the road they'd be traveling down after they came back from negotiating the deal on the kilos of cocaine. It was then Worth decided he was going to carry out the hit on the road. So, from there, they discussed an idea of exactly how Worth was going to handle things going forward, since he knew that Baby Boy and Latrell were going to be there.

"You know what? I think I will take a slice of that pizza." Baby Boy rose to his feet, looking at Worth opening the pizza box, and taking out a slice. Baby Boy had been chopping it up with Worth for a while, and in that time he'd naturally grown hungry. "Thanks." Baby Boy accepted the slice of pizza on a napkin. He took bites of it, as he followed Worth to the door. Worth unlocked and opened the door for Baby Boy. They dapped up, and the little nigga went on about his business.

King Rich hit up Baby Boy while he was on his way home, requesting to see him. Baby Boy was about to tell him to go fuck himself, but he felt that may ruin his plans. With that in mind, he told him he'd be there in twenty minutes. As Baby Boy zipped through the opening gates of his father's mansion, he could see his old man's silhouette standing at the bottom of the steps of his home. He had his hands on his hips and his head was bowed. It was from this stance that Baby Boy could tell that he was thinking about something serious.

Baby Boy's car jerked as it came to an abrupt stop beside his father. With one hand, he jumped out of his Benz and pointed his remote control at it to lock it. He sauntered over to King Rich. The kingpin suddenly grabbed him and hugged him tight.

"I love you, boy. You hear me? I love you with all of my heart." King Rich swore. He hated himself for losing his cool and putting his hands on his son. He loved both of his boys dearly, and prided himself having raised them without ever physically disciplining them. "I'm sorry for hitting you. You forgive me?"

Standing there, in his father's embrace, Baby Boy rolled his eyes. He then took a deep breath and said, "Yeah, I forgive you, pop. And I'm sorry for disrespecting you. That shit shoulda never happened. You're my father, and I should have more respect for you than that. I'm sorry."

"I forgive you, son." King Rich kissed him twice, on different areas on the side of his face. He continued to hold Baby Boy in his *arms for a while longer. Diabolic came down the steps and threw his arms around them both, in one, big group hug. King Rich kissed him on the side of his head as well. He told him that he loved him too, and Diabolic reciprocated the words to him.*

Baby Boy quickly sat up in his chair, and yanked the necklace containing the urn from around his neck. He pulled open the top drawer of his desk, and dropped the necklace inside it. He then pulled out his burn-out cellular phone, and switched the SIM card with another cell phone that he had. Lastly, he powered the device on and dialed up his brother, Diabolic.

Diabolic picked up on the third ring, "What up?"

"That thing we discussed earlier, I want it handled tonight."

"Say less." Diabolic disconnected the call.

Tranay Adams

Chapter 5

Four black-on-black Chevrolet Suburbans with pitch- black tinted windows, rims and tires, drove up the street, one after the other. Each SUV was filled to capacity with killaz wearing ski-masks and dressed in all black, from head to toe. Their gloved hands held tight to AK-47s, with one-hundred round drums attachments. Every man accounted for was either wrapped in his own thoughts, or staring out of the windows of the bullet-proof vehicles. In the Suburban leading the pack, in the front passenger seat, holding his AK-47 between his legs, was the masked-up goon leading the mission. He stared through the tinted window glass, out into the street, with his gold crucifix pinched between his index finger and thumb. Once the driver turned onto the grounds the wedding reception was being held, the goon leading the mission shut his eyelids, and said a silent prayer, which he did before every mission he went on. After he'd finished his prayer, he kissed his crucifix and tucked his necklace inside his shirt. He then opened his eyes. The SUV he was in had just pulled up to the curb outside of the tenement, with two of the Suburbans pulling up behind it. The fourth and final Suburban ventured off on its own, disappearing on the side of the building, to tend to a mission of its own. The lead goon, who was riding shotgun in the lead Suburban, placed his finger to the ear-bud in his ear, and contacted the other killaz in the other vehicles.

"Alright, gentlemen, let's move!" the lead goon gave the order, and jumped out of the Chevrolet Suburban. Hunched down, with their assault rifles gripped expertly, the killaz moved in on the building stealthily. They were as quiet as an army of ghosts floating through the grounds of a cemetery. The lead goon stopped at the opened door of the facility. He could hear the loud music coming from behind the doors of the ballroom. He held up his gloved hand, which signaled for them to halt. They did just as he commanded. The lead goon took a cautious peek inside the doorway. He looked up and down the hallway, clocking two armed security guards on duty. One of the security guards was busy texting on his cellular, while the other was fixing his hair, staring into a hand-held mirror. Both were so engrossed in their activities that they hadn't noticed that the premises were under siege.

The lead goon held up two fingers, to let his killaz know that there were two security guards on deck. Hearing someone coming in over his ear-bud, he pressed his finger against it, and listened closely. He'd just been informed that there were four security guards on the opposite side of the building, which had already been dispatched with deadly force. The lead goon responded back, reporting that there were two security guards on their side, and that they were moving in to dispatch them. He then glanced back inside the doorway, to find the security guards still occupied with their vices. He gave the hand signal, to let his killaz know he was moving in. Right after, he hoisted up his AK-47 and moved in skillfully. He turned to his right and squeezed off two shots, blowing up half of the face of the security guard who was on his cell phone. The lead goon didn't wait for the security guard's body to drop, before he turned down the opposite end of the hallway. He was just in time to see the other security guard dropping the hand-held mirror, and reaching for his holstered handgun. The security guard had cleared his gun halfway, before he was met with rapid gunfire. Chunks of bloody flesh and broken skull went flying everywhere, when the top half of the security guard's head exploded. The security guard's lifeless body dropped to its knees and then fell on its side. His blood poured out of what was left of his head, and coated the floor.

The lead goon motioned for the rest of the killaz to follow him inside the hallway. They poured in behind him. One half took a set of double doors, while the other side took the other set of double doors. The lead goon looked down the hallway, at the other goon manning the other set of doors. They exchanged nods. They then barged through the double doors. Instantly, they were hit with Juvenile's "Back That Ass Up", and bathed in light. The lead goon spotted the bride, Starr, who was Montray's niece. He saw Starr looking back at the groom, Jody, grinding her big booty against him. Jody had a big smile stretched across his face. His arms were held up. He was snapping his fingers. Occasionally, he'd use his handkerchief to wipe the small bubbles of sweat that covered his bald head and forehead.

Montray stood off to the side with a glass of champagne, which he occasionally sipped from; as he watched the newlyweds get their grooves on, on the dance floor. A smile was plastered on his face, and he was standing beside a very attractive woman. Montray was a six-foot-tall dude who wore his hair in a close fade. He had hazel eyes. A scar he'd gotten during a knife fight in prison stood out on his left cheek; the scar had healed into a keloid. The thick goatee he flossed showed signs of graying.

Montray was wearing a black V-neck shirt under a suede gold, black, and royal blue Versace blazer, black slacks that stopped above his ankles, and sported black suede Versace shoes with gold Medusa heads on them. A gold diamond-studded necklace hung around his neck. An icy gold presidential Rolex watch with a black face adorned his wrist. On his pinky finger was an icy gold ring with an "M" on it that spun. On his opposite wrist he wore an icy gold diamond-studded bracelet, identical to his necklace. He rocked big diamond earrings that twinkled in his earlobes, underneath the light shining out from the dance floor. The young caramel-complexioned woman beside him wore her reddish brown locs in a bun. Her ears, neck, wrists, and fingers were dripping gold and diamonds. The royal blue dress she had on was form-fitting, and showed off her large bust, and a big old ass you couldn't get down in the Dominican Republic. The young lady was drop-dead gorgeous, and just one of many babes Montray had at his disposal. He was a playboy millionaire, so women as fine as her came at a dime a dozen for him.

Surprisingly, none of the guests at the wedding had noticed the killaz had entered through the doors of the ballroom. The lead goon scowled and smiled devilishly behind his ski-mask when he spotted Montray. He took aim with his AK-47 just as an older man rose to go to the men's room. His actions blocked the lead goon's line of vision, and when he pulled the trigger, the older man winded up getting chopped down. He fell hard to the table, and then rolled off, hitting the floor. His wife hollered aloud and looked to the lead goon, taking in all of the masked faces of the killaz, her eyes widening, her heart filled with terror. Right then, everyone whipped around to the entrances of the ballroom. The lead goon chopped the wife down. Then, he turned his AK-47 on Montray, pulling the trigger. Montray pulled his lovely date before him, using her as a human-shield; bullets blew off her face and breasts. Her blood dotted up Montray's face and shirt.

Montray let his date's dead body drop, and pulled his gun from out of his blazer. He walked backward, gun pointed, firing again and again. His bullets slammed into the chest of one of the killaz, dropping him to the floor. By this time, the entire ballroom was in pandemonium, with guests zig-zagging back and forth across the floor, screaming and hollering. The killaz scattered throughout the ballroom like roaches, spraying their assault rifles, chopping mothafuckaz down, and leaving them with horror etched on their faces, the victims lying in pools of their own blood. Montray looked around for his niece, eyes sweeping over the crowds of people running around him. He finally found his niece lying on the floor and coughing up blood, as she lay in her husband, Jody's arms. There were several holes in her torso. Blood was spreading all over the center of her white dress. Jody stared down into his wife's face. His eyes were pink, and big teardrops were falling from them, splashing on the love of his life's bloody dress.

"Please, don't leave me, baby! Please, I can't live without chu, Starr! I can't live without chu!" Jody said louder and louder, watching his wife's eyelids flutter. Finally, her eyelids stopped fluttering. They were wide and vacant. She released her last breath. Her body went limp in Jody's arms, and her head leaned off to the side, blood droplets dripping from the side of her mouth. Before Montray knew it, Jody was getting chopped down by automatic gunfire as well. Still holding Starr in his arms, Jody slumped over his wife with the back of his head blown out. Blood poured out of his open mouth and splashed on the floor, creating a small puddle.

Montray's eyes grew as big as tennis balls. He couldn't believe what had occurred before his eyes. He turned around and opened fire on the masked-up nigga that had laid down Jody. He popped him in the chest twice and sent him flipping over the table, knocking over all of the wrapped wedding gifts on top of it. Right then, a few of the killaz set their sights on him. They turned their guns on him. Out of nowhere, Montray's personal bodyguards appeared. They were a couple of shady-looking characters dressed up in black suits. They had tattoos on their necks and hands. There were also ear-buds in their ears, with what looked like a swirling telephone cord attached, which led around to the back of their necks. The bodyguards stepped forward with their automatic handguns drawn. The first one sent fire at the killaz, while the other attended to Montray.

"Boss man, gon' and get up outta here, we'll lay down some cover fire!" the bodyguard told him. Montray nodded and patted him on the shoulder. He then took off running. As soon as he did, the bodyguard that had told him what to do, stood side by side with his partner, firing shot after shot. They managed to hit a couple of the killaz, but they were all wearing bullet-proof vests; so it didn't matter. The killaz returned fire and chopped the bodyguards down swiftly. One by one, the bodyguards went down in a bloody mess, bleeding on the floor.

Montray, still running, stopped occasionally to fire at the killaz. In the midst of this chaos, more and more bodies began to gather on the floor. The killaz were laying his family and loved ones out, and coming after him. Montray let off three more shots, before his gun clicked empty. He threw it aside, and kept running for his life. When he looked ahead, he found double doors in front of him that he knew would lead out into the hallway. Montray charged forward, leaped up, and kicked the double doors open. He hit the floor, tucking and rolling. As soon as he got back up, he kept on running.

"*Haa! Haa! Haa! Haa! Haa! Haa! Haa!*" Montray huffed and puffed, as he bent the corner of the corridor, running as fast as he could. His eyes were bucked and his nostrils were flaring. Sweat slid down his face and drenched the middle of his back. Montray occasionally looked over his shoulder to see if the masked up goons were on him, and they were. He could see their shadows cast against the wall as they poured out of the ballroom. He could also hear the reoccurring sound of automatic gunfire, and the horrified screams of his loved ones as they were being cut down. Before Montray knew it, the goons were bending the corner and heading in his direction. Their boots made screeching sounds as they ran on the shiny, waxed floor. "Oh, shit!" Montray shouted when he saw the goons like a lynch mob on his heels. Whipping his head back around, Montray sighed with relief when he saw the green exit sign over the double doors ahead. Picking up speed, he leaped up into the air and kicked the double doors open. He tucked and rolled on the ground with bullets whizzing over his head. Down on his knees, he looked over his shoulder and saw the double doors closing and the goons still coming after him, firing their AK-47s.

Montray scrambled up on his feet and made hurried footsteps towards the stretched Mercedes Benz that had driven him to the reception, breathing heavily. He wiped the hot sweat that trickled from the corner of his brow, with the back of his hand, and snatched open the backdoor of the limousine. He quickly jumped inside and slammed the door behind him. He then looked over his shoulder out of the rear, black tinted window to see the double doors of the ballroom flying open and the goons spilling out, looking left and right for him.

"Oh, fuck!" Montray blurted when he saw them. He then whipped his head back around and knocked on the tinted window glass that separated the backseat from the front seat, calling up front to the chauffeur. "Vernon, man! Vernon, start this mothafucka up and get us the fuck from outta here!" Montray waited for a response, but he didn't receive one, so he rolled the window down, finding Vernon, the chauffeur, with his back to him. "Vernon? Nigga, you hear me?" Montray stuck his hand through the partition and nudged the man that had been his chauffeur for the past fifteen years. Vernon slumped in the driver seat, and his lifeless eyes reflected in the rearview mirror, making contact with Montray's eyes. Looking at Vernon through the rearview mirror, Montray took note of a river of blood pouring down his forehead. Right then, Vernon slid to the right and Montray spotted a huge hole at the back of his head. Montray's eyes darted to the windshield and that's when he noticed there was a single bullet hole in it surrounded by breakage.

A terrified Montray hopped out of the limousine, and left the door open. He looked to his left and saw Trevante, who was leading the goons, point in his direction and wave for them to follow him. Trevante and the goons took off, running after Montray, firing their AK-47s at him. Montray ducked his head and zig zagged as he ran for his life, bullets flying around him. One bullet blew off the side view mirror of the stretch Mercedes Benz. A second one grazed his arm and tore the fabric of his blazer. A third bullet ripped through Montray's calf muscle, and he threw his head back hollering, scrunching up his face. He fell to the ground with a thud, and slowly pulled himself up to his feet. He hobbled forward, bleeding at the back of the leg, and glancing over his shoulder. When he saw Trevante and the goons closing the distance on him, he knew that he was in grave danger, and nothing could save him short of a miracle. And that miracle came in the form of a black Astro van.

Skrrrrrt!

The van swung around diagonally, and the side door was pulled open. A masked-up nigga stood in the doorway, firing his automatic handgun at Trevante and his goons. A few of the goons crumpled to the ground, howling in agony, having been struck down by the rapid gunfire of their fearless enemy. This masked gunman was a part of Montray's security team. Montray was a very wealthy man, so there was always someone out to get him. That's why he employed a band of hittaz to follow him wherever he went, to watch his back, specifically for situations like this.

"Come on!" the masked-up nigga extended his leather gloved hand. Once Montray grasped his hand, he pulled him inside the van. While this was going on, bullets were whizzing through the air, striking the van, and sending shrapnel flying. After Montray was safe inside, the masked gunman knocked on the inside of the vehicle and hollered up front to the getaway driver, who was also masked up. "Let's go, let's go, let's go!" he called out over the loud gunfire, ducked, and dodging the bullets that were meant to take his life. The van sped off, making a screeching sound once again. The masked gunman that had pulled Montray safely inside, hung out of the open door of the van, and fired a few rounds in the opposition's direction.

Blowl, Blowl, Blowl, Blowl!
Ratatatatatatatatatatat!
Blowl, Blowl, Blowl!

The masked gunman ducked back inside the van and pulled its sliding door shut. The driver hightailed it out of the parking lot, with police car sirens wailing in the distance; the law was hastily approaching.

"Man, what the fuck took y'all niggaz so long? Them niggaz out there almost had my ass." Montray said from the floor of the van, while removing his blazer. Once he'd done this, he tore off the sleeve of his Versace shirt and tied it tight around his calf to slow his bleeding, gritting.

"Yo', The Boys are on our ass!" the masked driver announced from behind the wheel. He'd just glanced in the side view mirror and saw the red and blue flashing lights of the oncoming police cars speeding up behind them.

"Alright," the masked gunman called up front to the driver. He then switched hands with the handgun, and pressed his finger to the earbud inside his ear, contacting the chopper that was supposed to pick them up. "Yo, we're coming up, so have yo' ass there. Okay."

The masked gunman then removed his backpack and got down on his knees, sitting his handgun down beside him on the floor. While he was doing this, Montray was wincing in pain and pulling himself up on his feet. He looked around inside the van. Suddenly, something occurred to him, causing his brows to furrow. He then looked up to the masked gunman, who was pulling a magnetic explosive from out of his backpack and placing it against one of the backdoors of the van.

"Where are Kyng and Major?" Montray asked, with one hand placed against the wall of the van, leaning against it.

"Where's who?" the masked gunman asked, with his focus on the explosive. The device beeped with each button that he pressed. His back was to Montray, oblivious to whatever he may or may not be doing behind him.

"The other mothafuckaz I hired witcho ass to watch my back," Montray said, as he slowly picked up the handgun from the floor of the van.

"Oh," the masked gunman said, after having armed the explosive. He then rose to his feet and turned around to Montray, smiling, boasting his rose gold and pink diamond teeth. He slid his tongue across his top row of teeth and then bit down on his bottom lip, smiling again. "I killed them." As soon as he said this, Montray pointed the handgun at him, prepared to squeeze the trigger. The masked gunman then pulled off his ski-mask, revealing himself to be Diabolic. "Surprise, surprise."

Montray's eyes dilated in shock and he clenched his jaws, pulling the trigger of his handgun. *Blowl, blowl!* The handgun went off, sounding like thunder erupting inside of the van. Two empty shell casings dropped to the floor of the van, but Diabolic was unharmed. He slowly walked toward Montray, pulling a small knife from his sleeve, swiftly. Montray's face balled up further, and he looked at the handgun warily. He then pointed it back at Diabolic. The handgun went off two more times, and then four times again, but Diabolic kept on coming. A demonic expression was written across his face. He looked like the Devil himself.

"It's loaded with blanks, asshole! You've been played." Diabolic gritted, clenching the small knife tighter. "This is for my father, cocksucka!" He jabbed Montray in the left eye and caused him to howl in agony. He dropped the handgun, and grabbed his face with both hands, staggering backwards. Diabolic walked up on him again, and this time, he jabbed him in the side of his neck. Pain masked his face, and veins bulged on his forehead as blood sprayed from out of the side of his neck, slicking the wall of the van. Montray made a move to grab Diabolic, who took a step back, looking at him with an evil grin. Montray fell to the floor of the van. Holding his hand against the wound in his neck, Montray crawled towards Diabolic, trying to grab his leg. The further he moved toward him, the more blood he lost. Shortly thereafter, he found his vision growing blurry. He then collapsed, lying with the side of his face against the floor. His eyes were wide open, and so was his mouth. The blood continued to flow from the hole in his neck, coating the surface like burgundy paint. Diabolic stared down at his deceased enemy, seeing his reflection in his blood.

"Is that mothafucka dead?" the driver, Trevante, asked, glancing up at the rearview mirror.

"As a doorknob," Diabolic confirmed, as he pulled his ski-mask back down over his head and adjusted it so he could see out of the eye holes. He then kneeled down to Montray's limp body, and grabbed his hand he wore his ring on. Diabolic cut off Montray's finger and stood upright. He then pulled the severed finger free of the ring, and spat it on the floor, pocketing the ring.

"Yo, the 'copter's 'bouta land!" Trevante said, having seen the helicopter through the windshield. It was whirring loudly as it hovered near the middle of the street.

"Alright," Diabolic said.

A few minutes later, the van came to a halt, five feet away from the helicopter. Trevante was the first to hop out of the vehicle, grabbing his AK-47. Diabolic was next. He slid open the side door of the van, and jumped down onto the middle of the street, pulling out the detonator to the explosive he'd planted against the wall inside the van. The police cars were closely behind him, sirens wailing, lights still flashing. Diabolic walked towards the helicopter, which Trevante had just climbed aboard. As he pulled up the antenna of his detonator, he narrowed his eyelids into slits, to stop the debris from getting into his eyes, as the helicopter's propeller was blowing trash all around from its spinning.

Seeing the police cars coming to a halt behind Diabolic, Trevante rose to his feet and took aim with his AK-47, bracing its stock against his shoulder blade. He pulled the trigger of the deadly weapon, and it rattled to life in his gloved hands, spitting hot fire. The jacketed bullets shattered the windshields of some of the police cars, and left holes in their hoods. Once his banana clip had been spent, Trevante reloaded and motioned for Diabolic to *come on.*

"Come on, man!" Trevante called out to him over the loud whirring of the helicopter's propeller. He then outstretched his hand for Diabolic to take it. Diabolic ran forward, and grasped his comrade's hand. Trevante pulled him inside of the helicopter, just as the police were jumping out of their vehicles and drawing their handguns from out of their black leather holsters.

"Take off, take off!" Trevante told the helicopter pilot, motioning with his hand. Instantly, the pilot took the bird up into the air. The police stood around the van. They pointed their handguns up at the helicopter and opened fire. Their bullets pinged and panged off the bottom of the bird. They also struck the aircraft's propellers, causing sparks to fly.

The helicopter was about twenty feet into the air when Diabolic peered down at the police. Some of them were firing the last of their bullets up at him, while others were reloading their handguns. Diabolic held up his detonator and waved goodbye to them, smiling devilishly behind his ski-mask. He pulled the button on the detonator, and the van exploded into flames and burning wreckage. The impact from the blast sent the police flying every which way.

The flames from the wreckage shone in Diabolic's pupils. He was still smiling devilishly because he got a kick out of putting it work. His eyelids narrowed, and he placed his right-hand above his brows, staring ahead. The very bright spot lights of a police helicopter was shining in on him.

"This is the police. Lower your bird to the..." the voice of the police helicopter's pilot came over the loud speaker, as the bird hovered in the air. He went on speaking, but his command fell on deaf ears, because Diabolic had stepped aside. As soon as he did, Trevante stepped up with a rocket launcher. He pressed the button that made its sighting pop up, and squinted, as he took aim at the police helicopter. The police helicopter pilot's eyes bulged, and his mouth dropped open when he saw the lethal weapon in the young criminal's hands. When he swung his aircraft around, Trevante pulled the trigger of the rocket launcher. The rocket ripped through the air, loud and threateningly, leaving smoke behind in its wake.

Ka-boom!

The police helicopter exploded into a cloud of black smoke and flames. Its burning remains rained down upon the streets below, along with its pilot's sooty, severed body parts.

A grinning Trevante lowered the rocket launcher, and took the time to look at his handiwork. He then dapped up Diabolic, and they sat down on their seats inside of the helicopter, lighting up a blunt and sharing it between them.

***

The night was cold and silent until the sound of a whirring propeller filled the air. Shortly thereafter, a helicopter made a gentle landing on the helipad. The pilot, a Caucasian man by the name of Jeffrey, killed the controls, and the propeller of the bird slowly came to a stop. As soon as it did, Jeffrey removed his headphones and pulled out a small vial of coke from his breast pocket. He removed its cap and tapped some of the powdery white substance on his hand, before totting it up his nose, and throwing his head back. With his eyelids shut, he snorted like a pig and licked his lips. A slight smirk emerged on his lips as he enjoyed the sensation that *The Girl* brought him. When he peeled his teary eyes open, his pupils moved to their corners and found Diabolic staring at him in utter disgust.

"You needa leave that shit alone, bruh. It's gonna turn yo' mind into fucking hamburger." Diabolic blew hot air and shook his head, as if to say, *you pitiful, mothafucka*. He and Trevante then grabbed their respective duffle bags and hopped out of the aircraft. The two of them were dressed in a fresh set of clothing. Their duffle bags contained the ski-masks and clothing they'd worn on their mission, as well as the guns they'd used. Diabolic and Trevante made their way toward a sexy, royal blue 2020 Ferrari F8 Tributo, which boasted peanut butter leather interior.

"Yeah, we made it safe and sound. How're thangz on your end? Everyone there and accounted for? Smooth. I'll holla at chu later! Out!" Diabolic took his finger from the ear-bud inside his ear. He'd just finished talking to one of the lieutenants of the troops that had massacred the entire ballroom.

Seeing Diabolic and Trevante were about to leave without paying him for his services, Jeffrey opened the door of the helicopter and stood up, looking over the windshield of the aircraft. "Heyyyy," Jeffrey called out to Diabolic, which made him stop and turn around, raising an eyebrow, like, *what's up?* "You didn't pay me!" said Jeffrey.

"Gon' pay the man," Diabolic told Trevante, before dumping his duffle bag into the hood of the Ferrari, which is where the trunk was actually located. Trevante approached Jeffrey, unzipping his duffle bag and dipping his hand inside it.

"I hope you brought cash 'cause I don't accept checks." Jeffrey snorted and pinched his reddened nose, which was starting to drip blood from all of his years of bumping coke. Feeling something wet on his upper lip, Jeffrey swiped his hand across it, and his fingers came away bloody. His brows furrowed, and he said: "What the fuck?" When he looked back up, he saw Trevante pulling out something short and black, with a silver silencer on its barrel. Instantly, Jeffrey's eyes bulged and his mouth dropped, stomach twisting in knots. He pleaded for his life, but by that time, he was already getting acquainted with some hot shit.

Choot, Choot, Choot!

The quiet bullets escaped the muzzle of the black handgun and entered Jeffrey's chest. He yelped as he fell to the ground, groaning in pain, face twisted in agony. A heartless Trevante walked up on him and gave him two more in his forehead, saying, "Keep the change." He then threw the murder weapon beside Jeffrey's body and walked back towards the Ferrari. The whip was idling, with Diabolic behind the wheel waiting. Trevante lifted up the passenger door and jumped into the front seat. Once he pulled the door down, the sporty vehicle sped off until its rear lights disappeared into the night.

Chapter 6

Shavon had successfully disarmed the alarm system to Onyx's baby mansion; she gave Latrell the thumbs up. Latrell went about the task of placing a glass-cutter against the window of the backdoor. He took his time carving a circle into the door's window glass, making a complete three-hundred-sixty degree turn. Carefully, Latrell pulled the glass-cutter from the window and removed the round piece of glass. He sat the glass-cutter aside on the ground, then motioned Shavon over to him. Once she'd come along, he snaked his arm inside of the hole in the window he created, and unlocked the door. Next, he pulled out his silenced handgun, and eased his way inside the house, with Shavon right behind him, gripping a shotgun.

Latrell and Shavon moved through the mansion cautiously, looking around and making sure there wasn't anyone in sight. The house was quiet, and the only light on was the one in the kitchen. The one inside the living room was out, and they were moving through it right then, hearing someone having sex upstairs, inside one of the bedrooms. Latrell led the way, making his way up the staircase, with Shavon creeping up the steps behind him. Together, they made their way down the hallway, with their guns leading the way.

***

Onyx was fucking Lyrica doggy-style on the bed, looking at himself in the mirror attached to the dresser. His eyes were fixed on her beautiful, pleasure-streaked face, with his jeweled hands gripping her shoulders firmly. Onxy was a six-foot-three nigga, with skin so black it looked purple, especially in the sunlight. His long, thick locs hung down his back and tickled his ass. He was clean-shaven, with big nostrils, and bigger lips. A platinum Cuban link chain hung down to his protruding belly. It held onto a tiger head medallion the size of a dinner plate. There were black diamonds in the eyes of the feline, and an even bigger black diamond clutched in its mouth. Onyx's wrists and fingers were dripping in platinum and black diamonds also.

Onyx breathed heavily as he pumped Lyrica from the back. Each time he thrust forward, his locs flew forward, and so did his Cuban chain. His pelvis collided with Lyrica's booty and made thunderous clapping sounds, and the smell of sweat and sex filled the atmosphere of the bedroom. Onyx slid his hands from little mama's shoulders, and palmed her behind with both hands. He then held Lyrica's ass cheeks apart. Looking down, he watched his thick, long dick going in and out of her gooey center.

"*Haa! Haa! Haa! Haa! Haa! Haa!*" Onxy breathed heavier as he lapped at her rear, hot sweat sliding down his face and dripping upon his nappy chest hairs. His fingers were molded onto Lyrica's buttocks as he pummeled away, causing that big old booty of hers to mash up and then return to form. Each time he crashed into her behind, her breasts jumped up and down on her chest. Big droplets of sweat fell from Onyx's brows and splashed on her back, as he moved forward and backward from her shaven sex lips. Lyrica squirmed and pulled at the sheets, balling them into her fists. Her face was balled up into a mask of euphoria, and her long cotton candy pink-colored hair matted onto her caramel face. Her sexual cries bounced off of the walls, and so did her fucker's grunts. The noises she made let him know that he was laying it down like a mothafucking boss!

"Uhn huh, me told ya me wuz gon' tear dis muddafuckin' pwussy up once me got it, right? Right?" Onyx talked cash money shit as he pounded away at Lyrica's rear end, sweat splashing on her back. *Smack!* "Ya hear me talkin' ta ya? Huh?" *Smack!* "When daddy talkin' ta ya, ya tawk back gatdammit!" *Smack!*

"Yes, yes, daddy! You told me, you told me. Now take this pussy, it's yours!" Lyrica whined as her pussy was getting beat up.

***

Latrell and Shavon placed their backs against the wall and crept down the corridor, holding their guns up at their shoulders. The closer they drew to the master bedroom, which was at the end of the hallway, the louder the sensual sound became. The hallway was dark, but the door of the master bedroom was wide open, its light shining out into the corridor.

Latrell stopped at the door of the master bedroom and poked his head inside the doorway. He found Onyx putting the pipe to Lyrica. Bubbles of sweat covered Onyx's face and his entire body. Some of the sweat dripped from his nose and he quickly wiped it away. Onyx was oblivious to the presence of Latrell and Shavon, and that's exactly how Latrell liked it. Latrell looked to Shavon and signaled to her that he was going in first, and for her to come in after him. Shavon nodded with a clear understanding of their roles in the plan. With a clear understanding of their roles, Latrell hunched over and crept inside of the master bedroom, gun held down at his side. As he made his way over to Onyx, the big man threw his head back with his eyelids shut, licking his lips and enjoying the sex he was in the throes of. When he brought his head back down and peeled his eyelids open, he saw a disguised Latrell in the mirror attached to the dresser before him. His eyes got as big as golf balls, and he said, "Oh, shit!" He went to dive for the chrome Desert Eagle .44 on the nightstand beside his bed, but before his hand could grasp it, Latrell sprung forward and clocked him upside the head.

Whack!

Onyx fell out of the bed onto the carpeted floor, wincing as he held the back of his head. He looked at his hand, and saw that the tips of his fingers were bloody. The little broad he was sexing screamed and scurried from off the bed, with the sheets held against her nakedness. Terror was in her eyes as she looked around the bedroom for somewhere to run. When her eyes landed on the bedroom's door, she dropped the sheet and went running toward it. She'd just reached the threshold, when Shavon popped up in the doorway, pointing her fat ass shotgun at her.

"Please, please, don't kill me!" Lyrica pleaded, with her trembling hands held high in the air. The tears in her eyes constantly poured down her face. Her heart thudded, as she wondered what was going to happen to her next.

"Shut up! *Shut your fucking mouth, right goddamn now!*" Shavon demanded, with murder bleeding from her pupils, as she spoke through clenched jaws, gripping her shotgun tighter. The threatening look in her eyes made Lyrica shut her mouth. She shut her eyelids briefly, as she swallowed the lump of fear in her throat and nodded. Lyrica continued to tremble, for fear of having her head blown off of her neck, but she didn't dare make a peep, for she knew that Shavon wasn't playing with her ass. "Good girl, now put your clothes on! Hurry the fuck up!" Shavon watched Lyrica closely as she hurriedly slipped on her bra and panties, and then the rest of her clothes. The young girl was slipping her clothing on so fast that she was putting some of it on backwards. This was because she was terrified that if she hadn't gotten dressed fast enough, Shavon would kill her.

"Do ya know—do ya know who ya jackin', huh?" a wincing Onyx asked, as he looked up at Latrell, from the floor, blood running down the middle of his back, from his head wound. Latrell picked the Desert Eagle up from off of the nightstand and tucked it on his waistline.

"Of course not, we just drew yo' name from outta fucking hat!" Latrell cocked his leg back and kicked Onyx in the stomach.

"Aaahh!" Onyx's eyes bulged and he grabbed his belly, squirming in pain. That kick had knocked the fucking wind out of him.

"What the fuck do you think? Yeah, I know yo' big, black ass!" Latrell told him. He stood over him with his handgun pointed down at him, threateningly. "Now get up on the bed, and lay spread-eagled, bitch!"

Onyx mad-dogged Latrell. He wanted to rush him, but he knew the odds were against him. He had him and his bitch to worry about. If one didn't put one in his ass, then the other one surely would. Angry, Onyx pulled himself up from off the floor, with the support of the bed. He then laid flat on his back, with his arms and legs stretched out. Once he'd done this, Latrell ordered Lyrica to tie his wrists and ankles to the posts of the bed. Lyrica rummaged through Onyx's dresser drawers until she found a pile of dress socks, which she used to tie him to the posts of the bed.

"Make sho' dem shits are good and tight on 'em too, yo' life depends on it!" Latrell told her. Once Lyrica was done, she took a step back, waiting for whatever was to come next.

"Now, where the money and the dope at?" Latrell asked him, still pointing his handgun at him. Onyx's eyes were focused on the black hole of the silencer which was attached to Latrell's gun's barrel. As he lay restrained in bed, he thought up ways to torture him and kill him, if he was to somehow get loose.

"It's in ya mudda's cunt, batty boy!" Onyx harped up mucus and spat at Latrell. The yellowish white goo splattered on his eyebrow and hung low to the floor, before eventually breaking off and landing on the carpet, by his sneaker. Seeing that Latrell was infuriated, Onyx threw his head back laughing maniacally. "Hahahahahahahahaha.!"

Onyx was a big time pill dealer that dealt in Molly and Xanax. He had a thing for swingers and sex parties. In fact, he threw the most lavishes sex parties in his neighborhood, where everyone—from weed peddlers to hot-shot attorneys and movie stars—attended. When Shavon used to turn tricks, he was one of her frequent customers and biggest tippers. She participated in orgies with him at several of the gatherings. Food, liquor, champagne, weed and cocaine were plentiful. One thing Shavon noticed about the rich people that attended Onyx's parties was that they loved cocaine. This was why Onyx made sure he had lots and lots of it whenever he threw one of his extravagant parties. He'd have the butt naked waitresses that worked the event serve sugar bowls of the shit to his guests. She recalled overhearing him brag to one of his guests that he kept at least ten birds on deck whenever he had a party. This was the knowledge that led Latrell and Shavon to Onyx's mansion tonight.

"Oh, you think shit is funny, huh? Well, here's where the laughing stops, asshole!" Shavon switched hands with the shotgun and propped her foot on the bed. She lifted the right leg of her jeans and revealed a sheathed hunting knife. She snatched the blade from out of its sheath, and a gleam swept up the length of it. A horrified Lyrica looked back and forth between Shavon and Onyx as she walked over to the side of the bed, placing her shotgun down on the nightstand. Shavon crawled into the bed with Onyx staring at her, wondering what kind of satanic thoughts were running rampant through her head.

"Wut—wut—wutta ya doin'? Huh?" A terrified Onyx looked down between his legs with beads of sweat running down his face. His heart thudded hard and he began breathing heavily. Shavon grabbed his flaccid penis and lifted it up, leaving his nut sack hanging. She then placed the tip of the knife at the entrance of Onyx's hairy asshole. The cold, sharp tip of the blade caused Onyx to jerk and lift his buttocks from off the bed. "Stop, stop, *stop! stop!*"

"If yo' chicken curry eating ass doesn't tell us where you keep that dope at, I'ma drag the knife from yo' asshole, up yo' sack, and leave it sitting in yo' belly. Now, get to talking, mothafucka!" Shavon demanded with a devilish look in her eyes. To let Onyx know that she wasn't bullshitting, she pressed the tip of her knife against his asshole and made a small bubble of blood to form. The bubble expanded until it eventually ran downward and disappeared in between his hairy butt cheeks.

Onyx's legs shook and urine threatened to spill from out of the pee-hole of his limp dick. He looked back and forth from the look in Shavon's eyes to the knife she held between his buttocks. He knew that she was as serious as cancer, and he'd better give up the whereabouts of that money and dope.

"Okay—okay—me tell you—me tell you," Onyx swallowed the lump of terror in his throat. He then went on to tell Shavon and Latrell where he had his money and dope stashed. "It's downstairs inside of me library, inna safe, unda da desk. Da combination is—" he went on to give up the combination to the safe.

"Good job, baby." Latrell walked over to Shavon and kissed her.

"Thank you, baby, I try." She smiled at him. Then he turned his scowling face back around to Onyx.

"I'ma go get this work. I'll be right back, hold it down fa me, lil' mama."

"You know I got cho back."

"And I got cho front, ma—always." Latrell dapped her up and bumped fists with Shavon. He then snatched the pillowcase from off one of the pillows on the bed, and left the master bedroom. When he returned he was ten birds and one-hundred thousand dollars richer.

"Was it all there, big poppa?" Shavon asked, when he entered the room, smiling behind the bandana covering the lower half of her face.

"And then some, lil' mama. Nigga hadda hunnit G-stacks in that bitch. Got us a nice lil' haul." Latrell cracked a fiendish smile as he held up the hefty pillowcase.

Latrell looked at Onyx, and for the first time, he noticed the icy jewelry around his neck, wrists and fingers. He then looked to Lyrica and ordered her to relieve Onyx of his drip. As soon as Lyrica approached him, Onyx turned his evil eyes in her direction, and clenched his jaws angrily.

"You fuckin' whore, you set me up!" Onyx said to her. He twisted and turned his body from left to right, trying to get free, so he could beat that little bitch to death.

"What!" Lyrica's eyes bulged. She couldn't believe he'd accuse her of setting him up for a lick.

"Yes, ya did! Me not stupid, bitch! Me sweah on me mudda's grave, if me live tru dis, me gon' cut cha heart out! Me promise ya dat!" Onyx harped up some more mucus and spat it at her, but she moved aside, and it missed her.

Lyrica broke down sobbing and crying, placing her hands to her face. She knew exactly how Onyx put it down. The man had a fierce reputation in Kingston, Jamaica; a reputation that followed him over into the United States. His level of violence was legendary, and even the roughest, toughest of gangstas bowed down to his G. So if he said he was going to cut her heart out, then he was literally going to do it. There wasn't any *ifs*, *ands*, or *buts* about it.

Shavon looked at Lyrica and shook her head. She then marched over to Onyx and slammed the butt of her shotgun down into his belly. The impact from the blow caused him to bend at the waist and cough violently. In fact, she struck the mothafucka so hard that a fart escaped his ass cheeks.

Shavon looked down at Onyx, watching him cough and look up at her with watering eyes. "From now on, you keep yo' goddamn mouth shut unless you're spoken to, Rasta man!" She then turned to Lyrica and said, "Now, relieve this dread of his jewels and shit! We don't have all fucking night!" She switched hands with the shotgun, and shoved Lyrica forward. Afraid that she'd be next, Lyrica removed Onyx's drip as fast as she could. Latrell held open his pillowcase for her to dump it all inside of it. Once she did, she went to stand back where she was before.

Latrell looked at Onyx, who was giving Lyrica the evil eye and gritting his teeth, flexing the bone structure in his face. He didn't know that Latrell was watching him as he mouthed verbal threats to her. A disheveled and crying Lyrica had her shivering hands together, silently pleading with him to spare her life.

"If you don't wanna worry about this nigga finding you and putting one in yo' head, then I suggest you get over here and handle yo' business," Latrell warned Lyrica with an authoritive voice. The sound of his voice startled Onyx and Lyrica. Lyrica looked to Latrell, who was pulling his handgun with the silencer on the tip of its barrel from off of his waistline. He motioned for her to come over to him. Right then, she knew what Latrell had in mind for her to do.

Lyrica wiped the dripping tears from her eyes and took a deep breath. She then walked over to Latrell, who ejected the magazine from out of the butt of his blower, leaving one in its head. Afterwards, he turned the silence gun over to her. Next, he stood behind her, teaching her how to hold the gun with both hands. Once Lyrica had leveled the gun up with Onyx's forehead, Latrell stepped away from her, watching her closely.

Onyx mad-dogged Lyrica from where he was bound in the bed. The vein on his temple pulsated, and his wide nostrils flared, his hairy chest rising and falling as he breathed. "Me see ya in hell, slut!" Those would be Onyx's final words. Lyrica pulled back on the trigger and a bullet ripped through the muzzle. A hole the size of a nickel appeared on Onyx's forehead and the back of his skull exploded, splattering brain fragments and chunks of bloody flesh against the headboard. Lyrica lowered the smoking gun and Latrell carefully took it from her. He tucked the gun back on his waistline. He then reached inside of the pillowcase and pulled out three stacks of blue face one-hundred dollar bills, which were all wrinkled.

"Here," Latrell extended the stacks of dead presidents out to her. Lyrica looked back and forth between him and the money, wondering if it was a trick. "I said 'here', take it!" he demanded of her. She took the money and grabbed her purse, stuffing all of the bills inside of it. "That money is yours to do with as you please. However, if I were you I'd change my lifestyle 'cause fucking with street niggaz will eventually put chu inna bad way. Now gon', get outta here!" His eyes followed her as she ran toward the door, but she turned back once he called after her. She looked at him like she hoped he didn't change his mind and was going to kill her. "That gun you used to pop this dread, I'ma hold on to it. So, if you think about running yo' mouth about what occurred here tonight, you'll go down as the sole killa. And if you think you're gonna take yo' chances and try to prove that it wasn't just you here—remember one thang, lil' mama, we know what you look like, but you don't know what we look like. You got that?"

"Yes—yes, I got it. And you won't have to worry about me saying anything. I'm going to think of this as one big nightmare, and put it all behind me," Lyrica swore to him, sniffling and wiping the wetness from her eyes.

"Good girl," Latrell said. He waved her on, and she hurried out of the master bedroom. He turned to Shavon, who sheathed her knife, and grabbed her shotgun from off the nightstand. "Let's get the fuck outta here."

Tranay Adams

Chapter 7

The game room inside of Baby Boy's mansion was dimly lit. Its walls were lined with portraits of legendary athletes. And in all four corners of the room there were glass display cases with sports memorabilia on each of their four shelves. In addition to that, there was a bar at the center of the room, with everything you could think of drinking lining the shelves behind it. There were also arcades off to the side of the room, across from the bathroom. There was Mrs. Pac-Man, Mortal Kombat, Street Fighter II, Streets of Rage, and Golden Axe. Baby Boy even had a glow in the dark pool table with colorful balls. As of right now, he was taking the occasional sip of cognac, walking around the pool table, and plotting on the next shot he was going to take. While he was preoccupied, breaking news came on the "65 flat-screen television mounted on the wall. He stopped in his tracks and took another sip, as he watched the scene that Diabolic and his crew created during their murder of Montray and his family at his niece's wedding. A devilish smirk curled the corner of Baby Boy's lips.

"The son of a bitch pulled it off," Baby Boy said to no one in particular. He watched a little more of the broadcast, before taking another sip of his drink and sitting it down at the end of the pool table. He then leaned over the pool table to take his next shot, teasing the Q-ball with the tip of his stick. He jabbed the pool stick at the white ball three times, coming close to hitting it, before finally striking it. The pool stick struck the Q-ball, and it collided with a striped orange ball.

Brack!

The ball dropped inside of the leather corner pocket. Baby Boy took a few more shots, knocking all of the balls into the pockets he'd set his sights on. He took another sip of cognac before picking up the small blue cube, and using it to sharpen the tip of his pool stick. Once he sat the blue cube down at the end of the pool table, he leaned over the table to take another shot. Again, he teased the Q-ball with the tip of his stick. Baby Boy was about to take his shot, when he heard a knock at the doorway. When he looked up, he saw the silhouette of a man. Right then, he stood upright. The man approached him, revealing more and more of himself until he was in full view. It was Diabolic.

Diabolic tossed Baby Boy something, and he caught it in his palm, balling his fingers around it. When he looked down and opened his fist, he saw Montray's icy gold ring with the spinning *M*. That's when he realized that the kingpin was dead.

"Does this belong to who I think it belongs to?" Baby Boy asked him, as he laid his pool stick down on top of the pool table, walking around the table to meet his brother.

Diabolic nodded as Baby Boy advanced in his direction. He wore a dead serious expression on his face, and an air of accomplishment surrounded him. Baby Boy hurriedly walked over to Diabolic, with his arms open for an embrace. He wrapped his arms tightly around his older brother, who wrapped his arms around him, too. Baby Boy broke down sobbing and crying, teardrops falling from the brims of his eyes. As he continued to sob, his body quaked, and Diabolic comforted him. He squeezed him in his arms tighter, and spoke into his ear.

"I got that mothafucka, bro—I got that mothafucka for us, for pops," a teary-eyed Diabolic said, before kissing Baby Boy on the cheek. "He can finally rest in peace now."

Baby Boy stared over Diabolic's shoulder with teardrops continuing to fall from his eyes. The trifling mothafucka even had the nerve to have a wicked smile etched on his face. He was one scandalous ass nigga, and he didn't give a fuck about anyone but himself.

Now, that I know fa sho' Montray is outta the way, I've gotta work on getting rid of yo' punk-ass.

"Ahem!"

Baby Boy and Diabolic broke their embrace after hearing someone clear their throat at the door. They wiped their tear streaked faces with the back of their hands, and the collars of their shirts. When they looked to the doorway, they found Trevante there.

"You didn't tell me you brought someone back witchu," Baby Boy said to Diabolic, looking back and forth between him and Trevante.

"My bad—but, yeah, I brought lil' homie along—I'm sure you'd wanna congratulate him personally for the good job he did tonight—My young nigga handled his business—Come here, Trevante," a prideful Diabolic said, as he extended his arm out toward Trevante, who was approaching him. Diabolic had handpicked Trevante out of a litter of pups himself. He saw great potential in the young street nigga, and he knew he'd be an asset to their organization, which was why he brought him in out of the cold. Trevante had become like a little brother to Diabolic, and he treated him as such. The two of them had been as thick as thieves since the youngster was fourteen.

Diabolic threw his arm around Trevante's shoulders and ruffled his head. He then shoved him back playfully, and they threw phantom punches at each another, horsing around like siblings do, laughing. Afterwards, Diabolic told Baby Boy how Trevante blew the police helicopter out of the sky that night, and how he handled the cokehead helicopter pilot. Having heard the news of how Trevante got down for him, Baby Boy gripped his shoulders with both hands, and looked him square in his eyes.

"I'm proud of you, young nigga. You went out there and you handled your business like a mothafucking man is supposed to." Baby Boy spoke to Trevante with serious, glassy eyes. "You made your bones, so that makes you officially a part of this family. And family takes care of family, you hear me?"

"Yeah, I hear you." Trevante nodded. He was looking serious as hell, too. Both of the young nigga's family was strung-out on dope, so his grandmother raised him. She was the only family he had until she died, and he ended up a ward of the state. Trevante ran away from the group home, and dove head first into the street life. He did whatever he had to do to eat. It didn't matter what it was. If it was going to put food in his belly and keep a roof over his head, then he was with it.

It was safe to say that Trevante didn't know what family was. It wasn't until he started rolling with Diabolic and his goons that he got a taste of what it was like, to have people that actually loved and cared about him. As soon as he got down with the family, Diabolic saw to it that he got a fully furnished apartment, a wardrobe of clothes, shoes and his own whip. All of his birthdays and holidays, he celebrated with Diabolic and his family. They showed him mad love, and he in return gave him his undying loyalty.

"Now, listen, bro was telling me about a lil' financial situation you were having," Baby Boy said to Trevante.

"Yeah, I'm tryna buy my girl a new car and droppa down payment on this crib I saw up in Ladera Heights before the baby comes."

"You did yo' thang tonight, so I'ma bless you."

Trevante looked back and forth between Baby Boy and his brother, smiling. "You gon' look out for real?"

"Yeah," a grinning Baby Boy assured him. "Like I said, you're family. And family looks out for family. Besides, kid, you earned it." He patted Trevante on his cheek like one of those old Italian mafia bosses do in the movies. Right then, Baby Boy's forehead creased, as heard a funny sound coming from Trevante. He narrowed his eyelids before looking down at his stomach and then back up into Baby Boy's face.

"My bad. That's my stomach. A nigga hungry as a mothafucka." Trevante smirked as he held his hand to his stomach. When his stomach growled, it sounded more like a fart; so he was a little embarrassed.

"Well, I'ma take care of that. Come on." Baby Boy threw his arm around Trevante's shoulders, leading him out of the room. "What would you like to eat? I'ma have my chef whip it up for us; my guy's a fool with those pots and pans."

"Mannn, it doesn't even matter. I'll putta hurting on anythang right about now. You feel me?" Trevante spoke truthfully. The young nigga had never met a meal he didn't like.

"Alright then, I've got just the thang for you to try," Baby Boy said as he, Diabolic, and Trevante disappeared through the doorway.

Baby Boy had his chef prepare smoked salmon, Spanish rice, and corn on the cob for dinner that night. For dessert they had slices of German chocolate cake. Afterwards, they indulged in Cuban cigars and sipped Louis XIII. They shot the shit about everything, from women to sports. It wasn't long before Diabolic was nodding off at the table. Baby Boy and Trevante got a really good laugh at his expense, hearing him snore like a pig and drool like a mentally challenged person.

Trevante switched hands with his cigar before leaning over and shaking Diabolic awake. "Say, bruh, wake yo' ass up!"

Diabolic looked around through narrowed eyelids and a scrunched up face. "Aaahhhhhh!" He threw his head back and raised his arms over his head, stretching. He looked down at his shirt. His face balled up with disappointment, when he saw that he'd burned holes in his shirt when he'd fallen asleep with the cigar in his hand. "Ah, fuck, man! This a five hunnit dollar shirt." He brushed the half smoked cigar and grayish black ashes from off his lap before rising to his feet. He continued to brush off his lap until all of the ashes were gone. Next, he picked up his glass of cognac and downed it, frowning as he swallowed the strong liquor. "Yo', you ready to slide yet?" he asked once he'd tapped Trevante to get his attention.

"Yeah, we can roll out," Trevante said as he mashed out his cigar, snuffing out its ember inside the ashtray. He then tucked the cigar behind his ear. Rising to his feet, he picked up his plate and glass to take them over to the sink. He was heading to the kitchen sink, but Baby Boy lifted his hand and stopped him.

"Don't worry about this. My maid will take care of it. It's all good." Baby Boy assured him as he sucked on the end of his cigar, making smoke swarm around him.

"You sure?" Trevante asked, still holding the plate and glass.

"Positive," Baby Boy replied, watching him sit the dishes back down on the table.

"Well, thanks for the meal and the hospitality. I really appreciate it." Trevante extended his hand. Baby Boy switched hands with his cigar and shook his hand firmly.

"Don't mention it. Look, lemme bestow that blessing upon you before you head out."

"Uhhhh," Trevante looked back at Diabolic and saw him yawning again. The nigga looked exhausted. "How about I come by and get it another time. The homie tired, and I don't wanna keep 'em from his bed any longer."

"Nonsense," Baby Boy said as he rose to his feet and mashed out the ember of his cigar into the plate of food he'd been eating from. At this time, the maid emerged and began clearing the table in the midst of them talking. "Bro can wait outside in the car. It won't take butta minute."

"Yeah, bruh, gon' and get that paypa—I'ma chill in the car 'til you come out," a sleepy eyed Diabolic told him, with a pat on his shoulder, before he made his way from out of the kitchen.

"Come on," Baby Boy motioned for Trevante to follow him, as he headed out of the kitchen. Trevante followed right behind him.

***

Trevante followed Baby Boy inside his study. He posted up beside his desk, watching Baby Boy sit down in his executive chair and pull out the top drawer of his desk. From it, he removed a check book and a golden ink pen. Trevante watched as he opened his check book and began jotting. Baby Boy then tore out the check and handed it to the young nigga, leaning back in his chair and closing his ink pen. He then crossed his legs and interlocked his fingers, resting hands on his kneecap. A slight smirk was on his face as he watched Trevante hold the check between his hands. The youngsta looked back and forth between Baby Boy and the check, with widened eyes. He couldn't believe the dough that Baby Boy had hit him with.

Trevante scratched the side of his head as he held the check. "You sure this isn't a mistake? I mean, this is a lotta gwap."

"Notta mistake at all," Baby Boy assured him, taking the liberty to fire up another Cuban cigar, and blow smoke up into the air. "Like I told you before, my young nigga, 'family takes care of family'."

"Aye, listen," Trevante began, pinching his nose, "I'ma pay this back as soon as I can. So don't even—"

Baby Boy threw up his hand, which stopped Trevante from talking. "How about you do a lil' something, something for me, and we call it even?" Trevante raised an eyebrow, looking at Baby Boy. He hoped that he wasn't trying to get him to do any homosexual acts for the money he'd just given him. Baby Boy chuckled, and blew a smoke ring into the air. "I've never been on no gay shit, my boy. I love pussy too much."

Trevante sighed with relief and wiped imaginary sweat from his brow. "My fault."

"It's all good."

"Well, what were you getting at?"

"I need you to take a nigga off the shelf, if you know what I mean?"

"You mean?" Trevante made his hand into the shape of a gun.

"Exactly."

"Who do you have in mind?"

With the question posed, Baby Boy turned around the framed portrait on the desk top toward Trevante. It was a photograph of him, his parents and Diabolic. The only ones alive in the picture were Baby Boy and Diabolic. So Trevante knew that Baby Boy meant for him to split Diabolic's wig. Trevante looked into Baby Boy's eyes, trying to see if he was reading him correctly or not. Baby Boy had a dead serious look written across his face, so he knew he was being straight up.

Trevante was at a loss for words. He felt awkward as hell. He hated Baby Boy had put him in this position. There was no way that he could see himself popping Diabolic for any amount of money. He had mad love for that nigga. The way he looked at it, if it wasn't for Diabolic, he'd still be that little dirty ass nigga with the nappy locs, nickel-and-dime hustling.

This nigga look dead-ass serious, but he's gotta be pulling my chain. This has gotta be a test, or some shit. That's it! He's tryna see how deep my loyalty runs, Trevante thought as he stood before Baby Boy's desk with the check still in his hand.

Suddenly, Trevante smiled and pointed a finger at Baby Boy. "You're fucking with me, right? This a lil' jokey joke?"

Right then, Baby Boy looked at Trevante, like, *Nigga, you must really think I'm playing.* He sat his burning cigar down in the ashtray on his desk top and pulled out the second drawer of his desk. Trevante watched as he pulled out a chrome .45 automatic handgun, and a black silencer. He screwed the silencer onto the tip of the gun. Next, he whipped out a handkerchief and used it to clean his fingerprints off the pistol before laying it down on the desk top.

Baby Boy picked up his cigar and took another pull from the end of it. Once he blew out the smoke, he began to talk again, "No jokes. No games. I'm not playing.You have him take you somewhere secluded and put a bullet in his brain, and the money is yours to keep. You know what? Fuck it! I'll throw in one-hundred gees. I know you got mad love for my brotha, so let's call that a lil' incentive." Baby Boy continued to smoke his cigar as he waited for Trevante's response. He could tell by the look on the youngsta's face that he was thinking it over. He only had to hope that the youth's greed would override his loyalty, and he'd carry out the hit.

Trevante took another look at the check in his hands, and took a deep breath. He was holding a lot of money in his hands. And Baby Boy was offering even more if he was to knock Diabolic's head off his shoulders. Still, Trevante would rather commit suicide then betray his friend. He knew niggaz that would splash their mother's head for the grips Baby Boy was putting up for Diabolic's hit. But he couldn't bring himself to do it; niggaz like him didn't get down like that.

Trevante walked up to Baby Boy's desk. And to his displeasure, the young nigga placed the check he'd written him on the desk top and slid it before him. A disappointed look came across Baby Boy's face right then. He knew that by Trevante refusing his money, he'd just created another problem that he'd eventually have to take care of.

"I'll have to respectfully decline your offer," Trevante told him, straight up. "Yo' brotha is as good as blood in my eyes. He's like family. I couldn't live with myself if I was the one behind the trigger that presented him with his demise."

Baby Boy mashed out his cigar in the ashtray as he watched Trevante head toward the door. Suddenly, Baby Boy threw his head back, laughing heartily and clapping his hands. His actions caused Trevante's face to frown up, and he turned around. He saw Baby Boy doubled over laughing with one hand on his stomach, while his other hand smacked his desk top, hysterically. Trevante's face frowned up further, wondering what was so funny.

"What's so funny?" Trevante inquired.

"You—you fell for it, man," Baby Boy brought his head back up, wiping the teardrop of laughter that threatened to fall from his right eye. "You really thought I was finna have you knock off big bro? Dawg, I was totally fucking witchu. You shoulda—you shoulda seen your face." He chuckled, and looked to Trevante who'd managed a weak smile.

"Yeah, you got me. You looked convincing as a mothafucka. That moment was awkward as hell." Smiling, Trevante was relieved. He had planned on telling Diabolic what had happened, as soon as he dropped him off at the house. Next, he was going to pack him and his girl's shit, and they were going to get on the first thing smoking out of Cali. Trevante was aware that the bomb he'd drop on Diabolic would surely cause a war between he and his brother. And if that happened, he knew without a shadow of a doubt Baby Boy would send some head hunters after him. Now don't get it fucked up! The little homie would bust his gun. He was a gangsta's gangsta. But what really was his one gun going to do against an entire fucking army of niggaz who were about that life? He was a G, but the streets didn't raise a fool.

After having calmed down from his laughter, Baby Boy picked up the .45 automatic handgun from off his desk top, and screwed the black silencer from off its tip. He put the gun and the silencer back inside the drawer and pushed it shut. He then picked up the check he'd written and walked over to Trevante, handing it to him. Baby Boy threw his arm around Trevante's shoulders and walked him toward the door.

Grinning, Baby Boy said, "That's all yours, baby boy. Don't even worry about shooting that back to me, all right?"

"Are you sho'?" Trevante asked, looking up from the check.

"Yeah. Remember what I said?" Baby Boy raised an eyebrow questioningly.

"Family takes care of family."

Baby Boy chuckled and then smiled, stopping at the door. "That's right. Take it easy."

"You too, and thanks again." Trevante slapped hands with Baby Boy and embraced him. He then walked out of the study, making his way down the corridor.

Baby Boy leaned up against the doorway, with his arms folded across his chest, watching him. The smile that was just on his face disappeared once Trevante was out of his sight. His face balled up with anger and he rushed back inside of his study, pulling out his top desk drawer. Baby Boy pulled out his burn-out cellular phone, and switched the SIM card with another cell phone that he had on deck. He powered the device on and dialed up a contact of his.

"Detective Breedlove," Baby Boy greeted his contact as soon as he picked up. "I needa favor . . ."

Chapter 8

"Home sweet home," Diabolic said to Trevante as they sat in the underground parking level of his condo. Trevante lived in a black high-rise building in downtown Los Angeles on 3rd and Vermont. They were idling just outside the entrance of the tenement. In fact, Diabolic could see through the front glass windows of the dwelling. Although the complex was composed of condominiums, its lobby was dressed up like a very exquisite hotel. There was a snazzy dressed clerk at the front desk. He was a tall Caucasian fellow, who wore glasses. His hair was shaved on the sides and slicked to the left, with a part on the right side. The burgundy blazer he was in hung loosely off of his wiry frame. Right then, he was in the middle of calling up a tenant, to let them know they had a visitor downstairs for them.

"Alright, my nigga, I'ma gon' and get upstairs to my family and shit," Trevante told Diabolic. He then switched hands with the bouquet of roses he'd bought for his lady, and dapped him up. "Love you, fool."

"Love you, too, big dawg." Diabolic tapped his fist to his chest. "Tell wifey I said, what up?"

"Fa sho'," Trevante said, as he stood outside the foreign vehicle, holding the door up. He shut the door and knocked on its roof, signaling for Diabolic to pull off, which he did. The glass double doors of the building parted as Trevante made his way toward them, pulling out his keys to his spot. "What's up, Niv?" he hollered at the clerk standing behind the desk. Niv, who was still on the telephone, glanced up with a smile, and gave him a slight wave of his hand. Niv seemed like a straitlaced white dude, but that couldn't be further from the truth. The truth was, he'd recently gotten out of federal prison after serving time for credit card fraud. His aunt and uncle owned the condominiums, so that's how he was able to get his foot in the door for the position he held. Niv was mad cool! On his breaks he'd come up to Trevante and his girl's crib to blow trees and play Madden.

Trevante switched hands with the bouquet of roses, and pressed the up button for the elevator. There was an instant *ding,* and the doors of the elevator opened. Trevante made his way inside the elevator, and held the door open for the man that was waiting at the desk while Niv was on the telephone. The man gave Trevante a slight smile and a nod, as he entered. He pressed the button to the floor he was going to and Trevante pressed the button to his floor. The double doors pulled shut, and the elevator ascended.

***

Trevante walked inside his condo and shut the door behind him. Outstretching his arms, he said, "Honey, I'm home!" His voice resounded. A moment later, his pregnant fiancée, Jada, came waddling from out of their bedroom, with a manicured hand on her protruding belly. She boasted a small gapped-tooth smile that seemed to grow wider and wider the closer she got to the love of her life. Jada was a light-skinned number, with bleach-blonde locs that tickled her shoulders and back as she walked. She had a diamond stud nose piercing in her right nostril, and a white-gold, 5 karat engagement ring on her right ring finger. *Trevante* was inked on the side of her neck. Jada was wearing a yellow sundress with flowers on it, which showed off her roundabout stomach and ample ass.

"Hey, handsome," Jada greeted her man.

"Hey, beautiful, I got cha something." Trevante smiled as he handed her the roses.

"Awww, thank you, baby . . . they're beautiful," Jada said before shutting her eyelids and inhaling the scent of the lovely roses.

"You're welcome, baby."

"Lemme put 'em in some water." Jada headed inside the kitchen, rocking from side to side. She retrieved a clear, glass flower vase from underneath the kitchen cabinet and filled it halfway with water. She then placed the roses inside the vase, and spread them out to her liking. Afterwards, she made her way across the kitchen floor, bypassing the refrigerator, which had pictures of them at various locations, with refrigerator magnets stuck to them. Jada made a place at the center of the kitchen table for the vase. She then took a step back from the table, placing her hands on her hips, admiring the vase of roses, with a smile plastered across her face. While she was doing this, Trevante came from behind her, wrapping his arms around her, staring at the roses, with his chin resting on her shoulder.

"Mmmmm," Trevante said, with his eyelids shut briefly, taking in Jada's scent. "You smell good, boo." He swept her locs away from her neck and inhaled the fragrance expelling from her. "What chu got on, babe?"

"Guilty Gucci," she replied with a smile, enjoying the delicate kisses he placed on her shoulder and the nape of her neck, as he rocked her from side to side.

"Shit smell bomb as fuck," he said, kissing her behind her ear, and then nibbling on her neck.

"Stop, babe, before you get something started." She smiled harder.

"What, you aren't ready for that?" He lifted his head back up, wearing a smirk at the corner of his lips.

"Oh, I'm always ready, boo. And from the feel of it, you are, too." She looked over her shoulder at him, feeling his hardened dick pressed up against her booty.

"My bad. That's my strap." He pulled out his handgun, which was tucked in the front of his jeans, and laid it down on the kitchen table. He then kissed softly on her neck. She grabbed his strong, masculine hands, and placed them on her protruding belly. She then shut her eyelids and basked in his affection.

Jada gasped, feeling her pussy getting wet from Trevante's touch. While kissing her neck, he kept one hand on her belly, and used the other to dip underneath her dress. She had gone commando, so the tiny hairs on her vagina felt like peach fuzz. Trevante curled his middle finger inside of her hot, moist pussy, making sure to coat it with her natural juices. He then coated his index finger and used them both to massage the small flap of meat nestled between her pussy lips. Turned on, Jada moaned sensually. She began groping her breasts and grinding up against him. Again, she could feel his hardness pressed up against her buttocks.

"Babe—Baby," Jada called out to Trevante as she breathed heavily.

"Huh?" Trevante said between the kisses he was placing against her spine. He was slowly moving down her back, taking his time. He wanted her so aroused that she couldn't take it anymore, and she started begging for the dick.

"Is that—is that another gun?"Jada asked, as she rubbed the back of his head with one hand. She then propped her bare foot upon the kitchen table, so he'd have little trouble pleasuring the petals of her delicate flower.

"Nah, baby, that's all me!" Trevante swore. Right then, his jeans dropped in a pile around his ankles, exposing his hairy buttocks and his fat, vein-riddled dick. His shit was so hard that it was throbbing. A clear fluid and something white oozed out of his pee-hole, and threatened to drip to the floor.

Jada reached around and grabbed Trevante's dick. Its width, accompanied by its thick veins, drove her wild. She wanted him inside of her, real deep inside of her. Lately, he'd been treating her like she was fragile, when it came to their sex. She could tell that he was making love to her. Yes, it was good. But tonight she didn't want that. Nah! She wanted to be fucked like a no good, dirty, trifling whore.

"I want chu, daddy! I want chu so fucking bad!" Jada told him over her shoulder. She pulled his head around, and they kissed hungrily. You could hear the saliva swishing around inside of their mouths as they French-kissed long, deep and lustfully. Jada sucked on Trevante's tongue as if it was a dick. She then sucked on his bottom lip, and pulled on it gently with her teeth, before going back to kissing him again. "I want that dick in me, Trevante! I want chu to long stroke this pussy, you hear me, baby?"

"Yes!" he responded as he pulled back from her and slipped his shirt from over his head, tossing it aside on the kitchen floor.

His five-foot-nine stature was defined by muscles, and covered in tattoos. Quickly, he pulled off his Jordans and removed his jeans from around his ankles. He was now as naked as the day he'd been pushed out from between his mother's legs. The only thing he had on was socks.

"Bend me over, Trevante—Bend me over this kitchen table and fuck the shit outta me! Right now, right goddamn now!" Jada commanded. Trevante granted her wish. Taking charge, he forcefully bent her over the kitchen table, and hiked up her sundress. Jada spread her legs apart and tooted her ass up in the air. Trevante spat in his palm and used his saliva to lubricate his dick, stroking it up and down. Looking down at Jada's pussy, he could see her pinky entrance. Using his thumb, he guided himself inside her inviting opening. An icy chill slid down his back as he felt her gooey hole. She fit him like a catcher's mitt, and she was warm. It was as though someone had taken a part of the sun and placed it at the bottom of her pussy.

Trevante grabbed Jada's meaty buttocks and spread them apart. Staring downward, he pushed and pulled himself in and out of her. He watched his dick disappear and then reappear with each and every thrust.

"Harder, babe, *harder!*" Jada demanded, with her hands planted firmly on the kitchen table. Her eyelids were shut, and her blonde locs were bouncing up and down each time Trevante collided with her from behind.

With the order having been given, Trevante, with his dick still inside of Jada, forced her with the side of her face down on the kitchen table. He placed her hands behind her back, holding them in one hand. He then started lapping her from the back, sending ripples up her ass every time his nappy pubic region crashed into her behind. Trevante's face was twisted into a scowl, and his jaws were locked. His face and form shined from perspiration, as he fucked Jada like a savage.

"Uh, uh, uh, uh, uh!" Jada hollered aloud, eyes rolled to their whites, mouth hanging wide open. Trevante was giving her that long dick action, like only he could. There was a loud clapping sound whenever their wet flesh connected. Beads of sweat oozed out of Trevante's pores and ran down his face and back, disappearing in between the crack of his ass cheeks. "Uh, uh, uh, uh, uh!" Jada continued to holler aloud. Trevante was slamming into her so hard that the table was backing up and making screeching noises across the floor. The glass vase containing the roses fell over, spilling water which dripped on the floor. Next, one of the chairs toppled over.

Sweat trickled from the corner of Trevante's brow and splashed like raindrops on Jada's buttocks. Swiftly, he wiped his forehead with the back of his hand, and kept at it, fucking her like a mad man.

"You wanted to get fucked hard, huh? You wanted to get fucked hard?" Trevante said through clenched jaws.

"Oh, god, yes, *yes!*" Jada admitted.

Trevante released her hands from behind her back. He then grabbed a fistful of her locs and pulled her head back. He pounded her from the back violently, while holding her hair and occasionally smacking her ass. She cried for more, enjoying the pain and pleasure he was dishing to her.

"This yo' pussy, babe! It's yours, it's all yours!" she swore.

Trevante threw his head back as he continued to put in work. He felt his nuts swelling, and he knew he was about to bust, but he was trying to hold out because the pussy was fire. Realizing he was fighting a losing battle, Trevante announced that he was about to cum. He kept long stroking Jada from the back until the last minute. Abruptly, he pulled himself out of Jada, and pumped his dick up and down. She looked over her shoulder at him, licking her top lip and twerking that bodacious ass of hers.

"Awwwww, fuck! Here I cum! Here I—fucking—cum!" Trevante called out, as his eyelids fluttered and he jacked his dick. He grunted. Then, warm string after warm string of semen erupted from out of his pee-hole, and painted Jada's ass cheeks. An exhausted Trevante laid his sweaty face and body down against Jada's back. His eyelids were narrowed into slits as he breathed huskily. A smile was stretched across Jada's face. Her husband-to-be had put on one hell of a performance and satisfied her.

"Babe?" Jada called out to Trevante.

"Yeah," Trevante replied, still lying against her.

"That's shit was fire, right?"

"That shit was all that, lil' mama, my baby got some good pussy."

"And my boo got some good dick. Now, gemme kiss." She looked over her shoulder and he lifted his head. They kissed again.

Trevante helped Jada out of her sundress, and they headed inside the bathroom. They turned the shower on, and adjusted the temperature to their liking. They then climbed inside the tub and took turns soaping each other up with a loofah. They kissed under the spray of the water and allowed the hot liquid to rinse the suds off their bodies, the suds disappearing by degrees down the drain. Their kissing eventually turned into sucking, and then fucking. Once they came again, they washed up and dried off outside the tub.

**

Quantavious sat at the bar hunched over a glass of Hennessy. He was a tall, caramel-skinned man with light brown hazel green eyes. His short locs spilled out from underneath his powder blue Tennessee Titans cap. He had a cross inked between his eyes, and three teardrops leading down his left cheek. His slender frame was draped in a matching Titans football jersey, which showcased his tattooed arms. A gold cable hung around his neck, and was attached to an icy capital Q. An icy gold Rolex of coruscating brilliance hung around his wrist.

Quantavious was in deep thought as he nursed his drink, taking the occasional sip of his alcohol beverage. He was stressed out as a mothafucka, which explained why he was only twenty-seven-years-old and already growing gray hairs. No matter how many times he plucked the grays out of his mustache and chin hair, they'd grow right back. On top of that, his hair was falling out. A bald spot was quickly expanding at the back of his head, and his hairline was receding. This was why he'd made it his business to always rock a baseball cap, hat, or beanie of some sort.

Quantavious had also lost forty pounds in the last two weeks, taking him from a solid two hundred and ten pounds to a measly one hundred and seventy. He'd inherited black rings around his eyes, and his eyes had become sunken in, giving him the resemblance of a zombie. The people he knew from around the way swore to God he was fucking with that *Girl*, but his homies and his relatives knew better. Quantavious may blow a little weed here and there, but he damn sure wasn't playing with his nose. You know, fucking around with that nose candy, snorting it to get high.

Quantavious had a very good reason to be as worried as he was. As a teenage boy he'd developed the taste for underage flesh. He'd molested his three and five-year-old female cousins, and a few girls half his age around his neighborhood, but his father, who was a Supreme Court judge, was able to grease the palms of the parents to keep things quiet. His old man believed that his boy would grow out of his sick addiction; but, unfortunately, he was sadly mistaken. Quantavious never stopped his despicable acts, and his old man always managed to sweep his disgusting deeds under the rug. But this time, his old man wouldn't be alive to pull his ass from out of the fire, since he'd died from colon cancer.

Although Quantavious came from a well-off family, he had always been intrigued by the street life, which was why he dove into the game head-first. He was inducted into the life by Keyonte. They robbed niggaz together. Overtime, the bond between them grew considerably. They became best friends. Keyonte loved and trusted Quantavious like a brother. Which was why, when he was sentenced to fifteen years flat for a body, he entrusted Quantavious with taking care of his family. Big mistake!

Once Keyonte was out of the picture, Quantavious didn't waste any time getting his baby momma hooked on heroin. He made sure she got as much dope as she desired. That way, he was free to do with ten-year-old Isis as he pleased. The sick bastard ended up getting her pregnant. And when DCFS found out, they snatched Isis up, and threw her mother in jail. Now, with a warrant for his arrest, Quantavious was on the run. Moreover, word was out that Keyonte had heard about his erstwhile friend molesting his daughter, and had put a bag on his head.

Quantavious hated himself for not being able to control his sexual cravings for young girls. He knew that if he had been able to keep his dick in his pants, he wouldn't have been in his current situation. But it was far too late to take things back now. He'd have to deal with it. He not only had to worry about the law, but a killa coming for his ass as well. Quantavious wasn't a bitch. He stayed strapped. But he knew he'd have better chances staying alive if he had a couple of hittaz watching his back while he moved through the streets. That was why he hired two of the baddest, gun-toting mothafuckaz from the eastside of Long Beach to watch his back. The hittaz were brothers that had just gotten out of jail from fighting homicide charges, and they needed the capital to keep their heads above water, since no one was trying to employ a couple of niggaz suspected of murder. Having them around made Quantavious feel a little better, but not too much. For some reason, he couldn't shake the feeling that he was living on borrowed time.

Quantavious swallowed what was left of his drink and sat the glass back down on the bar top. The bartender went to refill his glass, but he smacked his hand over the top of it. He held up his left hand and shook his head, letting him know that he was good.

"I've hadda 'nough, OG," Quantavious told the graying-haired bartender. "One more drink, and my chaperones will have to have me carried out of here onna fuckin' gurney."

"Alright—Lemme get that tab for you," Nigel told him, before smacking the bar top and walking away. He was an older man that rocked a small afro, and didn't have a hair out of place. He was dressed in a white button-up shirt, black tie, and black vest. His sleeves were rolled up, which allowed his old gold watch to be seen. The old man walked with a slight limp since he'd gotten crippled in a shoot-out that had taken place inside the bar some time ago.

Once Nigel had disappeared, Quantavious pulled out a Newport and stuck it between his lips. He then pulled out a lighter and tried to strike a flame to light the tip of his cigarette, but the damn thing wouldn't ignite. He shook it up and tried again, but to no avail. Right then, one of his bodyguards, who was sitting on the stool to the right of him, tapped his shoulder. When he turned to him, the bodyguard lit his square with his trusty Zippo-lighter, then flicked it shut.

"Good lookin' out, my nigga Poobs." Quantavious thanked him, and got a nod in return. Nigel reappeared and dropped the receipt for all of his drinks on the bar top. Quantavious switched hands with the cigarette and picked up the receipt. He then pulled a knot of dead presidents from out of his pocket and peeled off a one-hundred-dollar bill. He passed it to Nigel and told him to keep the change, for which the old head thanked him. Nigel went on about his business, and he stuffed the knot of white men back inside his pocket.

Quantavious took the time to smoke his Newport, blowing out smoke clouds into the air. He looked up into the wall-length mirror behind the bar, and noticed the slight outlining of the bullet-proof vest underneath his jersey. He also made note of the Glock .40 on his waistline. Then, he looked to Poobs, who was still sitting on the stool to the right of him, and then to JaCoby, who was sitting on the stool to the left of him. These men had bullet-proof vests strapped to their bodies, just like he had, as well as Tec-9s with seventy-two round drum attachments, which they kept within the confines of the trench coat they were wearing. Right then, Quantavious realized he was as safe as he was going to get. This gave him the nerve to move around more confidently than he had been since he'd gotten the word that he was a hot boy in the streets.

Quantavious mashed out what was left of his cigarette inside the glass ashtray on the bar top, as he blew out smoke from the side of his mouth. He then tapped Poobs and told him that he was

ready to go. Quantavious bid Nigel farewell, before he and his
bodyguards rose from their stools and moved toward the exit of
the bar that was known as *The Bar Fly*. Poobs and JaCoby made
sure to move strategically and keep a close eye on things as they
moved about. The bodyguards were the first ones through the
double doors of the establishment, while Quantavious stayed
behind. They wanted to make sure the perimeter was safe before
they escorted their client out to his vehicle.

Poobs and JaCoby looked around for anyone or anything that
may pose a threat to them or their charge. They didn't see
anything at first, but the whining of a speeding motorcycle coming
from their right stole their attention. They craned their necks and
squinted, trying to see what was coming at them as they reached
inside their coats for their Tec-9s. They were about to draw down
on whoever it was, until they saw that it was a black leather-clad
man wearing a helmet, and the man seemed to be minding his
business. The man popped a wheelie on his motorcycle. He
brought the motorcycle back down and zipped down the street,
disappearing into the night. Once he was gone, the bodyguards
ushered Quantavious from out of the bar. They were about to step
off the curb and head toward the bullet-proof black-on-black
Excursion parked across the street. It wasn't until the bodyguards
heard the whining of the motorcycle again that they froze where
they were. They looked to their left, and saw the black leather-clad
motorcyclist again. He reached over his shoulder and grabbed the
handle of something that was sheathed on his back.

Snikt!

The leather-clad motorcyclist drew his katana, and a gleam
swept up the length of it. The bodyguards shoved Quantavious
hard to the street. They reached for their Tec-9s, but before they
could pull the guns, the motorcyclist whipped past them, causing
the collar of their coats to flap against their chin. The motorcyclist
zipped down the street, with his motorcycle still whining. A
shaken Quantavious scrambled to his feet, dusting the dirt off his
jean shorts. He looked at the bloody scrape he'd gotten on his
elbow when the bodyguards shoved him to the pavement. Then, he

looked up at Poobs and JaCoby. They were as still as statues, and wore solemn expressions on their faces. Suddenly, thin red rings slowly appeared around their necks, and blood ran from out of them. Poobs and JaCoby's heads dropped to the surface like basketballs, and tumbled forward. Right after, their headless bodies fell to the street.

"What the fuck?" Quantavious's eyes were as big as baseballs, and his mouth hung open. He couldn't believe what he'd just witnessed. He believed that he was experiencing a nightmare, so he pinched himself to try to wake up. It didn't work. That's when he knew that he was wide awake, and this was real fucking life. Having come to that conclusion, Quantavious pulled his Glock from his waistline. When he turned to his left, he saw the motorcyclist coming at him full speed ahead. He pointed his blower at him as the rider popped another wheelie on his motorcycle. Quantavious finger-fucked the trigger of his handgun and flames spat from its barrel.

Blocka, Blocka, Blocka, Blocka, Blocka!

Sparks flew as bullets ricocheted off of the bottom of the speeding motorcycle. The motorcyclist threw his katana back over his shoulder. And just as he brought the motorcycle down, he swung his katana with all of his might, and continued on down the block.

"Aaaaaaah!" Quantavious screamed to high heaven as his severed hand, which was still clutching his Glock, fell at his sneakers. Blood sprayed out of his stump, and then spurted a few times before it eventually stopped. Quantavious looked at his bleeding stump in shock. Hearing the whining of the motorcycle at his back, he looked over his shoulder to see the motorcycle coming back at him. The motorcyclist flipped the katana over in his black leather gloved hand, and rocketed at him. Seeing that homeboy was on him like stink on shit, Quantavious took off, running as fast as he could. He was sweating profusely, and starting to turn pale from his wound and the amount of blood he was losing. He felt woozy, but that didn't stop him from running.

As soon as the motorcyclist was close enough to Quantavious, he swung his katana with all of his might. It whistled as it cut through the air, slicing through the flesh, tendon, and bone of his victim's leg. Quantavious's severed limb went high into the air and dropped to the ground, leaking blood. The poor bastard fell back hard on his back. He looked down at what was left of his leg, and then the other half, which was lying in the middle of the street. The motorcyclist swung his motorcycle sideways and brought it to a complete stop. He brought the kick-stand down, and leaned his motorcycle against it. Next, he dismounted his bike and casually made his way toward Quantavious. He swung his katana downward and sent the blood on it flying toward the pavement, splashing against it.

Quantavious lay on the ground with his eyes rolled to their whites and his mouth stretched wide open. His body shook like crazy, going through convulsions. The motorcyclist was sure Quantavious was going through cardiac arrest, but he didn't give a rat's ass. Switching hands with his katana, he yanked the gold cable from around Quantavious's neck. Then, he removed his Rolex watch. He placed the items deep within the recesses of his duster. Later, he'd fence the jewels along with others to an older cat he knew downtown. The motorcyclist straddled Quantavious. He unbuckled his belt, unzipped his jeans, and pulled them down around his thighs. In doing this, he revealed his nest of nappy brown pubic hair, and his flaccid dick. The motorcyclist grabbed Quantavious's penis and stretched it as far as he could. He then drew his katana back, and swung it with all of his might, severing the penis from his nut sack. Afterward, he wiped his bloodstained katana on Quantavious's jersey and sheathed it on his back. Switching hands with the severed dick, he stuffed it as far as he could, inside of his victim's mouth. He then pulled a rose from the recesses of his duster and laid it down gently on a dead Quantavious's chest. Standing upright, he took the time to look over his handiwork before jumping back on his motorcycle and speeding off down the street, vanishing into the night like some sort of magic trick.

***

Worth ripped up the street, turning the lines in them into blurs. He was going so fast that the end of his duster flapped behind him like the American flag on a very windy afternoon. A crowd of black, gray, and brown pigeons pecked at what was left of a stale cheese burger, which was inside a yellow wrapper, flapping their wings sporadically. Worth flew through the birds, and they flew away, leaving feathers floating in the air. Looking ahead, Worth saw police cars with their red and blue sirens blaring, heading in his direction on the opposite side of the street. The police cars flew past him, like he wasn't even there. Realizing that he was the least of their concerns, Worth made a turn off the road and into a wooded area, where a moving van was waiting for him. Emblazoned on both sides of the vehicle was the name and logo of the moving company, *Joe's Movers*. A beautiful dark-skinned sister, with her hair styled in micro braids, which spilled out from a navy blue cap that was pulled low over her brows to conceal her identity, stood beside the huge vehicle. She was smoking a cigarette and tapping her booted foot impatiently. The chocolate goddess was dressed in a navy blue jumpsuit, and her name –Amari –was stitched on the pocket of her uniform. She came alive when she saw Worth headed in her direction. She threw down the square and mashed it out underneath her boot, opening the shutter of the van and pulling out the ramp. Amari stood aside as Worth rode up inside the van, and used his outstretched foot to turn his bike around so he'd be facing out the back of the vehicle. Worth hurriedly got dressed in a matching cap and uniform that resembled the one Amari was wearing, before jumping down to the ground. He then jumped into the front passenger seat and slammed the door closed. Shortly thereafter, Amari put the ramp back up, and jumped onto the bumper of the van, pulling down the shutter. Once she jumped down from the van, she ran around to the driver's side and hopped it. Amari then fired up the van and drove off.

Chapter 9

The next night

Jada stood at the kitchen counter singing Nivea's "Don't Mess With My Man", while whipping up batter for the cornbread she planned on cooking that night. Behind her, on the stove top, were two small pots with steam fogging the inside of their glass tops, as something cooked inside them. Jada had her locs pulled back in a ponytail. She was fitted in Capri jeans, tan UGG boots, and a plaid button-down shirt of Trevante's, the sleeves of which she had rolled up. The apron she was wearing had food stains on it. Also, there were smudges of flour on her face and clothing from her seasoning and flouring the chicken, which was sitting inside a red ceramic bowl on the counter top beside her. By the side of the bowl were the seasonings and flour she'd used to prepare the chicken.

While Jada continued with her whipping of the cornbread batter and singing, Trevante emerged from out of the hallway, slipping a black thermal over his head. He stopped at the beginning of the corridor and slipped his arms inside the sleeves of the thermal. After straightening the wrinkles out of it, he leaned up against the wall inside the hallway, and folded his arms across his chest. A smile spread across his lips as he stared at Jada—his future wife, and the mother of his unborn child. He couldn't stop thinking of how lucky he was to have found her. It's crazy because she was supposed to have been just another fuck, but she ended up becoming so much more to him. Never in a million years would he ever think that he'd find his soul mate within an exotic dancer. But fortunately he had.

Jada had been down for Trevante when he didn't have shit; living from pillar to post and committing every sin known to man to get by. The two of them slept in seedy motels, gas station bathrooms, and sometimes even in the back of his old '79 Impala SS. Times got so bad that they found themselves eating out of trash bins, inside of the alleys, of Chinese take-out restaurants.

They would even loiter around fast food restaurants and eat whatever leftovers they found. Trevante knew that he was in a fucked up situation, and he couldn't stand to see his woman suffering with him. He tried to get her to leave him, but she wouldn't hear of it. There were a couple of times he left her while she slept, but she would determinedly go looking for him, finding him later. She was sort of like a lost dog that managed to somehow always find her way home. The realization that Jada wasn't going anywhere without him forced Trevante to step his game up. Together they formulated a plan. Jada would lure in big time dope boys and ballers, and set them niggaz up to be jacked by Trevante. It wasn't long before Diabolic recruited him into the joint operation he ran with Baby Boy. From there, things started looking up for them.

Trevante had promised to give Jada the world, for sticking by his side when he was down and out. But she wouldn't hear of it. All she wanted was him. Still, he gave her his word, so he was going to make good on it by any means necessary, because little mama deserved it all, and then some.

"I thought I heard an angel singing from the bedroom," Trevante said as he left the hallway wall and approached her.

Jada looked up at him, smiling from ear to ear. Little mama was glowing, and the glow wasn't just from the baby either. It seemed like she'd been living a fairytale since she and Trevante had been together. Sometimes she found herself pinching her arm to see if she'd wake up and it all be a dream. But that wasn't the case. No! The love she always wanted from the man she desired was a reality. They say if something is too good to be true, then it probably isn't. But Trevante McBride had convinced her otherwise. And for that she was thankful.

"Babe, stop. You're making me blush," a blushing Jada said, as she poured the cornbread batter inside a pan. She'd just placed it inside the pre-heated oven and shut the door, when Trevante eased up from behind her. He kissed on her neck and wrapped his arms around her waist, causing her to smile harder.

"What chu up in here whipping up, Queen?" Trevante asked from over her shoulder, watching her check the fire from under one of the pots, and remove the glass lid to check the other.

"A feast for my King," Jada said as she turned the fire from off a pot of rice. "We're having black beans, yellow rice, cornbread, and for dessert, peach cobbler."

"You're cooking all of my favorites? Girl, you must want that thang to be put on you again." He smiled and swept her locs aside, kissing her neck.

Jada smiled and said, "I don't want anything in return, baby. You've treated me like I was spawned from a royal bloodline, and I want to return the favor." She told him how she truly felt. "It's not always women that want to be catered to, but men also. Men deserve to be made to feel special."

"You make me feel that way every day, baby. Thank you." His tone of voice was serious and emotional. Suddenly tears welled up in his eyes, and he sniffled. A concerned look came over Jada's face, and she turned around to face him. She looked up into his eyes, as tears slid down his face unevenly, caressing the side of his face with her hand.

"No. Thank you, Trevante, for having accepted me for me; my flaws and all. Thank you for accepting my past, showing me the meaning of true love, giving me a family, and eternal happiness the day you got down on one knee and asked me to be your wife." She spoke sincerely; tears sprang in her eyes and flooded her cheeks. She and Trevante wiped the tears from each other's eyes, and kissed romantically.

"Oh, shit!" Trevante's eyes got big and his mouth hung open. He looked down at Jada's round belly, and then up at her. He'd felt the baby kick. "Did you feel that?" A smiling Jada nodded. She put her hands on her hips as Trevante got down on his knees and laid his head against her pregnant belly. "Hey, princess, are you getting jealous with all of the attention I'm showing mommy? Huh?" Jada rubbed Trevante's head as he continued to talk to their unborn baby. She loved hearing her future husband interact with the life growing inside of her. "Don't be jealous, princess; you know you'll always be daddy's favorite." Jada playfully shoved Trevante, and he smiled, looking up at her. He then kissed her belly and rubbed it affectionately.

Right then, there were knocks at the door that broke up their special moment. Trevante stood upright. Jada looked back and forth between him and the door, creases on her forehead.

"Who is that, babe?" Jada inquired curiously.

"It's that nigga Diabolic, Niv just told me he's on his way up," Trevante told her, smacking her on her ass playfully when she turned around. She smiled and giggled as she grabbed the bottle of canola oil, and screwed the cap off of it, pouring her desired amount into a black skillet.

Trevante opened the front door and found himself standing before Diabolic. Diabolic switched hands with the guitar case he was carrying, and slapped hands with Trevante, patting him on the back. He then shut the door behind him and passed the guitar case to Trevante, before making a beeline toward Jada.

"You're getting big, Jada. How far along are you?" Diabolic smiled and placed his hand to Jada's belly. She'd just turned around, twisting on the cap to the bottle of canola oil.

"Eight months," Jada said.

"One mo' month and lil' mama will be scot-free," Diabolic said. "You gotta name for her yet?"

"Not yet," she said, turning the fire under the skillet so the oil could get hot. "I gave up tryna think of a name for her, so I left that up to ya boy." She nodded with a smirk to Trevante who was standing at the kitchen table, unlocking the guitar case.

"Oh, alright," Diabolic responded, then looked over the food she was cooking on the stove top. "What chu cooking up in here? Nigga hungry as a hostage. I ain't ate shit all day. I've been out here making moves." He went to lift a lid off of one of the pots, and Jada popped his hand playfully.

"Ouch!" Diabolic frowned and rubbed his hand, looking at Jada like she was crazy. Their bond was just as tight as his and Trevante's. While he looked at Trevante as a little brother, he looked at Jada as a little sister. They were as good as blood in his eyes. Family.

"Aht, aht, aht! Dinner isn't ready yet. It will be in a few minutes." Jada smiled. "You're more than welcome to stay, and join us."

"About that, babe," Trevante said, glancing over his shoulder as he held the guitar case open.

Jada was in the middle of placing some of the floured chicken into the hot oil. But hearing her man about to delay their dinner plans, she sat the bowl of chicken down and turned around to him. She had one hand on her hip, and her weight shifted to her other foot, with her face displaying mad attitude. "Lemme guess y'all inna rush so you want me to save you a plate for later, right?"

Trevante stopped and turned around to her. "Yep, we'll sit down and eat together once I get back."

"See, Trevante, this the type of shit I've been talking about. You run the streets so much that you don't even spend time with me and the baby." She fumed, moving her neck like ghetto chicks do when they're hotter than fish grease.

"Don't start now, babe, we've been doing so good," Trevante told her. Although they'd gotten along most of their relationship, he and Jada had been getting into it quite often since she'd been pregnant. She was super emotional and aggressive. But he put up with it because he knew it was her hormones that had her acting irrational. Well, that—and the fact that he loved her more than life itself.

"Whatever, Trevante." Jada went back to placing the chicken inside the skillet. The hot oil sizzled and popped with each piece of the bird she laid down in it.

A frowned up Trevante waved Jada off, and focused his attention back on the guitar case. Inside, he found a beautifully crafted oak wood guitar polished to a high shine and lying snuggly in a cushiony bed of red velvet. "Yo', what the fuck is this? I thought you said you had a 223 assault rifle you wanted me to check out," Trevante said to Diabolic as he approached.

"I do," Diabolic said. He then pressed a small black button that was in between the locks of the case, and the cushiony bed of velvet lifted the guitar up, on some Desperado type shit. The guitar was just a disguise to hide what the case was really concealing: a dismantled high-powered 223 sniper rifle. It was equipped with a silencer, a scope and infrared laser sighting.

"Now, that's some Double O-7, James Bond type shit right there, my nigga," a smiling Trevante turned to Diabolic and dapped him up. He then went about the task of assembling the lethal weapon and aiming it at different pieces of furniture, vases, and framed portraits that made up the living room. Behind the trigger of the high-powered rifle, he imagined himself blowing his enemies' brains out. "This bitch right here is gorgeous. I'ma fa sho' make her prove her worth tonight." He dapped up Diabolic again.

"That's what I'm counting on," Diabolic told him. He then threw his arm around his shoulders, pulled him close, and told him in a hushed tone: "Look here, why don't chu gon' and straighten Jada out before we raise up outta here. I know you not tryna come home to a nagging woman."

Trevante looked over his shoulder at Jada, and he could still see that she was pissed. He then focused his attention back on Diabolic and said, "You right." He glanced at the black digital watch that adorned his wrist, checking the time. "Gemme 'bout ten minutes, then we can gon' and go."

"You got it, big dawg." Diabolic dapped him up. He then watched Trevante disassemble the 223 sniper rifle and place it back inside of the guitar case. He closed the guitar case shut and locked it.

Diabolic's eyes followed Trevante as he grabbed Jada by the hand and took her toward the hallway, leading her toward their bedroom. He had it in mind to fuck the attitude right up out of her. It was nothing like a good dick down to get her to act right.

"Where are we going?" a frowned up Jada asked, but allowed herself to be led along.

"In the bedroom, so I can get you that act right," Trevante informed her. He then looked over his shoulder at Diabolic. "Yo', keep yo' eyes on that chicken for me, fam!"

"I got chu faded," Diabolic replied. Once he saw the couple disappear inside of their bedroom and heard the door slam, he made his way inside the kitchen to tend to the chicken. Making sure there wasn't anyone around to see what he was doing, he removed a small transparent tube from his pocket, the tube looking like it could be used to smoke crack. It contained cyanide. Diabolic poured some of the liquid onto the chicken that was cooking inside of the skillet. He then turned off the fire on the beans and poured some inside there. Next, he poured some inside the pot of rice. Once the chicken was done cooking, he placed the last pieces of it into the skillet, which caused the hot oil to sizzle loudly. Once the sizzling calmed down to a shimmer, Diabolic poured what was left of the cyanide onto the chicken. Just as he was slipping the empty tube back inside of his pocket, Trevante's bedroom door opened. Trevante came out tucking his gun on his waistline. Right behind him was a Jada. Her locs were wild and her clothes were wrinkled. She wore a smile of satisfaction on her face.

"You ready to go, big dawg?" Trevante asked Diabolic. He was leaning up against the kitchen counter, trying to act natural. You know, like he wasn't just doing something to the food that Jada was cooking.

"I stay ready, young nigga," Diabolic replied.

"Alright then, let's roll." Trevante grabbed the guitar case by its handle and headed for the front door. He stopped in his tracks, once Jada called after him. She'd just finished taking the last of the chicken from out of the skillet, and sitting it on a bed of paper towels to absorb its oil.

"I know your trifling ass not leaving up outta here without giving me a kiss," Jada said, acting like she was mad, one hand placed on her hip.

Trevante smiled as he turned toward her and switched hands with the guitar case. He made his way over to her and pulled her close. They shut their eyelids, kissing each other intensively. When Trevante tried to pull away, Jada held him longer, prolonging their kissing. Finally, he broke their lip-locking, and turned to walk away, with her holding on to his hand.

Then she told him: "Hurry back to me, baby. Don't keep your Queen waiting."

"I won't, Queen, I promise," he said, and she released his hand.

Jada stood where she was, watching her man walk toward the front door. Once again, she called out to him and he turned around. "What's up, babe?" he asked, with a raised eyebrow.

"I love you so much," she spoke from the heart.

He smiled and responded with, "And I love you so much more."

With that exchange having been made, Trevante and Diabolic disappeared through the door of the condo. Jada turned around, sniffling and wiping away the teardrops that fell from her eyes, with her fingers. With her being madly in love with Trevante, plus pregnant, she was highly emotional.

Jada used the collar of her shirt to dry her eyes. She then fixed herself a plate of food, and poured a glass of Minute Maid fruit punch. She sat down at the kitchen table, said grace, and dug into her plate.

***

Tyrell sat in the front passenger seat, taking an occasional glance at his cell phone, as he'd been at the meet up spot far longer than he'd expected. Diabolic had arranged to meet him at MacArthur Park, to give him the fifty thousand dollar bag he'd earned when he'd given Baby Boy the whereabouts of the niggaz that stole the shipment of cocaine. Diabolic was supposed to have been there a half hour ago, but he'd yet to show his face.

"Where the fuck is this nigga at, man?" Tyrell said to no one in particular as he sat beside Whitney, who was holding the bluish yellow flame of her lighter to the tip of her crack pipe, causing the rocks in it to sizzle and crackle. Whitney sucked on the end of her glass dick, and drew the smoke into her lungs. Shutting her eyelids, she took the pipe from out of her mouth and blew smoke up, toward the ceiling. She passed the lighter and crack pipe to Tyrell, for him to take a blast. He was about to fire it up, when he was suddenly bathed in the headlights of an approaching vehicle. Right then, he passed the pipe and the lighter back to Whitney, and took his blower from underneath his seat. He then tucked it into his waistline and hopped out of his whip, shutting the door behind him.

Diabolic stopped his SUV ten feet away from Tyrell, and jumped down. He flicked to the ground what was left of the cigarette he'd been smoking on the way over, and mashed it out beneath his sneaker. He stole a glance back at Tyrell, who had his arms folded across his chest and was keeping an eye on him, but he didn't say a word. Diabolic made his way to the hatch of his truck and opened it. He pulled a duffle bag into him and poked his head out from the side of the enormous vehicle, motioning Tyrell over.

Come here? Why the fuck didn't this nigga just bring the bag or whatever he has the money in over? I wonder if he remembers who I am—and if this is a set-up—Well, if he does any crazy shit, I'ma puff homie's wig out and get the fuck from outta here! Hell, I plan on doing that anyway, Tyrell thought before glancing over his shoulder at the pick-up. He found Whitney hanging out of the window, looking at him.

"What's up, babe? Is everything cool?" Whitney asked him, worry lines creasing her forehead.

"Yeah, everything is straight, I'm finna go get it now," Tyrell assured her.

"Okay. I love you." She kissed the palm of her hand and blew him a kiss, smiling sweetly.

"I love you, too, ma." Tyrell said with a crooked grin. He kissed his two fingers and threw his hand up at her.

Tyrell ran as fast as he could, tucked and rolled. Coming back up, he aimed his blower at the shadowy figure hidden within the trees and pulled the trigger, rapidly.

Blowl, Blowl, Blowl, Blowl!

"Aaaaaaaaah!" The sniper fell from out of the tree, and finally collided in a heavy thud with the ground. After he'd dispatched the sniper, Tyrell sent some fire at Diabolic, which caused him to duck back behind his truck. Tyrell then ran alongside his whip as Whitney drove beside him. Keeping one hand on the steering wheel, Whitney leaned over into the front passenger seat, and pushed open the door. The door swung open, and Tyrell dove into the front passenger seat, leaving his legs hanging out of the vehicle before he eventually pulled himself inside of the whip, closing the door behind him.

"Oh, my god, babe, are you okay?" Whitney asked Tyrell, looking between him and the windshield.

Tyrell, panting, out of breath from running, looked to his woman and said, "Yeah, I'm straight. I shot that bitch-ass nigga that was busting at me from outta that fucking tree."

Blocka!

The back window of the vehicle shattered as a bullet whizzed through it and peppered the seats with broken glass. The bullet slammed into the back of Whitney's skull, and her head ricocheted off the steering wheel, settling against the driver's window. Her eyes were as big as golf balls, and her mouth was stretched wide open. Her face wore the expression of death as her vacant eyes stared off at nothing. Dots of blood covered a shocked Tyrell's face, as he ducked low in the front passenger seat and grabbed the steering wheel, mashing on the gas pedal. The vehicle sped ahead, with more bullets coming through the shattered back window, slamming into the interior and damaging the upholstery. The other bullets slammed into the dashboard. Tyrell glanced into the rearview mirror, and saw Diabolic standing beside his truck, sending back to back shots at the whip as it sped away.

Tyrell's truck hurriedly crossed the massive lawn of the park, jumping off the curb. *Skirrrrrrrrrrrrrrrrrt!* The truck wailed, its tires engaging the ground in friction as it made a right in the middle of the street, with Diabolic busting shots at it until it disappeared. Once Tyrell's whip was out of his sight, Diabolic lowered his smoking handgun and ejected the spent magazine from out of the ass of it. He then pulled another fully loaded magazine from out of the front pocket of his jeans, and smacked it into the bottom of the handle of his blower, cocking it. His chest expanded and shrunk as he breathed, wiping the dripping sweat from the corner of his brow, with the back of his leather-gloved hand.

At this time, police car sirens could be heard far-off in the distance, but Diabolic knew that the pigs were headed to his location. With that in mind, he tucked his gun on his waistline. As soon as he had, he heard a pained voice calling out to him. When Diabolic looked over his shoulder, he found a wincing Trevante, who was wearing a ski-mask over his face. He was the sniper Tyrell had shot down from the tree.

Diabolic took a deep breath as he stared at him, shaking his head, pitifully. Kneeling down to the young nigga, he pulled a bandana from out of his back pocket and held it over his nose and mouth.

Diabolic had just pulled up outside of his father's mansion, when the front door opened and an overweight Caucasian man shambled out. He stopped at the top step and took a long drink from his flask. The fellow had a receding hairline, cherry blonde hair and a five o'clock shadow. The top button of his dress shirt was unbuttoned, due to his neck being too thick to fasten it. This was Detective Breedlove. Diabolic had seen him more times than he could count. He was one of his father's contacts down at the seventy-seven police precinct.

If this nigga came to holla at bro, then its bad news, Diabolic thought. Baby Boy had hit him up that night and told him to come to the mansion because he wanted to discuss something that he couldn't over the jack.

Diabolic's eyes followed the roundabout detective as he jumped behind the wheel of his shitty Buick LeSabre and slammed the door shut behind him. A moment later he heard the vehicle start up and drive away, heading toward the large double gates of the estate. Diabolic killed the engine of his whip and jumped out. He stuck his handgun at the small of his back and jogged up the steps of the mansion, knocking on the door with the brass knocker. Shortly, the butler opened the door and greeted him, before standing aside to let him inside of the dwelling.

"Where's my brother?" Diabolic asked the butler as he crossed the threshold.

"He's in the kitchen, suh," the butler responded in his thick British accent. He then shut the door behind him.

Diabolic made his way across the foyer and then the living room, before he crossed the threshold into the kitchen. He found his younger brother, Baby Boy, sifting through the cabinets above him. On the island behind him there were two glasses filled with ice, and a folder loaded with paperwork. Baby Boy took down a half a bottle of Russian Vodka. When he turned around, his eyes were swollen and the brims of them were red. From the looks of him, Diabolic could tell that he had been crying, but he wondered from what though.

"What up, bro?" Diabolic approached the island with a concerned look.

"You're gonna wanna have a drink for this one," Baby Boy assured him as he filled the glasses halfway with the clear alcohol. He picked up one glass and extended the other to his brother. Diabolic reluctantly took the glass from his sibling, eyeballing the folder of documents on the island. The brothers touched glasses and said "Salud," before taking a sip of the foreign liquor. Their faces balled up from the Vodka washing down their throats. The alcohol stung like a scorpion's tail. They swallowed it down, hissed, and then took another sip. After indulging in the Russian liquor, Baby Boy handed the folder over to Diabolic. As soon as he took it, he sat his glass down and opened it. Baby Boy watched as Diabolic opened the folder. The first document had a mug shot photo of Trevante paper-clipped to it. Diabolic glanced up at Baby Boy, seeing him closely observing him as he sipped Vodka.

Diabolic read through the paperwork inside of the folder, and with each sheet he read, he felt his heart break more and more. The documents detailed accounts of several crimes and illegal activities that he and the young nigga, as well as others, were involved in. Trevante had even told about the massacre that took place back at the ballroom, when they'd laid the murder game down on Montray and his people.

Diabolic's eyes were glassy and red-webbed when he looked back up at his brother, holding up the folder. A single tear slid down his cheek. It hurt like hell, knowing Trevante had turned rat. He'd taken the youngsta under his wing and groomed him himself. He believed he was from an Ilk like his, but the documents he'd just read through proved otherwise.

"Did Breedlove just drop this off here?" Diabolic asked, but feared to hear what his brother had to say. Baby Boy regretfully nodded. Instantly, Diabolic's face contorted into a mask of rage. He grabbed his glass so tight that a fracture line formed in it and the Vodka slowly spilled out. His eyebrows slanted and his nostrils flared. He bit down hard on his bottom lip and threw the glass into the wall with all of his might. The glass exploded, and alcohol and broken glass rained down to the kitchen floor. Right then, Baby Boy turned his back to his brother and continued to drink, a wicked smile forming on his lips.

"You know what's gotta be done now, right?" Baby Boy asked him, without turning around.

Diabolic wiped his dripping eyes and looked up at his brother. He sniffled, nodded, and said, "Yeah. I know."

"Look, I brought lil' homie in, but we both loved 'em like family. He may as well have had the same blood pumping through his veins." Baby Boy spoke to his brother from over his shoulder, still holding the drink in his hand. "Knowing the relationship that the three of us had, I wouldn't dare put the burden on your shoulders of taking him out. I'm thinking we have Huge, or maybe that new nigga take . . ."

"Nah," Diabolic shook his head as he looked up at his brother. "It's like you said, 'I brought Trevante into this thing of ours', so I've gotta be the one that takes him off his feet."

"You sure?" Baby Boy asked as he turned around to face him.

"Yeah, I'm sure. I'm supposed to have 'em roll with me tonight to drop homeboy off that paypa for that lil' tip he gave us. I'll take care of 'em tonight," Diabolic said in a cool monotone, like it wasn't going to be a big deal to knock Trevante's head off. He was fronting though. The thought killed him, which is why he finished off his drink and poured another one.

"Alright. Lemme go get that bag for homeboy that gave us that tip." Baby Boy finished off his drink and sat his glass down on the island. He walked by his brother and patted him on his shoulder affectionately, letting him know he felt his pain. Diabolic didn't acknowledge the gesture, as he continued to indulge in the foreign liquor. The teardrops continuously fell from the red brims of his eyes. Realizing that the glass of alcohol wasn't going to be enough to ease his pain, Diabolic picked up the bottle of Vodka and took it to the head. His Adam's apple rolled up and down his neck as he drank from the bottle.

Trevante struggled to breathe as he clawed at Diabolic's arm, to no avail. Hot tears stung Diabolic's eyes. He couldn't bear to see Trevante's final moments, so he looked away, shutting his eyelids. Tears instantly spilled down his cheeks, and left wet streaks behind. Once he had succeeded in suffocating Trevante, Diabolic stuffed his bandana back into his back pocket and pulled the ski-mask off the youngsta's head. He found his pupils staring out the corners of his eyes, and his mouth hanging open in a grotesque manner. Diabolic crossed himself in the sign of the crucifix, stood upright, and trekked back to his SUV.

***

With no time to waste, Tyrell slid into the lap of Whitney's lifeless body, and took hold of the steering wheel. The Toyota swerved from left to right, before he regained control of it and sped down the street like a bat out of hell. He wiped the bubbles of sweat that had formed on his forehead, with the back of his hand, and glanced up into the rearview mirror, to see if Diabolic was on his ass. He wasn't. When he looked ahead, Tyrell saw the blue and red blaring lights of police sirens heading his way. Looking to his right, he spotted a gray cat with black stripes running from out of an alley, chasing after a fat ass rat. He sped up the truck and made a sharp turn inside the alley. Tyrell then killed its engine and lights. When he glanced up into the rearview mirror again, he saw the blaring emergency lights of the police cars whipping across the entrance of the alley. Once he was sure they were gone, he slid over into the front passenger seat and pulled Whitney over into his arms, cradling her head in his arms. Blood and pieces of her brain fragments oozed out of the back of her head, and stained Tyrell's hands and shirt. Tears accumulated in Tyrell's eyes as he rocked back and forth, making an ugly ass face. He became overwhelmed with emotional turmoil, tears flooding down his cheeks.

"Whitneeeeyyyyyy!" Tyrell threw his head back and hollered aloud. He bowed his head, and big teardrops dripped from his eyes. His entire body shook as he sobbed uncontrollably. He sniffled and gathered himself as best as he could, wiping his wet face on his arm. He then looked at Whitney's face and shut her eyelids with a gentle brush of his hand. Afterward, he opened the passenger door and carried her out, laying her limp body on top of a pile of black garbage bags. He kissed her on her lips tenderly, and told her that he loved her.

Tyrell ran back to the Toyota, and grabbed his crack pipe and lighter. He stuck the crack pipe into his pocket and used the lighter to ignite the seats. He did this to destroy all of his fingerprints inside of the vehicle. Once Tyrell saw that the fire was spreading throughout the stolen truck, he ran to the end of the alley. He looked up and down the street to make sure there wasn't anyone in sight, before he took off running down the block.

"Haa! Haa! Haa! Haa! Haa! Haa! Haa!" Tyrell huffed and puffed as he ran down the sidewalk, cutting across the street. A

moment later, there was a loud explosion, and fire spilled from out of the alley. Tyrell ducked and threw his arms over his head, squeezing his eyelids tight and hoping not to be struck by shrapnel from the blast. He kept on running, and he bent the corner, placing his back up against a liquor store that was currently closed. Right then, a police helicopter flew above and cast its bright spotlight over the street and into the alley. *"Haa! Haa! Haa! Haa! Haa! Haa!"* Tyrell breathed heavily with his back still against the wall, and his head turned to the side. Once he heard the whirring sound of the ghetto bird's propellers growing smaller and smaller, he continued on his run.

Three hours later, Tyrell was crying and smoking crack in the corner of Ms. Pearl's basement. His face and body were covered in bubbles of sweat that had oozed out of his pores and slid down his body. His perspiration left dark sweat stains on the waistband of his light-gray Fruit of the Loom boxers. "I'ma get 'em back for you, baby—I'ma get that mothafucka back—First, he took my son from me, now you—He's gotta die," Tyrell said to no one in particular, before sticking the glass dick back into his mouth and holding the flame of his lighter to the tip of it. He sucked on the end of the L-shaped see-through tool, drew smoke into his body. The flame of his lighter cast a golden illumination on his face. The higher he got the better he felt. Tyrell fell asleep on the mattress on the floor, with the side of his face lying against it. The tears on his cheeks dried up and turned white. His last thoughts were of how he was going to avenge Whitney's murder.

***

A lifeless Jada sat hunched over her plate of food, with her jaw full of chewed up chicken. Her pupils were blue and cloudy, while her complexion was food stamp blue, due to her having been dead for hours.

Chapter 10

Sheila made his way out of his luxurious condominium complex, with his handbag hanging on his bony arm. His head was tilted aside as his ear was pressed against his cellular phone. At the moment he was in the middle of talking to one of his friends about the dinner party that they both were on their way to. Sheila was a six-foot-two homosexual with a scrawny body. He had long hair that was laid to the gods. He was dressed in a cheetah print silk shirt, which was opened to show his bare chest, and the two diamond-studded necklaces that graced his neck. He wore black Capri pants, which were held up by a cheetah print belt, and showed off the diamond-studded ankle bracelet on his right leg.

"Girl, I'm on my way now. You just make sure yo' ass is ready," Sheila told his best friend, Twan, as he walked across the parking lot floor, toward his black-on-black Mercedes-Benz C-Class. "I just got off the elevator, I'm on my way. Bye, ho!" He laughed and disconnected the call, dropping the cell phone in his handbag. His vehicle chirped as he unlocked it, and he snatched the door open, planting himself behind the wheel. Next, he slipped on his oversized designer shades and popped a strip of Winter Fresh gum inside his mouth. After strapping on his safety belt, Sheila fired up his Benz, backed out of his parking space, and sped out of the underground dwelling. The gate rose and he drove out, disappearing into the night.

Sheila didn't have to lift a finger. He was paid to do absolutely nothing, except stay away from his family. Sheila's father, Wesner, was one of the wealthiest cocaine peddlers in East Oakland. Ashamed of his son's "lifestyle", he set him up with his own place, wheels, and an allowance that was deposited into his bank account every two weeks. Old Wesner called it an allowance, but it really was his way of paying his only son to stay away. The kingpin didn't agree with his teenage son being gay. To him, he was a disgrace, and brought great shame to his family. Still, Wesner loved "Wesley" with all of his heart. The young man was his flesh and blood.

The only time Sheila was to come into contact with his family was on holidays, birthdays and other special occasions. This was fine by him because he didn't want to be around anyone that was ashamed of the way he was living his life. On top of that, he was welcomed with opened arms by the LGBTQ community. They treated him like family. Besides, the twenty grand he got every fourteen days was enough to dry his tears on.

Sheila descended the windows of his whip and let the night's fresh air inside. The cool air rushed inside, causing his hair to drift, and ruffling the collar of his shirt. Sheila cranked the volume up on Beyonce's latest album and sang along. He dipped in and out of lanes, going way over the speed limit, and running lights just before they turned red. He knew he was going mad fast, so he adjusted his rearview mirror, and looked into it to see if there were any police around. The coast was clear, so he continued to speed, causing the hand of the speedometer to turn up several notches. Unbeknownst to Sheila, the headlights of a car that was tailing him popped on. He hadn't noticed it because the lights were out, and the night was as dark as his complexion.

From the corner of his eye, Sheila saw his cell phone light up as it rang, then he grabbed it and looked at its display. It was Twan. Old boy he was talking to earlier, before he left his condo. He lowered the volume on his stereo and answered the call.

"Aye, I'm finna hop on the freeway, I'll hit chu up once I'm outside your—" Sheila jerked forward and dropped his cellular phone, as he was crashed into from the rear. He looked up into the rearview mirror and saw the car he hadn't noticed had been tailing him. Sheila's face formed a scowl. He immediately let down the window and stuck his arm out of it, motioning for the driver of the car that had hit him to pull over. "Pull over, pull over right now!" He focused his attention back on the road and made a right turn at the corner, glancing into the rearview mirror to make sure the driver who'd hit him was following behind. He was. "None driving mothafuckas out here, done hit my mothafucking shit!"

Sheila drove down a residential block and pulled over, parking along the curb. He grabbed his cell phone and told Twan what had happened, before disconnecting the call. Quickly, he threw open the door of his ride and hopped out. The headlights of the car that had hit him were beaming brightly on him as he approached the rear of his vehicle. Sheila's eyes grew big and his jaw dropped when he saw the damage done to the back of his Mercedes. "Oh, hell, nawww! I hope yo' ass got insurance 'cause the money it's gon' cost you to fix this gon' set chu back." Sheila waved his right jeweled hand wildly as he advanced in the driver's direction with one manicured hand on his hip. His movements were really fluid and feminine. His tall, scrawny ass was sassy as fuck. "Get out the car, bitch! Get up out the mothafucking car so you can see what chu did!" Sheila demanded of the person that hit his whip. He was now hunched over at the driver's window, knocking hard on the glass. He was shouting so hard and loudly, that his breath fogged up the window's glass and left specs of spit on it.

Suddenly, the driver's window descended, and she blew a glittery, white powdery substance into Sheila's face. Sheila stumbled backwards, coughing and blinking his teary eyes. He desperately tried to wipe the powdery substance from out of his eyes, but no matter how hard he tried, the shit wasn't coming out. He was blinded, but he could make out the driver stepping out of the car with something in her hand. Sheila knew that his life was in danger, and he had to defend himself. With that in mind, he dipped his hand inside his pocket and pulled out a barber's razor. He slowly backed away from the driver, swinging the razor blindly, while narrowing his eyelids, trying to see where the driver was coming from.

The driver, Shavon, pressed a button on the baton she grasped in her leather gloved hand. Instantly, the baton extended sixteen inches. Cautiously, Shavon approached Sheila, moving as agile as a cat. She ducked, dodged, and jumped back from the swing of the lethal razor, narrowly missing being cut. Sheila took a good, hard swing with the razor at Shavon's head, which she ducked. Shavon followed up by bringing the baton down on Sheila's wrist, with all of her might.

"Aaaaaaaah!" Sheila threw his head back, hollering. He dropped his barber's razor to the ground and grabbed his aching wrist. Now that he was unarmed, Shavon took full advantage of him. Using the baton, she struck him in the back of his kneecap which brought him down to one knee. She followed up by striking him on his shoulder, and then whacking him across the back of his head. The blow knocked him out cold and left him on the asphalt, snoring like a big ass grizzly bear. Seeing Sheila lying at her feet, Shavon closed up the baton and stuck it into the waist of her jeans. At that moment, Latrell hopped out of the car and ran over to Sheila. He zip-tied his wrists behind his back, and pulled a black pillowcase over his head.

"Baby, pop the trunk of his car," Latrell told her. Once Shavon carried out his orders, she ran back to the whip they'd driven there and got something out of the backseat. Latrell deposited Sheila into the trunk of his Benz. He turned around to find Shavon approaching him with an oxygen tank and mask, which she placed inside of the trunk beside Sheila. Afterward, Latrell slammed the trunk shut. He then told Shavon to follow him, before jumping in behind the wheel of the Benz. Once he slammed the door shut, he picked up Sheila's cell phone, and saw that he had four missed calls from Twan. Latrell strapped on his safety belt and pulled away from the curb, making sure Shavon was following him. He looked back and forth between the windshield and Sheila's cell phone, scrolling through the contacts. Once he found a number listed as Daddy, a smile stretched across his face.

***

Inglewood Park Cemetery

The night was dark and cool. Latrell was perched on a tombstone, with his gloved hand holding Sheila's cellular phone to his ear, and a voice distortion device inside of his mouth. In his other gloved hand he held a can of red spray paint. His shirt and jacket hung on the shaft of a shovel, which was planted standing up in the ground. Smudges of dirt covered his bare upper body. Latrell's locs were sprawled wildly on his shoulders. There were bubbles of sweat covering his forehead, and his face was shiny, as well as the rest of his form. He was hot as well; digging a grave was a lot harder than he'd realized. He was used to killing a mothafucka and leaving them wherever he caught them slipping. Not long ago, he buried Sheila six-feet-deep inside the ground, on the opposite side of the tombstone in which he was seated upon.

"This is not a game. This is notta joke," Latrell assured Wesner over the cell phone. He was using a voice distortion device to speak through because he didn't want Wesner to recognize his voice. Latrell used to work as a hired gun for Wesner back in the day. That was how he knew that he was pushing big time dope and making major grips in East Oakland. Seeing he and Shavon needed one-hundred bricks to get Mank back, he felt that Wesner would be the perfect victim to fill such a tall order. "If you ever wanna see your son again, I want you to deliver one hunnit birds to the address I just gave you. Keep in mind that he's buried in the ground and he has about," he took the time to glance at the time on the cell phone's display, "two hours worth of oxygen left. Once that oxygen is gon' you're gonna find yo' self with a dead body on yo' hands and I'm sure you don't want that—Look, nigga, fifty of them thangz isn't gonna be enough. I wanna hunnit. You either make it happen in the time I gave you, or prepare to make funeral arrangements." Latrell disconnected the call and stuck Sheila's cellular into his pocket. He then removed the voice distortion device from his mouth, and placed it into his pocket as well. Next, he pulled the cover off of the can of spray paint, and shook it up. Kneeling downward, he marked the back of the tombstone with a big, red X. Afterward, he slipped his shirt and jacket back on. He grabbed the shovel from out of the ground, hoisted it over his shoulder, and ambled back to Sheila's vehicle.

***

One Hour Later

Shavon stood posted up beside a white 2019 Lincoln Navigator that she'd procured on her way over to the vacant warehouse, in which she was standing in. A hood covered her head, black sunglasses shielded her eyes, and a bandana was down around her neck, concealing her identity. There wasn't any way to tell who she was, thanks to this disguise, and that's exactly the way she wanted it.

Shavon took casual puffs of her withering Newport cigarette, and occasionally glanced at her watch for the time, as she waited for Wesner to arrive. She started pacing the ground as she sucked on the butt of her square, and blew out a cloud of smoke. Shavon kept her hand tucked inside of the pocket of her hoodie, where her gloved hand gripped a black .45 automatic handgun. If shit got funky, then she was going to lay Wesner the fuck out, and get from out of there.

This nigga needa hurry up 'fore he finds his son dead by the time he gets to 'em, Shavon thought, as she continued to pace the ground. As she moved back and forth, she didn't notice the fat gray rat that scurried her sneakers. Hearing the sounds of vehicles approaching, she dropped what was left of her Joe, and mashed it out underneath her shoe. Once she blew out the last of the smoke from between her lips, she pulled the bandana that was around her neck over the lower half of her face. Right then, she was bathed in beaming headlights as two whips entered the empty warehouse. Droplets of brown dirty water fell from the ceiling and splashed on the ground below.

Shavon made note of the vehicles: a stretch Mercedes-Benz, and a big black Suburban, which turned around and backed up. The Benz and the Suburban turned off. Not long after, two thuggish-looking men hopped out of the truck, wearing serious expressions. The thugs tucked their handguns into the front of their jeans as they walked to the back of the SUV. One was wearing a dark gray sweatshirt, while the other was wearing a black tank top underneath an opened hoodie. Once the thugs opened up the back of the Suburban, they grabbed two big ass duffle bags. The duffle bags looked heavy as shit, but the thugs were muscular, so they didn't have any trouble lifting them. As the thugs advanced in Shavon's direction, Wesner's chauffeur jumped out of the Benz and opened the back door for him. Wesner, a tall, burly man, with a big, bald shiny head, emerged from out of the luxurious vehicle. He was smoking a fat ass cigar, which caused smoke to waft around him. His extra-large frame filled out a white tuxedo, over which he wore a black overcoat. Just as the thugs dumped the duffle bags at Shavon's feet, Wesner approached Shavon.

"They're all there. One hundred bricks of the purest cocaine that money can buy," Wesner said. He was putting extras on the coke though. The shit was decent, but it wasn't as fire as he was claiming it was. "Now, where is my son?" He dropped the cigar at his black leather dress shoe and mashed it out, extinguishing its ember.

Shavon pulled a voice distortion device from out of the pocket of her hoodie and placed it to her mouth, speaking from behind the bandana. "Slow your roll, pops, how am I supposed to know there's a hundred birds right there?" She pointed to the duffle bags. "Pull them shits outta the bag and count 'em up."

Wesner pulled back the sleeve of his coat and glanced at his AP Rolex watch. A line formed across his forehead and he looked back up at Shavon. "Are you fucking kidding me? We're already pressing for time." He spat angrily.

"I'm not fucking around. So, I advise you to have yo' goons put a rush on it and start counting 'em birds. Or, don't, I don't give a fuck! It's your faggot-ass son that's gon' die, not mine."

The thugs looked back at Wesner, waiting for his response. Frustrated, the kingpin ran his hand down his face and blew out hot air. If it wasn't for the fact that Shavon had taken his son hostage, he would have ordered his goons to put a few bullets in her for her slick mouth. But in this situation, she and Latrell had him by the balls, so he didn't have any choice but to comply for his son's sake.

Wesner gave the thugs a nod. Instantly, the thugs unzipped the duffle bag and counted the bricks, which were wrapped in scotch tape, one by one. Shavon counted the number of bricks they had, inside of her head. Once they'd finished, she knew that there were indeed a total of one hundred birds.

"Satisfied?" Wesner asked Shavon with his arms folded across his chest. She nodded. He then motioned with his finger for his thugs to load the duffle bags into the back of the whip Shavon had driven there. The thugs stuffed the bricks back inside of the duffle bags, zipped them up, and followed Shavon around to the back of the Lincoln Navigator. She opened the hatch of the enormous SUV and stepped aside, letting Wesner's thugs load the duffle bags. She shut the hatch and approached Wesner. She unzipped her hoodie and pulled out a folded map, which she passed to him. When Wesner opened the map he saw an area on it that a red X was drawn on.

"That map is a layout of the Inglewood Cemetery," Shavon spoke through the voice distortion device. "The red X is where your son is buried. On the back of that tombstone you'll also find a red X spray painted. The tombstone is marked Terrance McGowan—1985-2011." She glanced at her watch before looking back up at Wesner. "If I were you I'd hurry, you've got forty-five minutes left before junior runs outta oxygen."

Shavon watched as Wesner motioned for the thugs to follow him. He jumped into the back of the stretch Mercedes-Benz and slammed the door shut. The limousine pulled off in a hurry, with the Suburban following closely behind. Once they'd gone, Shavon hit up Latrell and confirmed that she'd made the drop. She jumped behind the wheel of the Navigator and fired it up. She drove out of the warehouse, removing her sunglasses and pulling her bandana down around her neck.

"Yeah, I'm on my way to you now. Okay. I love you, too, bye." Shavon disconnected the call and sat her cellular down on the console.

***

Boom, Boom, Boom, Boom!

Several tombstones broke into pieces as the speeding stretch Mercedes-Benz plowed them over. Time was running out. They had twenty minutes left to dig up the grave that Sheila was buried in.

Wesner's gaze moved back and forth between the windshield of his car and the map Shavon had given him. His face frowned up and he narrowed his eyelids, seeing a tombstone coming up ahead that had a red X spray painted on it. "There it is, up ahead," he pointed out the tombstone to his chauffeur. "Step on it!"

The limousine bounced up and down as it flew up manicured lawn on the resting grounds, with the Suburban following closely behind it. The limousine stopped a few feet before the tombstone. Wesner hopped out of the luxurious vehicle, and so did the driver, who quickly removed his cap and jacket. He ran over to the tombstone that Sheila was buried in, and started digging as fast as he could. By this time, the Suburban pulled up beside the stretch Mercedes-Benz and the thugs hopped out. They removed their hoodie and sweatshirt as they raced to the back of their truck. Once they opened it up, one of them grabbed a shovel for himself and tossed his partner the other. They ran over to the grave that the chauffeur was digging up, and began digging up the ground alongside him. The headlights of their respective vehicle shone on them. Wesner stood off to the side, tapping his foot impatiently and glancing at his watch ever thirty-seconds.

Fuck, fifteen minutes left, Wesner thought as he paced the ground and rubbed on his bald head. The thugs and his chauffeur weren't even halfway down into the six-foot-deep hole, and he was afraid they weren't going to make it in time to save his son. Turning toward them, he clapped his hands and shouted, "Come on, come on! Pick up the pace! Hustle, hustle, hustle!" He commanded with strong claps of his palms. The thugs and the chauffeur were covered in smudges of dirt and beads of sweat.

They breathed heavily and grunted, as they dug up the land and tossed piles of it aside. Their hearts thudded and they felt hot, but they were determined to get the job done.

One hour later, the thugs and the chauffeur, whose shirts were drenched in sweat, found themselves standing on top of a pine box scarcely covered in dirt. When Wesner saw that they'd reached the lip of the pine box, he quickly stripped down to his wife beater. The chauffeur tossed him his shovel. He switched hands with the shovel and grabbed the chauffeur's hand, helping him climb out of the grave. Once he was out, together, they helped the thugs out. Afterward, Wesner jumped down inside of the grave. He glanced at his time piece and saw that ten more minutes had passed.

"Oh, God, please let 'em be alive, please!" Wesner stabbed the shovel into the slight opening of the lid and pried it open. When he lifted the lid he found Sheila inside wearing a see-through oxygen mask over his nose and mouth, with a gray and green oxygen tank that read *zero*. On top of that, Sheila was scarcely covered in dirt and there was also dirt inside of the pine box. Sheila's eyes and mouth were shut. It looked like he wasn't breathing. Seeing his son like this caused Wesner to panic. He threw his shovel back upon the surface. Next, he removed the oxygen mask from off his face and struggled to pull his limp body from out of pine box. He found himself hot and sweaty. With a grunt, he hoisted Sheila over his shoulder, holding him upward for his thugs to grab him. "I got chu, I got chu, son. Just hold on, hold on."

Once the thugs pulled Sheila upon the surface, they laid him flat on his back. The chauffeur then pulled Wesner out of the six-foot grave, by his hands. He ran over to Sheila and got down on his knees. He placed two fingers to his neck, but couldn't feel a pulse. Next, he placed his ear to his chest and listened for his heartbeat. He couldn't hear it!

Without another minute to waste, Wesner went right to work performing CPR on Sheila, breathing into his mouth and pumping his chest. He performed this procedure three times, and was starting to give up hope. The thugs tried to pull him away from

Sheila's body, believing that he was dead. But he wouldn't allow it; he fought them off.

Wesner went on to perform the procedure again, talking to Sheila and begging him to come back. Wesner's eyes turned pink and pooled with water. Shortly thereafter, his cheeks were flooded with tears. "Please, son, don't leave me! Come back to me! I love you, I need you!" He continued to breathe air into Sheila's lungs and pump his chest. Seeing that he wasn't getting any reaction, Wesner bowed his head and dropped his arms at his sides. Big teardrops fell from his eyes and splashed on the ground. The thugs and the chauffeur hung their heads, and crossed themselves in the sign of the crucifix. They didn't know how it felt to lose a child, but they felt sorry for their boss.

Wesner leaned over and laid his head against Sheila's chest, silently crying. Abruptly, his eyelids popped open. He'd heard Sheila's heart thumping. He picked his head up from his chest. The moment he did, Sheila started coughing hard. His eyelids peeled open, and he looked around like he didn't know where he was. When his eyes settled on his father, he was surprised to see him, especially crying. For as long as he'd been alive he'd never seen his old man cry. He was also an Alpha Male. He was very strong, aggressive, and masculine. Sheila couldn't think of a time where he'd showed any kind of affection, or even said that he loved him. So, to see him on his knees before him now was shocking.

"Oh, thank God, it's a miracle! Thank you, thank you, Lord!" Wesner said as he looked up at the sky, with his fingers interlocked. The tears continued to pour down his cheeks, and slick his face wet. Wesner wiped his dripping eyes with the back of his hand, and crawled over to Sheila. He pulled him close and wrapped his arms around him. He kissed him on the cheek and hugged him tight, sobbing aloud.

Unbeknownst to Wesner, his thugs and chauffeur, Latrell and Shavon were in the Lincoln Navigator outside the cemetery, watching them through binoculars. Once they saw Wesner had revived Sheila, Shavon fired up the truck and drove off.

***

A bare chest Latrell sat before the two big ass duffle bags on the table top, removing the kilos from them. He stacked the blocks neatly on top of one another. While he was occupied doing this, Shavon returned to the kitchen, toting the pillowcase containing the birds, jewelry and money they'd jacked Onyx for. She sat the pillowcase down on the table top, and began removing the bricks from it, stacking them neatly as Latrell did. Once Shavon finished stacking the bricks they'd gotten from Onyx, she went on to stack the money they'd gotten from the lick aside. Afterward, she put the pile of jewelry in a pile by itself. Shavon then reached across the kitchen table to grab one of the bricks from out of the duffle bag that Latrell was grabbing from. She accidentally knocked one of the bricks he'd stacked from off the table. When it fell to the floor, she went to pick it up, and noticed a white substance had spilled from out of it. The substance resembled sugar to her. This was a major problem because cocaine is not like powdered sugar. It's not even powder until it is cut down. Pure or mostly pure cocaine is a solid, dense, somewhat crumbly substance, especially once it's compressed. It will absolutely stick together in a single piece until it's cut with other substances, and then cut up or crushed.

Latrell stopped stacking the bricks up, once he noticed Shavon staring down at the kilo she'd dropped on the floor. He watched as she picked the key up and stuck her finger inside of the small hole at the corner of the package. She stuck her finger inside the hole, and when she pulled it out, she stuck it inside her mouth, tasting it. Shavon's forehead crinkled and her eyelids narrowed, as she tasted something sweet. She looked up at Latrell, and he frowned up, wondering what she'd discovered.

"What? What's up?" Latrell questioned, with a furrowed brow. Shavon didn't respond. She handed him the kilo and he tasted it, just like she had. He was surprised too. "It's sugar!"

Latrell sat the kilo of sugar down on the table top and raced inside the kitchen. He came running right back out with a big ass butcher's knife, and started opening up the kilos. Following his lead, Shavon unsheathed her knife from where it was strapped, on the lower part of her leg. She and Latrell stood side by side, opening up the kilos Wesner had hit them with. They found that brick after brick was filled with sugar. By the time they were done, there were grains of sugar covering the floor, along with torn strips of scotch tape. Their chest rose and fell with each hefty breath they took. Their forehead, shoulders, and chests were shiny from perspiration. Their heads were bowed, and their hands were planted on the end of the table. They'd discovered that only fifty of the kilos were actually cocaine, which made sense because Wesner had informed Latrell that he couldn't fill such a tall order of one hundred keys in such a short time.

Hearing Shavon whimpering, Latrell looked to find her shoulders shuddering and big teardrops falling from the brims of her eyes, splashing on the table top and the floor.

"I'm sorry, baby. I'm so, so sorry," Latrell said, affectionately placing his hand on Shavon's shoulder.

Shavon looked up with a face twisted with hostility. Her eyes were pink and her cheeks were full of tears. Suddenly, she exploded like a powder keg. Enraged, she stabbed her knife into the table top with all of her might and flipped the kitchen table with a shout. Latrell jumped back as the table crashed to the floor, spilling the bricks, stacks of money, and jewelry. Shavon dropped to her hands and knees. Her head bobbed as she sobbed hard and loudly.

"They're gonna kill 'em, they're gonna fucking kill 'em!" Shavon said over and over again, sniffling and crying. "They're gonna kill 'em and it's my fault."

"No." Latrell got down on his knees before Shavon, and cupped her face in his hands. He looked her square in the eye, with seriousness bleeding from his pupils. "I am not gonna let Mank die, you hear me? I'm not gonna let them mothafuckaz kill 'em! We're gonna get up these bricks, and we're gonna give 'em to them and get my nigga back. You understand me?" he asked her, watching the tears slick down her cheeks. He hated when she cried. It hurt him. She was hurt. Shavon nodded, and Latrell went on: "I need you to say 'Baby, I believe in you, we can do this. I got cho back and you got my front.'"

She looked him in the eyes and said, "Baby, I believe in you, we can do this. I got cho back and you got my front."

"Good." Latrell kissed her lips twice and hugged her. She tightened her arms around him. In that moment, she felt confident and relieved. And it was all thanks to him.

Latrell got up on his feet and helped Shavon up to hers. Together, they set the kitchen table back up and placed all the items that had fell back on it. Latrell stood, looking over the kitchen table at all of the *real* bricks they'd obtained from the lick, with his hands on his hips. Shavon walked over to him and wrapped her arms around his waist. He threw his arm around her shoulder, and together, they took stock of everything they had.

"Alright, we've got fifty birds from the ransom." Latrell pointed at the stacks of bricks they'd secured from Sheila's kidnapping. He then pointed to the ten bricks, which was stacked up on the side of the fifty bricks. "Ten bricks from the Onyx lick, plus, the seventy gees in cash, and the jewelry. Hmmm." He lowered his eyebrows and massaged his chin, as he thought about something. "Hopefully, I can get about, sayyyyy, a hunnit kay off those jewels, once I fence 'em. Then, I can cop, like, four birds with that seventy bandz we got. The dude I know usually slangs 'em for, like, twenty, twenty-five racks, but he owes me a favor, so I figure I can talk 'em into givin' nem to me for fifteen a piece. If so, I'ma see about getting, like, ten of them shits with this paypa I got set aside. So, that'll bring us up to seventy-two birds. We'll only need twenty-eight mo' to pay this nigga and get Mank back."

"I gotta few dollars too, baby. I can pitch in." Shavon looked up at him, still holding him around his waist.

Latrell looked down at Shavon. "What chu got, slim?"

"I got sixty bandz put up, and I can slang my car. I figure I can get, like, twenty-five, maybe twenty-eight, for it. I mean, it's a 2018 Chevy Impala."

"Okay, we can possibly get six mo' with that."

"That'll leave us with twenty-two mo' bricks to come up with," she said. "We can get the rest of 'em up by kicking in niggaz doez and snatching up dope boys."

"You're right." Latrell told her. "We just gotta go hard, real hard. And we can pull this shit off!" He slammed his fist into his palm for emphasis, looking over the kitchen table full of the items from the lick again. Seeing Shavon's movements from the corner of his eye, he turned around to find her pulling out her cell phone. Then, while she was scrolling through her contacts, Latrell asked: "What chu up to, babe?"

"I'm finna call this fool Tyrell again," she informed him, before putting the cellular to her ear. "If what Korey said about 'em having the shipment being true, maybe I can talk 'em into giving us the other twenty-two birds we need."

Latrell nodded as he thought, *She must be crazy if she thinks that crackhead gon' give her any parts of that dope back. If we catch up with this nigga, I'm putting that ass in the hurt-locker for the whole lot of the shit. Then, I'ma make sho' his ho-ass get flat-lined for putting my young niggaz, Mank and Korey's lives in jeopardy!*

"Good idea, baby. If he'll shoot us the twenty-two we need, we can drop that shit in Baby Boy's lap and get Mank back," he told her as he folded his arms across his chest, watching her as she listened to the telephone ring. The longer the phone rang, the more the disappointment spread across Shavon's face. Finally, the answering service picked up. She left a message for Tyrell, telling him that it was urgent that he called her back. What she didn't know was, Tyrell had seen her calling, and put his cell phone on silent.

Seeing the defeated look on Shavon's face, Latrell threw his arm around her shoulders, trying to comfort her. "Look, don't wet that shit. Even if he doesn't hit chu back, we still gon' do what we needa do to get what we needa get." His voice sounded reassuring. She was looking down at her fidgeting hands, so he tilted her chin upward, with his curled finger. "You feel me?" She nodded. "Gemme some lip then."

Shavon, still holding her cellular, threw her arms around Latrell's neck. She kissed him passionately. He then scooped her up into his arms and carried her to their bedroom.

Chapter 11

The day was warm and cozy, with the occasional breeze, when Shavon pulled up alongside the curb and killed the engine. Latrell popped open the glove box and removed a satchel. He unzipped it and looked inside at the jewelry. Once he zipped the satchel back up, he kissed Shavon and told her he'd be right back. As he opened his door, a black motorcycle pulled up a few feet behind them, and its rider got off, rocking a black helmet. The motorcyclist flipped his visor to reveal his eyes, and continued down the sidewalk, carrying a pouch. Latrell was just a few feet behind him, taking in the scenery of downtown Los Angeles traffic.

Latrell noticed that the motorcyclist was headed toward Cooper's pawn shop, which was the exact place he was headed to fence the jewelry he'd gotten from the Onxy lick. The motorcyclist removed his helmet and looked up at the intercom. He held down the button on the small, scarred, yellowing box and told whoever was listening, what he was there for.

Worth, the motorcyclist, tucked his helmet underneath his arm. A moment later, the door buzzed, and Worth opened it with his black leather-gloved hand. Latrell came behind him, and went through the same procedure. Once he crossed the threshold inside of the establishment, he walked to a metal gate, where he was buzzed inside. On the other side of the gate, Latrell took in everything the pawn shop had to offer. The place was made up exactly like your ordinary pawn shop. For the most part, Cooper's pawn shop was a legitimate business, but its owner had some shady dealings as well. He dealt in stolen jewelry, cars, boats, planes, amongst other things. These illegal goods brought everything from thieves to dope boys to Cooper's to do business. He had a long list of clientele that he fucked with when it came to his illicit business. But with his legit business, he dealt with his average patrons straight up. This was how he was able to stay under the radar of the law for so long, and make as much money as he had. As quiet as it's kept, old man Cooper was a low-key millionaire.

Behind the glass display case, where all of the silver, gold, and platinum diamond jewelry was stored, a young African American woman stood holding a clipboard and an ink pen, going over the inventory that they had in stock. Her name was Veronica. She chewed on bubble gum, and occasionally blew a huge bubble until it exploded. She then went right back to chewing the gum. The youthful looking woman had a mahogany skin tone. She wore her hair in a fade, and it was the color of red brick dust. Underneath her black Cooper's pawn shop logo T-shirt, she wore a Kevlar bullet-proof vest. On her right hip, she had a holstered, black handgun.

Latrell watched as a brute of a man lifted a wooden partition that separated the sales floor from everything behind the counter. The enormous man went by the name Caleb, and he had a body covered in muscles. He possessed a pale complexion and freckles that ran from his forehead to his cheeks. He rocked his long, rich auburn hair shaved on the sides, while the top of it was pulled back in a bun. His thick, lengthy beard reached his chest. And his jade green eyes shone like emeralds in the beaming sun. The stick of a cherry sucker hung from the corner of his thin, pink lips. His broad chest stretched the fabric of the black Cooper's pawn shop logo T-shirt he was wearing. Over his back, and around his shoulders, were leather copper brown twin holsters containing two black handguns.

Caleb stepped aside and allowed Worth to cross his path, and then he closed the partition behind him. Afterward, the six-foot-three man approached a metal door, and pressed the button on the intercom beside it. There was a static sound, like someone attempting to talk over a walkie talkie, and then someone spoke.

"Yeah?" Cooper spoke from the other side of the door.

"You've gotta custy out here, Coop. Fella by the name of—" He looked to Worth and waited for him to give him his name. Once he'd given it to him, he turned back around to the intercom. "Says his name's Worth."

Right then, the heavy locks came undone, and there was a buzzing sound. The man pulled open the door and Worth walked inside. He then closed the door behind him.

Latrell busied himself looking at things around the pawn shop, while he waited for Worth to come out of the backroom. He picked up a pair of shades with the tag hanging from the right arm of them, and turned to the full body length mirror. As he looked himself over, he saw the door to Cooper's office open, Worth strolling out, with his motorcycle helmet tucked under his arm. Once he was out of his line of vision, he approached Caleb, so he could see Cooper. It wasn't long before he entered the old man's office. Latrell looked over the small office. There was an aquarium behind him, with baby sharks swimming through the prettiest blue water he had ever seen. The liquid was the color of Listerine. It had seaweed and black rocks at the bottom of it. A "32-inch flatscreen was above Latrell's head, and a basketball game was on. There was a water cooler in the corner, which was sitting beside a table. On the table there was a coffee maker, stacks of Styrofoam cups, a box of creamers, and a box filled with small packets of sugar. A black leather sofa was against the walls on the left and right sides of the room.

Latrell and Cooper exchanged pleasantries, dapping one another up. Latrell and Cooper went way back. They'd been doing business since Latrell was a little nigga running wild in the streets, tearing shit up and sticking up everything moving. Whatever valuables he'd come up on, he'd come holler at Cooper to fence the shit for a profit.

"What chu got for me there, Jack?" Cooper asked Latrell, eyes on the satchel in his hand. He was in the middle of taking another look at the merchandise, when Latrell entered his office. Old man Cooper was a rotund man with dirty blonde hair, which he wore slicked back to cover a bald spot at the top of his scalp. He had a hairy chest, and hairy, meaty hands. Several gawdy gold necklaces were around his neck, and he had gold rings on every finger. He wore a black shirt with tan stripes on each side of it. He wore his shirt open to show off his chest hairs and jewelry. His black leather jacket hung off the back of the chair that he was sitting in.

"Gon' check it out, OG," Latrell passed him the satchel. Cooper sat the piece of jewelry Worth had brought in aside, on top of the small mountain of other merchandise he'd brought in. He then sat his loupe aside and took Latrell's satchel, dumping its contents out on a violet velvet cloth. While Cooper busied himself looking over Latrell's jewelry with the loupe, an impatient Latrell eyed the small mountain of jewelry he'd slide aside, which Worth had sold him. The gold, platinum, diamonds and rubies of the jewelry sparkled. They were very appealing to the eyes, but Latrell's main focus was on the gold locket. That locket resembled the same one that was snatched off of King Rich's neck after he was bodied.

"May I?" Latrell pointed to the gold locket on top of the small mountain of alluring jewelry.

"Sure, go ahead," Cooper told him, before going back to examining the jewelry that Latrell had brought him, with his trusty loupe, which was a small magnification device used to see small details more closely. The old man was using it to check the clarity of the diamonds in the jewelry.

While he was doing this, Latrell was picking up the gold locket. At that moment, the only sound he could hear was that of his heart, thudding wildly in anticipation of what he may discover. Latrell hesitated opening the locket as he held it in his hands, for fear of the truth that it may bring forth. Finally, he took a deep breath and opened it. His heart skipped a beat once he saw there was a picture of King Rich and his family inside of it. His eyelids peeled wide open, and his mouth hung ajar. He couldn't believe it. The mothafucka that had just fenced the jewelry was connected to whoever popped King Rich. It was either that, or he was the trigger man. Either way, Latrell couldn't let homeboy slip through his fingers. He had to catch up with him to see what he knew.

"Fucks the matter witchu?" Cooper looked at Latrell with a raised eyebrow. He could tell by the expression on his face that something was troubling him.

"Huh? Uh, nothing, I'm good," Latell told him, as he closed the locket, which made a click sound. He then held it up by its necklace, like it was the tail of a dead rat. "However much you're slinging this for, take it outta whatever you're gonna lay on me for the merch I brought in." Cooper nodded and went back to closely examining the diamonds in the jewelry. Latrell watched him impatiently, tapping his foot on the floor, and hoping that Worth hadn't gotten too far away. For the first time, he noticed the surveillance monitor on Cooper's desk top. It allowed its viewer to see the outside and inside of the store. Latrell took note of Worth still being inside the shop; he was looking over a row of katanas, which were on placements on the wall. The hit-man unsheathed one of the swords, and practiced using it with expertise. Veronica stood behind the counter, watching him excitedly.

"Alright, I'll give you one hundred grand for this haul; that's, with the locket included," Cooper told him as he leaned his hefty frame back in his executive office chair, waiting to see what Latrell would say about his offer. He was a notorious cheap skate that loved to haggle. Latrell knew this more than anyone else, but he didn't have time to bargain with him today. He had to get to Worth before he slipped between his fingers.

"Sold!" Latrell told him. He knew Cooper was beating him with his offer, but he was in the rush to get out of there and catch up with Worth. Latrell continued to tap his foot impatiently as he watched Cooper crack open his safe again. Homeboy grabbed a few blue faces from out of the safe, threw it shut with a bump of his arm, and stacked the dead presidents on top of each other before Latrell. Latrell hurriedly tossed the blue faces inside of his satchel and hauled ass out of the back office, shutting the door behind him. When he looked around the shop, Worth wasn't anywhere to be found. *Shit!* He tried to go through the gate, but it wouldn't open for him. Latrell turned around to Veronica and Caleb. She threw up one finger, signaling for him to give her a minute before pressing a button that activated the lock of the gate. The gate made a buzzing sound before clicking unlock. Latrell made his way outside. He looked left and then right, where he saw Worth halfway down the block.

Latrell jogged after Worth as he casually strolled down the sidewalk. He then slowed down and started speed walking behind him. He stopped in his tracks when Worth stopped and took the time to slide his motorcycle helmet over his head. Abruptly, he turned around and Latrell glanced at his watch, tapping his foot. He stuck his head out over the curb, looking up and down the street, pretending like he was waiting on a bus to pick him up. Figuring that's exactly what he was doing, Worth continued on down the sidewalk. Once he'd turned back around, Latrell continued to follow him. He watched as Worth made his way around the corner of a building and disappeared.

Latrell threw his hoodie over his head. He then looked around cautiously to make sure no one was watching him. He pulled a pair of gloves from the back pocket of his jeans and slid his hands into them, flexing his fingers inside them. Afterwards, he pulled the gloves down tight around his wrists. He took another cautious look around, to make sure there weren't any witnesses around to see what he was about to do. As soon as he confirmed that there wasn't, he pulled his handgun from the small of his back, and screwed his silencer on the tip of its barrel. Once he cocked the slide on it, he held the gun at his side, and out of view of watchful eyes.

Latrell placed his back against the building Worth had just disappeared behind. Carefully, he crept down the sidewalk with his eyes focused ahead. He slowly eased his head around the corner of the tenement and met the cold, black steel of Worth's gun. Latrell could see his reflection through the visor of the contract killa's motorcycle helmet. Latrell's heart thudded, and beads of sweat oozed from out of the pores on his temple and slid down the side of his face. His eyes were wide open as he swallowed the lump of fear in his throat, wondering if the next thing that was going to go through his chest would be a hollow tip bullet or not.

"Who are you, and why the fuck are you following me?" Worth spoke through the microphone inside of his motorcycle helmet. When Latrell didn't answer, he cocked the hammer on his blower. "You've got 'til the count of five to give me an answer, or your brain fragments are gonna be decorating the curb. One. Two. Three—"

Latrell slightly lifted his gun and pointed it at Worth's booted foot, pulling the trigger. A hushed bullet ignited from his gun's silenced barrel, and ripped through the contract killa's steel-toe leather boot.

"Aaaaah, mothafucka!" Worth hollered out in pain and dropped his handgun. He hopped back on one foot, dripping blood on the concrete sidewalk.

"Where'd you get this locket?" Latrell asked as he approached him. He held his gun on him while he used his other hand to pull out King Rich's locket.

Worth lunged forward just as Latrell pulled the trigger of his gun. The weapon fired, but Worth fluidly moved around it. The bullet slammed into a parked Subaru's back passenger window and shattered it. Worth moved like blowing wind, snatching the top off of Latrell's handgun and tossing it aside. Latrell looked at his inoperable weapon in shock, eyes wide, mouth open. An as soon as he was incapacitated, Worth took advantage of him. He chopped him in the throat, which caused him to drop his blower and wrap his hands around his neck, eyes bulging. The contract killa kicked Latrell in the stomach. Latrell doubled over. He was then rewarded with a swift kick square in the face, and then a round-house kick to the side of the head. The force from the kick slammed the side of Latrell's skull against the building. Dazed, he stumbled backward and crashed on the ground, groaning in pain. He looked to Worth and saw double as a sliver of blood ran from the side of his head, and dripped on the sidewalk. Latrell watched as the hit-man limped over to his gun, turned around and made his way back in his direction. At this time, there were bystanders looking on in awe, and vehicles flying up and down the street.

Some of them had even slowed down to see what was about to happen.

Seeing that he was being watched, Worth fired shots in the bystanders' direction and sent them scattering like mice. The sudden eruption of gunfire even made the nosy drivers speed off. Once the coast was clear for Worth to lay down his murder game, he limped over to Latrell and pointed his gun down at him. The hitta could see his reflection in his potential victim's pupils as his finger curled around the trigger.

"Aaaaaaaaaah!" Worth threw his head back hollering in pain. He dropped his gun and collapsed to the sidewalk, falling on top of Latrell. When he fell, Shavon was within view, standing behind him with a taser. She shoved the taser into her back pocket as Latrell pushed Worth from off of him. Shavon extended her hand to Latrell and pulled him back up on his feet. He winched as he rubbed his head, looking down at Worth.

"Luckily, I came when I did 'cause homeboy was whipping yo' ass," Shavon said jokingly.

"Hahahahahahaha!" Latrell laughed at her sarcastically, still rubbing his head. "Look in the glove box and get me those zip-cuffs," he told Shavon. She went off to carry out his orders and he picked up Worth's gun, sticking it at the small of his back. Shavon passed him the zip-cuffs from over her shoulder, and he fastened an unconscious Worth's wrists with them. He then removed the contract killa's motorcycle helmet and cast it aside. "Open the trunk up," Latrell told Shavon, grunting as he lifted the much heavier Worth up in his arms. Shavon opened the trunk of their car and stood aside, waiting for Latrell to deposit Worth inside of it. Once he did, she slammed it shut, and they hopped inside the car.

"Where are we headed to now?" Shavon asked from behind the wheel as she pulled away from the curb and into traffic.

When she asked this, Latrell was peering out of the windows of the car. He saw the bystanders emerging from where they'd hidden when Worth fired shots into the air. One of them was even bold enough to run out into the street with an ink pen and piece of paper to jot down the license plate number of their whip.

Latrell settled back down in his seat, and said, "First, we've gotta get this car off the streets and get another one. The Boys are gonna be all over it. Next, we're gonna head where no one can hear homeboy back there scream." He threw his head toward the backseat, referring to Worth inside of the trunk.

"Okay. Cool." Shavon nodded as she switched hands on the steering wheel, to pull out her cell phone. "I'ma hit up Tyrell's ass this one last time. I hope he answers."

***

Tyrell climbed the steps toward his cousin, Fat Daddy's apartment door. Feeling his cell phone vibrate, he pulled it out and glanced at its screen. It was Shavon. He blew hot air and put the cellular into his back pocket. He didn't have shit to say to Shavon. He knew that she was more than likely hitting him up to try to get him to give her the bricks he'd stolen out of her garage from Mank and Korey. If she thought he was giving her that shit back, then she was out of her fucking mind. With that kind of weight in his lap, he could level up and get back where he used to be in the crack game. He'd be damned if he let anything stop him. He didn't give a fuck if her and her brother's lives depended on them getting that work back. That would just be something that they'd have to deal with.

Tyrell switched hands with the shopping bag containing the four birds he was going to hit Fat Daddy with. Once he reached his door, he knocked on it and waited for him to answer.

"Who dat, Blood?" Fat Daddy asked.

Tyrell replied: "Yo' mothafucking cousin, nigga! Tyrell. Open it."

Tyrell listened as the door was unchained and unlocked, then pulled open. He found himself standing before Fat Daddy. Fat Daddy stood all of five-foot-ten and weighed three-hundred-and-twenty-five pounds. He was a caramel complexioned cat that wore his hair parted down the middle, and braided down the sides. His body was covered in tattoos, but the most noticeable ones were the ones occupying his face.. *Westside* in fancy cursive letters on his left cheek, and *Junglez* in fancy cursive letters on his right. And last, but not least, "Killa Kali" on his neck, which covered most of it up. Fat Daddy was dressed in a wife beater which displayed his protruding belly, tan Dickie shorts, long socks and red Chuck Taylor Converses. A golden albuterol inhaler hung from his necklace. His left wrist rocked an icy gold Rolex with a Cuban link bracelet, while on his right wrist there was a diamond stubbed bracelet, and a huge icy gold diamond ring on his pink finger.

"What up, relative? Took yo' ass long enough, nigga," Fat Daddy slapped hands with Tyrell and embraced him with his jeweled hand over his shoulder. "Close that doe back foe me, loved one," he told him as he turned around to walk back to where he was sitting on the couch, watching a kick boxing match. It was then that Tyrell spotted the chrome handgun with the ivory handle tucked in the small of his back. Once he'd shut the door like Fat Daddy had instructed, Tyrell dropped the shopping bag of bricks on the coffee table. He then made his way over to the La-Z-Boy chair and plopped down. He glanced up at the television's screen, and then over at Fat Daddy, who appeared to be texting someone on his cell phone.

"This the shit right here?" Fat Daddy pointed to the shopping bag. Tyrell nodded. "Cool. I'ma gon' get that paypa fa you. My homie Rat finna come up here to check this shit out. If it's good, you can get cho loot and bounce."

"Fa sho'," Tyrell adjusted himself on the La-Z-Boy chair. He then leaned forward, with his neck turned, facing the flat-screen television. Fat Daddy disappeared through his bedroom door, shutting it behind him. A couple of minutes later, Rat came through the door. He was a medium-built nigga with all of the facial features of a rodent. With his beady eyes and big nose, he held an uncanny resemblance to the four-legged creature. He was wearing a red beanie and long-sleeved red T-shirt. The gun impression underneath his shirt let Tyrell know he was strapped. Before dapping up Tyrell, Rat threw his head back like, *What's up?* He then copped a squat on the couch, and watched the fight on the flatscreen.

Fat Daddy ambled out of his bedroom with a Nike duffle bag, pulling the door shut behind him. He walked over to the couch, pulled out his chrome handgun which had a silencer on the tip of its barrel, placed it on the coffee table and then sat down. A smile stretched across Tyrell's face as he observed Fat Daddy pulling stack after rubber band stack from out the duffle bag, and sitting them on the coffee table. Fat Daddy lined the stacks of money up in three rows, and sat them on top of one another. The stacks of blue faces were wrinkled, and some of them were either partially torn or missing some of their corners. The money was obviously drug money, but Tyrell didn't give a fuck because dirty money spent just as well as clean money did. And that was all that mattered to him.

"Yo', Rat, this the shit right here, Blood," Fat Daddy nodded to the shopping bag sitting on the coffee table. Rat tore his eyes from off the kickboxing match. He then took the shopping bag with the birds in it, and walked it over into the kitchen. He pulled out one of them, cut off its packaging with a butcher's knife, and then hacked off a corner of it. He then went about the task of making the corner he'd chopped off into a fine powdery substance, making sure to smoothing out the lumps in it. While this was going on, Tyrell sat on the La-Z-Boy. He pulled his crack pipe from out of his pocket, and held it up for Fat Daddy to see, posing a question.

"Say, cuzzo, a nigga antsy, you mind if I take the edge off?" Tyrell asked if he could smoke in his crib.

"Do you, my nigga," Fat Daddy answered before shaking up his golden pump and spraying it a few times inside his mouth. He then focused his attention back on the television screen, waiting for Rat to return with the results of the cocaine. Unbeknownst to Tyrell, he'd also texted Jayvon to come up stairs. There was a knock at the door. Rat stopped doing what he was doing, to answer it. Jayvon, a tall lanky brother, as black as twelve o'clock midnight, came in, then closed and locked the door behind him. He too was strapped. Jayvon followed Rat inside the kitchen.

Tyrell stuffed his glass pipe with off-white crack rocks. He then put the pipe between his big, ashy, white chapped lips, and struck a flame with his Bic lighter. A long flame appeared and licked the air. Tyrell brought the flame to the tip of his pipe. The flame licked at the tip of the scarred, beat-up glass pipe, causing it to turn black. The crack rocks slowly began to melt, and smoke manifested inside the pipe, fogging it up. With his eyelids closed, Tyrell sucked greedily from the opposite end of his smoking utensil, making small smoke clouds appear. Unbeknownst to him, Fat Daddy sat where he was on the couch, watching him with disgust. His face balled up with animosity. He snorted and shook his head. He hated the fact that his smoked out ass cousin came up in the game. Fat Daddy felt like he didn't deserve it. To him, Tyrell wasn't anything but a low, down, dirty, stinking, mothafucking crackhead that didn't need any bricks. If anybody should have those shits, then it should be him.

Rat held a small tube of clear liquid pinched between his index finger and thumb. Using a very tiny, white plastic spoon, he scooped up a small pile of cocaine and dumped it inside the tube. He then sat the tiny spoon down on the counter top and placed a small cap on the tube. Jayvon looked over his shoulder as he shook the tube up. The liquid inside the tube turned blue, which meant that the cocaine was pure. In fact, it was one hundred percent pure. Now, if the shit had turned purple, then it would have meant that the coke was garbage. Rat smiled and when he looked to Jayvon, he was smiling too. They headed back inside the living room, where Fat Daddy and Tyrell were.

"Yo', Blood," Rat called out to Fat Daddy. The big man turned around from where he was sitting, and looked over his shoulder. "This shit official."

"Good." He looked to Tyrell, who was as high as a fucking kite. He then looked to the stacks of dead presidents sitting on the coffee table. Then, back at Tyrell again. Right then, he had made up his mind. He wasn't about to give Tyrell's smoked-out-ass a goddamn thing.

Fat Daddy kept his eyes on Tyrell, who was oblivious of what was about to take place, as he motioned Rat and Jayvon over to do his bidding with his chrome piece. A scowling Rat and Jayvon approached Tyrell, cracking the knuckles on both of their hands. Rat smacked the glass pipe out of his mouth while he was firing it up. The pipe flew across the living room and deflected off of the wall. A frowned up Tyrell looked at Rat, like he'd lost his mind.

"Nigga, what the fuck is yo' problem?" Tyrell was about standing up, and Rat punched him in the jaw, causing him to stumble and crash through the glass coffee table. The glass coffee table exploded and sent shards flying everywhere. Rat and Jayvon moved in on Tyrell, punching, kicking, and stomping his black ass out. Tyrell tried to put up a fight, but to no avail. The homies had gotten the drop on him, so he was at their mercy. While Rat and Jayvon were busy giving Tyrell the business, Fat Daddy busied himself over at the closet. He slipped on an insulated suit, shoe coverings, latex gloves, and a square, see-through face mask that was designed to block blood splatter and other secretions. He looked more like he was going to do a surgery than to commit a murder.

"Y'all grab his ass and drag 'em inside of the other room!" Fat Daddy ordered his henchmen. He shut the closet door and stood where he was clutching his gun. He watched as Jayvon and Rat drag a barely conscious Tyrell toward the second bedroom. Jayvon, while holding onto Tyrell's leg, opened the door. Next, he flipped on the light switch. Fat Daddy followed them inside the bedroom, which was covered from floor, wall and ceiling with black garbage bags. Fat Daddy, still holding his handgun, opened the bedroom's closet door. He pulled the drawstring, and the light bulb came on. The closet was covered in black garbage bags as well. In fact, the only thing in it was the pole used to hang clothes hangers on, and a pair of handcuffs, which dangled from it.

Fat Daddy stepped aside and allowed his henchmen to drag Tyrell to the closet, where they handcuffed him to the pole. Tyrell hung there, bloody, battered and bruised. Blood oozed out of his nose, over his lips, and onto the collar of his white T-shirt, turning it pink. He looked up at Fat Daddy through a swollen eye that was on to its way to swelling completely shut. His eye was pink with red webs in it. His vision was blurry, and he saw double for a minute. After a while, his vision came back into focus. He winced in pain. His eyes grew big once he saw Fat Daddy approaching him with a handgun, with a silencer on the tip of its barrel.

"What the fuck, man? You're about to pop me over some dope? We're supposed to be family, Teddy! Cousins, bruh! What the fuck!" Tyrell hollered, with blood and spit jumping from his lips.

"Blood is thicka than water, relative, but four birds is four birds," Fat Daddy told him like it was. "Nigga, do you know how hard it is to come across four bricks of pure dope these days? Huh? A nigga will kill you over that shit. Hell, I'm fitsna kill you over it!" Right then, he cocked the slide on his handgun and pressed it against Tyrell's forehead. Tyrell squeezed his eyelids shut, and started hyperventilating. He was trying to work himself up for the inevitable. "Give my dead homies my regards." He went to pull back on the trigger, but what Tyrell said next stopped him.

"There's more, there's more!" Tyrell shouted over and over again. He seemed to have come alive under the threat of having his brains blown out of his fucking head.

"More what?" Fat Daddy asked.

"More keys!"

"This nigga fulla shit, Blood! He's just tryna save his ass!" Rat called out to Fat Daddy.

"No, no, no, no!" Tyrell hollered out. "There's ninety-six more kilos! Ninety-six more! I'll take you to 'em if you promise to lemme go!" He looked Fat Daddy in his eyes, chest rising and falling. His heart thudded out of control. He hoped that he believed him. That was the only card up his sleeve. It was his last saving grace.

Fat Daddy continued to hold his gun to Tyrell's forehead, watching sweat slide down the side of his face. From the look on

Fat Daddy's face, he could tell he was thinking it over. "Okay," Fat Daddy said, before removing the gun from Tyrell's forehead. Once he did, Tyrell's head dropped and sighed with relief. His cheeks swelled and flattened as he breathed in and out, happy to still have his life. "You take the homies to the rest of the shit, and I'll see to it that you walk. But," he scowled and pressed his gun to his forehead, "if I find out that yo' cracked-out-ass is lying to me, then I'm gonna have them split cho wig. Now, do we understand each other?" Tyrell nodded rapidly, and then said *yes*. "Good!" Fat Daddy took his handgun away from Tyrell's forehead again. He then turned to Rat and Jayvon and gave them some orders. Afterward, he handed Rat the key to the handcuff and walked out of the room, leaving them to attend to Tyrell.

As soon as Rat unlocked the handcuffs, Tyrell dropped to the floor of the closet. Rat and Jayvon pulled him out onto the black garbage bags. Next, they put a strip of duct tape over his mouth and duct-taped his wrists behind his back.

Tranay Adams

Chapter 12

That night

A naked Worth stood with his wrists tied to the necks of the shower nozzles on the left and right side of him. His head was bowed. His muscular arms and wide muscular back shone from sweat, as well as his face and chest. The foot that Latrell had shot him in was wrapped up in a bloody bandage. Worth's upper body was covered in numerous old scars. The scars were four minute slashes, with a slash going diagonally across them. Each row of scars equaled to five bodies. Five lives that he'd sent from this life to the next, under contract. Fifty grand a head was what he charged his employers. Half up front! And the other half once the job was done. That's right! Killing was his business. And business was good. But not tonight. Business was bad. Real bad. In his twenty years in the murder game, he'd never found himself in this predicament. Worth had a bloody, swollen face, a fractured nose and busted lips, thanks to the brutal beating that Latrell had given him. A combination of blood and perspiration dripped from off his brow and bottom lip, splashing on the filthy tiled floor. A fat gray rat wandered over and started licking his blood from off of the floor.

Worth had a headache that told him he'd need an aspirin the size of a hockey puck to get rid of. He threw his head back and looked around, groaning, pupils rolling around lazily. His vision came in and out of focus as he looked about, trying to figure out where he'd been taken. From the looks of it, he was inside the shower room of some middle school or high school. Worth could hear water dripping from somewhere inside of the dwelling. Its walls, ceilings, and floors were dirty. And there were also cobwebs in all four of its corners, which were occupied by spiders and whatever prey they'd managed to capture.

Having just finished beating the living shit out of Worth, and tying his wrists to the neck of the shower nozzles, Latrell casually walked toward Shavon, with his chest heaving up and down. His face and body oozed with sweat, which caused his blood-speckled wife beater to cling to him like a second skin. His fists were wrapped in bicycle chains which dripped with Worth's blood, splashing on the floor with each step that he took.

"A nigga parched, lemme get some of that H2O," Latrell told Shavon, who had been standing in the shadows with her arms folded across her chest, watching her man lay down his torture game. Latrell went about the task of unwrapping the bloody bicycle chains from around his fists as he watched Shavon kneel down to the worn, brown leather bag he'd brought with all of his tools of torture. She sifted through the bag and pulled out a long bottle of Smart Water, screwing off the cap. Shavon guzzled some of the liquid down before passing it to her man, who'd just finished removing the bicycle chains from around his fists, letting them drop to the tiled floor. He then took the Smart Water to the head, throat moving up and down his neck as he drank. Latrell took the bottle from his lips, and tilted his head back. Closing his eyelids, he poured the cold water on his hot, sticky face while shaking his head from side to side. The swift movement caused his locs to whip from left to right, sending water flying in every direction.

Latrell took another guzzle of water before handing the bottle back to Shavon. As she began to drink from the bottle, he kneeled down to his brown leather bag. He went through the items inside until he found a leather whip. Once he stood upright, he turned to his right and motioned for Shavon to step aside. As soon as she did, Latrell tested out the whip, which he hadn't used in a very long time. He threw his hand back and slung the whip with expertise. The leather whip unraveled in a hurry as it was thrust forward, whistling through the air. When it reached its full potential, it made a loud snapping noise and severed one of many shower heads from its nozzle. The metal shower head clinked to the floor noisily and rolled a foot away. Satisfied with his demonstration, a scowling Latrell turned back around to Worth.

Latrell told Worth straight up as he readied the leather whip: "I'll give it to you, my nigga. You got humongous balls, big, humongous balls. And I admire that." Shavon stood behind him, within the shadows, drinking water and watching everything from over his shoulder. "But cho punk-ass gon' tell me where you got that locket from, or I'ma beat chu to death in this bitch. You hear me? Huh? You fuckin' hear me?" Latrell barked loudly, spittle flying from his mouth, and veins bulging at his temple. He gripped the handle of the whip tighter, drew back and thrust it forward. It whistled through the air, moving fast like lightning, unraveling and lashing Worth across his back. The pain that shot up Worth's back caused him to jerk violently, and his eyes nearly leaped out of his skull. He clenched his slightly hairy buttocks. Veins bulged on his forehead, and his face turned tomato red. Blood ran from the area of his back where the whip had struck. Before he knew it, the whip was whistling through the air once more. He was lashed again, again and again. His back was now a beet red, with welts overlapping welts that eventually split open and ran wet with blood. Droplets of his blood flew from his tender, sore back, decorating the surface with burgundy dots.

Lash, lash, lash, lash, lash!

The leather whip came back-to-back, making Worth jump with each lash. His glassy eyes became red webbed, and he scrunched up his face to fight off the pain. As soon as he squeezed his eyelids shut, he threw his head back and hot tears ran out from the corners of his eyes, and dripped inside his ears, slightly distorting his hearing.

Lash, lash, lash, lash!

A gritting Latrell continued to unleash hell on the hit-man's back without mercy. He was covered in so much sweat that it was dripping from him like he'd just gotten out of the shower, exploding in small puddles on the surface below.

"Talk, mothafucka! Talk!" Latrell demanded of Worth. As he whipped him, he watched as he danced in place. It wasn't long before Worth checked out mentally and went somewhere inside of his head. His thoughts drifted to a happier time in his life. He couldn't feel the lashes anymore. He'd become numb to the pain.

Latrell hunched over with his hands on his knees, staring up at Worth and breathing hard. Droplets of sweat fell from his brows and chin. His arm was sore as a mothafucka from his whipping of Worth.

This is one tough son of a bitch, but on my momma, I'ma break his ass!

After having caught his breath, Latrell stood back up and walked over to Worth. He pulled the red-ball gag out of his mouth and grabbed him by the lower half of his face, causing his lips to pucker up in the pose of a kiss-ready mouth.

While this was occurring, Shavon sat the bottle of water down and picked up Worth's pants. She rifled through his pockets, and came up with a couple of loose dollar bills and some change, which fell to the floor.

"You ready to tell me what I wanna know, white boy?" Latrell asked him with a frowning face and clenched jaws. Worth nodded. Latrell released his face, and the assassin spat blood in his face. Latrell closed his eyelids tightly just as the blood splattered on him.

"Fuck you, motherfucker! I'm not telling you jack shit!" Worth spat, with hate dripping from his vocal cords.

Latrell nodded and hung the leather whip around his neck. He then pulled his handgun from the small of his back and placed it against Worth's temple.

"Okay," Latrell told him and his finger was on the verge of pulling the trigger, then Shavon's voice stopped him.

"Wait!" Shavon called out to Latrell, causing his head to snap around in her direction. He watched as she approached him, then lowered his blower at his side. She passed him Worth's driver's license and a picture of him, Amari, and their precious baby girl.

Holding the driver's license and the picture in one hand, Latrell turned to Worth. He looked back and forth between him and the picture. "I take it this is wifey and yo' lil' mama, huh?" Worth didn't say a word. He just stared at Latrell as blood and sweat dripped from off his battered and bruised face. "Yeah, this is yo' family. I can tell by the way yo' eyes lit up when I asked.

Here, baby." He passed Shavon the driver's license and picture, which she slid into her back pocket. Latrell then pulled a silencer from out of his back pocket, and screwed it onto the tip of the barrel of his gun. He handed the weapon to Shavon, who looked from it to him, like she wasn't sure what to do with it. "Check this out, homeboy, you're gonna tell me where the fuck you got that locket from, or I'm gonna have my lady drive over to yo' house and execute yo' baby and yo' baby's momma, you feel me, dawg? Now, I want some answers. So talk, nigga!" Latrell barked, spit flying from his lips.

"Kiss my pale, pasty, white ass!" Worth told him, before spitting blood on the wall in front of him.

"Alright, Mr. Bad-Ass, have it yo' way," Latrell told him with a serious face. He then looked to Shavon. "Drive up to this mothafucka's house and putta bullet in wifey and his lil' girl's head." He winked at her, to let her know that he was running game on Worth.

"No! Noooooooooo!" Worth cried out with a scrunched up face, twisting from left to right, trying to pull himself free from his restraints, all to no avail.

"What the fuck are you waiting for, Shavon? Do like I told you! Pop that bitch and her baby," Latrell shouted at her, causing a vein on his temple to pulsate. With that having been said, Shavon's face twisted in anger and she tucked the silenced handgun in the front of her pants, moving towards the exit sign over the door.

Worth looked over his shoulder, following her as she set out to handle her business. "Wait, what are you doing? Don't chu do it! Don't chu touch my family." His head snapped over to Latrell and he said, "Okay. Alright. I'll tell you, I'll tell you what chu wanna know!"

Worth looked over his shoulder at Shavon again. She was still walking toward the exit until Latrell called out to her, which stopped her in her tracks.

"Okay, talk," Latrell told him.

"I'm a contract killer. This black kid by the name of Baby Boy hired me to knock off his old man. A kingpin with a fierce reputation—" Worth spilled the beans. His revelation caused Latrell to frown up, as the day of King Rich's assassination played back in his head. That's when he realized that Worth had to have been the motorcycle helmeted killa that whacked him out.

"What was his name?" Latrell asked.

"I don't know his real fucking name, man! In my line of work they never give you their real names. All I know is he goes by Baby Boy."

"No, not him! The man that you were hired to hit."

"King—King Rich was his name."

"Uh-uh," Latrell shook his head. "Yo ass is lying. I don't believe you."

"No, I'm not! That's the truth, so help me God!" Worth swore up and down.

"Nah. What chu saying doesn't make sense. Why the fuck would Baby Boy have his own father clapped?" Latrell looked to Shavon. "Baby, make sure this white boy's family gets closed caskets." Shavon nodded and headed toward the exit again, but Worth's constant shouting stopped her.

"No, no! Wait, stop!" Worth shouted at Shavon, then looked at Latrell. "I swear on the lives of my wife and daughter—Baby Boy is the one that dropped the bag on the hit on King Rich. Why? If I had to fucking guess, it was because he wanted to reign over his empire."

Damn, it's a cold-blooded world, Latrell thought as he dropped his head and massaged the bridge of his nose. He definitely believed Worth now. It all made sense. He could see Baby Boy putting money on King Rich's head. The little mothafucka was always walking around like he was top dawg already, plus he was always had something slick to say about his father under his breath. Besides that, he had a feeling that Baby Boy was jealous of his brother Diabolic, since the old man was talking about letting him sit on the throne of his kingdom.

Latrell looked up from massaging the bridge of his nose, and locked eyes on the rose tattooed on Worth's calf. The inked rose changed back and forth to the rose that Worth had left on King Rich's body when he'd murked him. Homeboy was definitely the cat that put the love on him.

"Alright. You may have brought yo' family a pardon, but cho ass ain't getting outta this," Latrell told him straight up. He then looked to Shavon. "Baby, blow this nigga'z hairline back." He gave his boo the nod. With that having been said, Worth lowered his head and began to mouth a silent prayer to the Lord as he was about to meet Him.

Shavon walked up on Worth. She was about to splash his ass. Then the sudden ring of her cell phone made her hold back. She looked at her cell phone's screen and saw that it was Tyrell.

"Who is that?" Latrell asked, with a creased forehead.

"Tyrell," she told him, looking back up from the cellular's display.

"Well, answer it then. We needa see about getting that work from 'em."

Shavon nodded and turned her back to Worth and Latrell. She adjusted her Blue-Tooth on her ear as Latrell was placing the red-ball gag back inside of Worth's mouth. "Hello," Shavon spoke as she answered the call. Her face frowned up further and further the more she listened to the man that had given her her first child. "What? Are you serious?" At this time, Latrell walked up behind her, to see what was going on. He tapped her on the shoulder and threw his head back like, *What's up?* She looked at him and held up a finger which signaled that he should give her a minute. After she finished listening to a panicked Tyrell, she spoke again. "Listen, the only way we're coming is if you give us the rest of that stash. That shit belongs to some very powerful people and they want it back, or they're gonna close Mank's eyes forever. You feel me? Good. So do we have a deal? Alright then, now where are they taking you? Okay, we'll be there inna minute." She disconnected the call and told Latrell the deal. He was all for saving Tyrell's ass since it meant they were gonna be able to take those bricks off his hands.

Latrell moved out of Shavon's line of vision, which left her standing a few feet away from Worth. The battered hit-man wasn't saying anything. He was just suspended there, dripping blood and sweat in the drain. "Gon' and handle yo' business, mama." He spoke of her finishing off Worth.

"Nah, I've gotta better idea," Shavon told him.

"Oh, yeah? Well, what chu got in mind?" Latrell asked as he massaged his chin, curious as to what was on his lady's mind. She ran down the plan she'd come up with to him, and he was feeling it. "Okay, let's do it."

***

Tyrell lay on his side inside the trunk of Rat's 1987 Cutlass. His wrists were still bound behind his back, but the strip of duct tape hung off of his mouth. He'd jabbed his tongue against it until it came loose. Remembering Rat and Jayvon hadn't relieved him off his cell phone, he pulled it out of his back pocket and used his nose to dial up Shavon. He made up a deal with her. If she saved him from his impending doom, he'd give her what was left of the bricks.

Tyrell's eyelids narrowed into slits as he frowned up. Rat opened the trunk, and the light from the street lamp radiated down upon him. He had been inside the dark trunk for so long that the light felt like bee stings to his pupils.

"Ahhh, Blood, what the fuck?" Rat's face scrunched up as he reached down inside the trunk. He picked up Tyrell's cell phone and looked at it. While he was doing this, Jayvon was pulling Tyrell out of the trunk.

"What's up?" Jayvon asked as he held Tyrell tight.

"This smoked-out-mothafucka done called somebody, probably the goddamn police!" Rat exclaimed and dropped Tyrell's cellular to the street, stomping and mashing it into the surface. The screen of the device cracked into a spider's cob web.

"Turn this punk mothafucka around and hold 'em, Blood!" Once Jayvon granted his request, Rat grunted as he slammed his tattooed fists into Tyrell's stomach, which knocked the wind out of him. Rat then followed up by hooking him across the jaw, whipping his head around. Tyrell turned around, breathing hard, with bloodstained teeth. He then spat a mouthful of blood on the ground. "I should kill you, nigga." He lifted up his shirt and pulled out his blower, placing it at the center of Tyrell's forehead.

"Don't let cho emotions cloud yo' judgment, Blood, we've gotta get that weight—Think about the kilos first, the kilos first," Jayvon told him, as he stood behind Tyrell, holding him up.

Rat mad-dogged Tyrell while holding the gun to his forehead, nostrils flaring and jaws clenching. He had it in mind to pop Tyrell, but he realized that Jayvon was right. Fat Daddy had given them an assignment, and they were going to carry it out. One thing was for sure, Rat thought: he was going to put Tyrell's dick in the dirt once they collected what they'd come there for.

Having made up his mind, Rat tucked his blower back up. "Even if this bitch did call the police it'll still take time for them to catch up with us. Let's get this shit up outta here and raise up." He slammed the trunk shut and turned to Tyrell.

"That's what I'm talkin' 'bout," Jayvon said, still holding Tyrell.

"Alright. Who's all in the house?" Rat asked Tyrell.

"Ms. Pearl. My girlfriend's grandmother. She should be the only one up in there." Droplets of blood fell from Tyrell's bottom lip. "She should be sleeping at this hour. My girl kept an extra key under the welcome mat on the front porch. We can slip right in without waking her, get the dope and leave."

"Just as simple as that, huh?" Jayvon asked him.

"Just as simple as that," Tyrell said, glancing over his shoulder at him.

"Alright, let's move." Rat motioned for Jayvon to follow him. Jayvon followed behind him while keeping a cautious look on his surroundings, his handgun pressed against Tyrell's back. They entered the yard of Ms. Pearl's house, and made it upon the steps.

Rat lifted up the welcome mat and grabbed the copper key that was there. He placed his ear to the door to listen for anyone that might be moving around inside. Once he didn't hear anything, he unlocked the black iron door, and then the wooden door. He stopped as he reached for the doorknob of the wooden door, because he thought he heard something. He listened for the sound again, but he didn't hear anything. Rat shrugged and opened the wooden door. When they entered the house, every light was out, save for the one inside the kitchen.

"Alright," Rat began in a hushed tone, looking back at Tyrell. "Exactly where did you put that work up at?"

At that moment, Jayvon's eyes bulged, seeing a shadowy figure emerge before Rat, lifting up an aluminum baseball bat.

"Look out, Blood!" Jayvon called out to Rat. Instantly, Rat whipped around and pulled out his blower. Just as he pointed his handgun at the shadowy figure, it knocked the gun out of his hand and cracked him upside the head. Rat's gun flew across the living room just as his body hit the carpeted floor. The shadowy figure, which was Ms. Pearl, continued to beat Rat with the baseball bat as he lay on the floor, and he couldn't help but cover his head with his arms, holding up his leg.

"Ahhh, fuck, man! Fuck! Get this crazy ass old bitch from off me!" Rat hollered out.

"You lil' young hoodlum, I'll teach cho black ass to run up in my house!" Ms. Pearl shouted with sloped eyebrows and flaring nostrils. Her graying hair was pulled back in a ponytail, and she was wearing a white house coat with pink flowers on it. Her ashy feet were in a pair of slippers.

"Ah! Ah, Ahh! Fuck, Blood! Yo', Jayvon, shoot this old bitch! Blast her mothafuckin' ass!" Rat hollered out as he turned from left to right, covering his face so it wouldn't be assaulted by the swinging baseball bat.

Feeling Jayvon take the handgun from out of his back, Tyrell threw his head back as hard as he could. The impact from the blow broke Jayvon's nose and sent him slamming back against the wall, which caused him to drop his blower to the floor. As soon as

Jayvon collided with the wall, an old, gold framed portrait of Ms. Pearl, her husband and Whitney fell to the floor. Its glass cracked at its corner.

"Ya thieving bastard, I'ma beat cha to a bloody pulp!" Ms. Pearl swore as she swung the aluminum baseball bat with all of the might her scrawny frame could muster. The baseball bat whistled through the air as she swung it downward.

Whoomp, Poonk, Boomp!

The baseball bat came down on Rat again and again, making him holler louder and louder. "Ah, shit! Ahhh, Jayvon, get this crazy bitch off me, Blood!" Rat tried his best to block the onslaught of the aluminum baseball bat. All he could see was Ms. Pearl's shadowy figure and the metal blurs of the baseball bat: it was coming down so fast.

During this time, Jayvon was slumped up against the wall, in a daze, with his eyes rolling around in his head, moaning in pain. Seeing that he had the advantage, Tyrell bent down to pick up Jayvon's handgun, with his back to it. After several attempts, he decided it would be best if he freed his wrists from his restraints first. As soon as the thought occurred, Tyrell ran inside the kitchen as fast as he could, over to the drawer where he knew all of the knives were stored. Turning his back to the counter, he grabbed hold of the knob of the drawer, and pulled the drawer all the way out. There was a sound of clashing chaotic metal, with several steak knives, butter knives, butcher knives, spoons and forks hitting the floor. Tyrell kneeled down to the sharpened blades and searched the pile with his back to it. Once Tyrell got his hands on a knife to his liking, he used it to saw away at the duct tape that bound his wrists.

"Come on, come on, come on," Tyrell said to no one in particular as he desperately cut away at his restraints. While he was doing this he could hear all the commotion going on inside the living room. He'd cut halfway through the duct tape before he was able to pull his hands free from it.

Tyrell stood upright. He then pulled the ravaged duct tape from around his wrists and snatched the strip from off his mouth, taking some of the hair above his top lip with it. Tyrell dropped the strip of duct tape and gripped his knife tightly. He took off running toward the living room, with murder on his mind and every intention of carry a couple of them out. He'd gotten halfway across the kitchen floor when he heard Ms. Pearl scream, and something slamming into the wall. By the time Tyrell reached the kitchen door, Rat was picking up his handgun and standing to his feet. Jayvon was doing the same. The two of them stood side by side with their guns pointed down at Ms. Pearl.

"No, no, pleeease!" Ms. Pearl screamed as she held up her hands, covering her face. Her eyes were stretched wide open, as well as her mouth. She continued to scream over and over again, seeing the angered young thugs standing over her, with their deadly weapons pointed down at her.

"You crazy old bitch!" Rat called out as he stared down at her, with malice in his eyes. He and Jayvon pulled the triggers of their guns and hot slugs rang out, back to back.

Blowl, Blowl, Blowl, Blowl, Blowl!
Blowl, Blowl, Blowl, Blowl, Blowl!

Rat lowered his handgun to his side and touched the side of his head, finger tips coming away bloody. While he was doing this, Jayvon had pulled his bandana down from over the lower half of his face, revealing his bloody, gushing nose. The lower half of his face was completely covered in blood.

"Don't move, don't chu fuckin' move!" Rat said, pointing his gun at Tyrell. He hastily approached him, mad- dogging. Tyrell dropped the knife, and his hands shot up in the air. As soon as he did, Rat gave him a swift kick in the stomach, which caused him to double over, holding himself. Rat then followed up by whacking him across the head with his handgun. The sharp blow spilled Tyrell to the floor, wincing, while holding his stomach with one hand. "If it wasn't for the fact that we weren't tryna get our hands on them birds, I'd pop yo' ol' smoked-out-ass." Rat kicked Tyrell in the side, and then stomped his head to the surface. The assault left his ass snoring, knocked out cold.

Chapter 13

Tyrell gasped for air as he threw his head back, sending water flying everywhere. His eyes were as big as saucers, and his mouth was wide open. Water rolled down his face and dripped off his chin. His clothes were soaked, and small puddles of water were quickly expanding at his feet. Rat had just splashed him with a big ass bucket of ice cold water, which brought him back from his unconscious state. Tyrell blinked his eyes, as if he was waking up from a nightmare, chest rising and falling with every breath he took. He took note of his surroundings, seeing that his wrists and ankles were duct-taped to a chair. Looking back up, Tyrell saw Rat and Jayvon standing before him. Rat was sitting the bucket down on the floor, while Jayvon was standing there with his blower at his side.

Rat marched over to Tyrell and started smacking him across the face rapidly with both hands, simultaneously.

Smack, Smack, Smack, Smack!

Tyrell was taken aback by the assault. Rat then grabbed him by his shoulder and looked him square in his eyes. "Hey, can you hear me?" Tyrell nodded *yes.* "Are you with me?" He nodded *yes* again. "Good. Now, where the fuck are them birds?"

"There, up there!" Tyrell looked up at the ceiling and threw his head back at it. When Rat and Jayvon looked up at the ceiling, they saw a trap door that looked like it had been painted shut some time ago. As soon as they saw that door, they smiled from ear to ear, knowing their prize was stored behind it.

"Yo', watch this nigga, man—I'ma finna find something to put them thangz in," Rat told Jayvon. A couple of minutes later, he came back inside the kitchen with a khaki sack bag. The bag looked like one of those that Marines carried their belongings in when they came back home to American soil.

Rat smacked the flower vase off the table, sending it hurling down to the surface. Colorful flowers lay amid water and shards of vase. Rat then pulled the table out, so that it would be positioned below the door in the ceiling. Using a chair, he climbed up on the table and reached for the door in the ceiling, but he couldn't really reach it. Realizing this, Rat told Jayvon to give him a broom, which he did. Rat then jabbed the door in the ceiling with the broom, until it popped up from where it was placed. Next, the nigga grabbed the chair he'd used to climb the table, and sat it on top of it. He climbed upon the chair, and the table rocked back and forth, causing him to stoop downward, for fear of falling.

"You good, my nigga?" Jayvon asked, concerned, seeing that his comrade had almost fallen.

"Yeah, I'm straight—It's just this raggedy ass table," Rat admitted. He then removed the door and felt around inside of the ceiling, a concentrated expression written across his face.

"You feel anything up in there?" Jayvon asked him, anxious to see if there were as many bricks of yay-yo stored up there, as Tyrell said it was.

"Hold on, you impatient fuck, gemme a second," Rat told him. As soon as he said that, he came upon something, and a delighted look blessed his face. He pulled his hand from out of the opening, and came down with one of the birds, wrapped up neatly. He looked down at it, smiling before kissing it and showing it to Jayvon, who was also smiling. "Jackpot, baby, that's what I'm talkin' about," he said, before dropping the block of yay-yo into the sack. Rat continued to fill his sack until he heard something that grabbed his attention. Crinkles appeared on his forehead, and he looked down at Jayvon just as he placed another bird inside of the sack. "Yo', Blood, you hear that?"

Jayvon looked around, and then shook his head, saying, "Nah, I didn't hear shit. What was it?"

"I don't know," Rat said. They then stood there, listening for the noise that Rat had heard, but it never occurred again. Rat shrugged and said, "Fuck it, man. It's probably the weed I smoked on the way over here. I'm probably just trippin'." He continued to drop the blocks inside of his sack.

"I don't know why you smoked that shit before a mission, knowing it be makin' yo' black ass paranoid, Blood. When it comes to shit like this, we've gotta be on point." Jayvon chastised him.

"Shut up bitchin', nigga. We came up on some dope, you should be happy, hell."

"I'll be happy once we collect up all that shit and get up from outta here. How many mo' you got up there?"

"Almost all of 'em," Rat assured him, as he peeked down inside of the sack. He then went back to filling it with drugs. Once he'd had all the bricks inside the sack and accounted for, Rat pulled the drawstrings of the bag and closed it up. He was about to step off of the chair he'd stood up on to take down the yay-yo, when he heard the noise he had heard earlier. He stopped in his tracks, and his forehead crinkled. Rat looked from left to right, listening closely for the sound. When it didn't occur again, he looked at Jayvon.

"What's up?" Jayvon asked, concerned, brows furrowed.

"You hear that?" Rat inquired. He listened for the sound again, hoping it would reoccur.

"Mannn, get cho mothafuckin' ass from down there, so we can get the fuck from outta here! You needa leave that shit a—" Jayvon's rant was cut abruptly short by a chaotic sound—*Boom, boom, bwap!*—then the back door came flying open, hanging off of its hinges. Shavon, wearing black sunglasses and a bandana over the lower half of her face, ran inside the kitchen with black and metal handguns in each hand. Rat was turning his head around toward her, when she was lifting her guns up at him and pulling her triggers back to back. The deadly weapons played their funeral music.

Bloc, Bloc, Bloc, Bloc, Bloc!
Bloc, Bloc, Bloc, Bloc, Bloc!

"Ah, ah, ahh, ahhh, ahhhh!" Rat grimaced as bullets ripped through his body. He did a funny dance on the chair, and dropped the sack of bricks. His right leg went up into the air as he fell backwards, hurling downward. His body crashed upon the table top and broke it into halves, sending wood shards flying. The last thing to fall was the chair he was standing upon, which came down on his torso.

Having seen his comrade get cut down by gunfire, a pissed off Jayvon went to pop Shavon. He was about to pull his trigger, when Latrell came running inside of the kitchen. He was covered in soot, from having descended down the chimney. His disguise was the same as his ride-or-die bitch. He put the silencer of his handgun to the back of Jayvon's dome piece, which caused him to stiffen like a 2 X 4 floor board.

"Drop it before I drop you," Latrell told Jayvon coldheartedly. Jayvon obliged his command and lifted his gloved hands into the air. "You good, fam?" he asked Tyrell, without taking his eyes off the back of Jayvon's head.

"Yeah, it took y'all asses long enough," Tyrell said as he watched Shavon tuck her handguns inside her jeans and walk over to the pile of silverware on the floor.

"You know what, Tyrell? You're an ungrateful mothafucka, you know that?" Shavon asked as she picked up a butcher's knife from off of the floor, walking toward him.

"Girl, hurry yo' ass up and cut me loose," Tyrell urged her.

Shavon stopped before him with the butcher's knife and said, "Say please, rude ass."

Tyrell looked off to the side and took a deep breath before turning back around to Shavon. "Please. Now, come on. You hear them fucking sirens out there? The Boys are on their way." He heard police car sirens hastily approaching far off in the distance.

Shavon kneeled down to Tyrell's ankles and cut the tape loose from them. She then stood upright and cut the duct tape from around his wrists before tossing the butcher's knife aside. Tyrell quickly rose to his feet, pulling the tape from around his wrists and ankles. He picked up the sack of bricks and peered inside of it, making sure all of the packaged cocaine was there and accounted for.

"What y'all think we should do with this fool?" Latrell asked Shavon and Tyrell.

Shavon looked at Latrell and pretended to cut her throat, which was a signal for 'kill his ass.' Jayvon's eyes bulged, and his mouth hung open. He couldn't believe his eyes.

"Aww, come on, man! Y'all ain't gotta do me like that. Look, listen, lemme go and you'll never have to see my face again. I put that on everythang that I love! My right hand to God." Jayvon pleaded with a pair of sorrowful eyes, hoping that his life would be spared.

"Nigga, shut cho ho-ass up!" Tyrell smacked the dog shit out of Jayvon, bloodying his lips. The young hooligan licked his lips and spat on the floor. "Now, if you wanna keep yo' sorry ass life then you're gonna make this call, and tell this fat tub of shit exactly what I'm finna tell you." Tyrell threatened Jayvon as he rifled through his pockets until he came up with his cell phone. He searched through his contacts until he found the cellular number that he was looking for. Next, he told Jayvon exactly what he wanted him to say before dialing up Fat Daddy, and placing the device to his ear. The cellular rang four times before homeboy picked up.

"Blood, you're not gonna believe this shit," Jayvon told him. "Niggaz done caught a flat and we don't have a spare in the trunk. And we got all of this merchandise with us. Look, I need you to grab us tire for this mothafucka, or a donut drive out here with it. Blood, if I had Triple A, I wouldn't be callin' yo' ass, now would I? Man, we took care of everythang. Right now we're just sitting ducks. We need you, ASAP. Okay, bool." Having said that, Jayvon gave him the directions to where he and Rat were supposedly stranded. "Good lookin' out, my nigga. Alright, peace."

Tyrell disconnected the call and tossed the cell phone aside. He then nodded to Latrell, who in turn took his blower from the back of Jayvon's dome piece. "Gon' and get the fuck from up outta here, nigga."

Keeping his hands up in the air, Jayvon told him: "Nah, Blood. As soon as I turn around you gon' shoot me in my back."

Tyrell stepped into Jayvon's face, mad-dogging him. The throbbing vein on his temple twitched as he clenched and unclenched his jaws, balling his fists tighter and tighter. "My nigga, if you don't gon' and get the fuck from outta here, you won't have to worry about me shooting you in yo' back 'cause I'ma shoot chu in yo' face. Now, get, nigga! Bounce yo' ass from up outta here!"

Tyrell and Jayvon stared into one another's eyes for a while. Hesitantly, Jayvon lowered his hands and made a run for the door. He'd nearly cleared the threshold into the living room when Tyrell pulled Shavon's black handgun from her waistline and shot him in his back callously. Jayvon threw his head back and howled in pain as he fell to the floor with a sickening thud. The mothafucka's fingers were still twitching, so Tyrell walked up on him and finished him off.

Bloc, Bloc, Bloc, Bloc, Bloc!

Tyrell lowered the handgun at his side as he stared down at his handiwork, spitting on him. "I guess I'ma liar now, huh?" Tyrell passed the gun back to Shavon. Afterwards, he picked up Jayvon and Rat's handguns, and tucked them on his waistline. At that moment, they heard vehicles screeching to a halt outside of the house. Blue and red flashing lights shone through the sheer curtains of the living room window. Latrell ran inside of the living room and took a cautious peek through the curtains. He saw six police cars on the street and upon the curb, the colorful lights on top of their respective vehicles flashing noisily. Right after, the cops were hopping out of their cars and drawing their guns with alacrity. The first cop to get out of his whip brought a megaphone along with him. He placed the megaphone to his mouth and began to speak.

"This is the police, come out with your hands up and no one will be harmed!" the brazen cop spoke through the megaphone. His voice was loud and intimidating. It was like Almighty God was speaking from the clouds of Heaven.

"Where did y'all park?" Tyrell asked Shavon as the cop continued to speak over the megaphone. She told him in the alley.

"Good. Take this," he passed her the sack of bricks. "Y'all wait out there for me. I'll be out there in a hot one." He headed to the back porch, stopping once Shavon called for him, hoisting the sack over her shoulder. Tyrell threw his head back like, *What's up?*

"What're you gonna do?" Shavon inquired with a raised eyebrow.

"There's a gas-can in the back porch that I use to fill up the lawn mower to cut the grass. I'm gonna set a fire to create a diversion. Now, y'all gon' and get the fuck outta here!"

"Come on," Latrell tapped Shavon as he turned to head out of the kitchen. She reluctantly went along with him. Once she was gone, Tyrell grabbed the gas-can from the back porch. He listened to the commanding officer on the megaphone, as he screwed the cap off of the gas-can and began splashing the interior of the house with flammable liquid.

"You have 'til the count of five to throw down whatever weapons you may have and come out with your hands up," the commanding officer continued.

He splashed the walls, the floor, the living room furniture, as well as the curtains. Tyrell then cast the gas-can aside and pulled out a Zippo lighter, drawing a bluish yellow flame. While holding it in one hand, he carefully peered out of the curtains into the front yard. Tyrell saw the commanding officer lower his megaphone and signal for a band of cops to storm the yard. As soon as he gave the hand signal, the law moved in strategically, guns at their sides.

Seeing that the police were moving in on the house, Tyrell took a step back and tossed the lighter onto the drenched carpeted floor. Instantly, there was a—*froooosh!*—and the living room ignited, and reddish orange flames swept throughout the house. Tyrell listened closely as he heard several booted feet coming up the front porch steps of the house.

Badoom, Thoom, Thoom!

The front door rattled from brute force as the cops tried to kick it down. The reddish orange flames of the fire illuminated Tyrell as he ran towards the kitchen for the backdoor. He'd just cleared the threshold when he stopped cold in his tracks, having thought about something. He looked over his shoulder inside of the living room and saw Ms. Pearl's limp body lying in the floor as the flames of the fire danced all around her. Quickly, Tyrell darted back inside the living room and scooped his late girlfriend's grandmother into his arms. He turned his back and made his way back inside of the kitchen, stepping over Jayvon and Rat's dead bodies.

Boom!

Shards of wood flew as the cops finally managed to kick down the door. They came in covering their faces with their arms and backing away from the roaring fire. The officer ahead of the pack said something to the others and pointed in Tyrell's direction. He'd seen him heading out of the backdoor with Ms. Pearl in his arms. The other cops looked in Tyrell's direction and pointed their guns at him, firing. Tyrell ducked his head low and ran as fast as he could, with bullets whizzing over his head, barely missing him. The cops ran through the fire after him, bypassing the gas-can that was bubbling, being cooked by the flames. Suddenly, there was a loud explosion, and the cops flew everywhere, screaming. They flapped their arms and legs like wild chickens, trying to shake the flames from off of their limbs.

Tyrell continued on his way with Ms. Pearl in his arms. He made it out into the back yard, where he turned around and laid her down gently on the lawn, closing her eyelids with a brush of his hand. He kissed her on the cheek and said, "Rest in heaven, Ms. Pearl. God's got chu now, beautiful." Tyrell sprinted across the backyard and hopped the fence, landing on his bending knees. He hopped into the backseat of Latrell's whip and slammed the door. Instantly, Latrell drove off.

"You good back there?" Shavon asked him as she handed him a pair of gloves over her shoulder. He took them and slid them onto his hands, flexing his fingers in them.

"Yeah, I'm straight. And gon' be hella good once I give this fat, greasey mothafucka his issue." Tyrell took the two handguns she passed him, one by one. He checked the magazines of the toys and made sure they both had one in the head. "About that deal, Ladybug."

"What about it?" Shavon's face balled up angrily. If he thought he was going to back out of their deal, then he had her fucked up.

"I gotta way we can get Mank back, and I can walk away with them birds," he assured her.

There was silence for a moment, and then Shavon spoke again, saying, "I'm listening."

"First, you mind if I get my mind right before I handle this fool?" He held up his crack pipe. He watched as Shavon looked to Latrell, who nodded *yes*. She then gave the nod to Tyrell. "Thanks. You gotta lighter?" Shavon passed him a lighter and he lit up his crack pipe. Instantly, the high hit him and he blew smoke toward the ceiling. "Alright, tell me what chu think about this . . ." He went on to tell Shavon and Latrell the plan he'd came up with.

***

Fat Daddy was as happy as a fag with a bag full of dicks, once he knew Jayvon and Rat had secured the bricks. He'd had it in mind to slang the birds wholesale, so he could get rid of it faster and cake up. Because the way he saw it, the grips he'd collect from the weight would be all profit. Fat Daddy put those thoughts to rest when it came to him being the man in the streets again. The nigga loved the status that came with being top dawg in the drug game on his side of the city. That's when he settled on the idea of keeping the drugs for himself, and getting his crack houses twerking like they never did before. Fat Daddy was about to make it snow in the trenches and have shit popping like they were, back in Reagan's era.

Where the fuck these niggaz at? Fat Daddy wondered as he coasted down the street with his head on a swivel, looking for Rat's whip. A look of concentration masked his face as he kept a close eye out. When he didn't see Rat's car, he busted a U-turn in the middle of the street, and turned around to head in the direction that he'd come from. Still not seeing Rat's ride, he took two more puffs of his albuterol inhaler and picked up his cellular phone. He hit up Rat, but he didn't answer. So he dialed up Jayvon next, and his shit went straight to voicemail. Right then, he decided to leave him a message. "Blood, where the fuck y'all niggaz at? I'm out here and I don't see y'all and its dark as fuck. Hit me back, dawg." He disconnected the call and tossed his cell phone into the front passenger seat. At that moment, he was blinded by twin orbs which were shining so brightly that he squinted his eyelids, frowning up his face. The orbs were actually the headlights on an oncoming car, and it was coming at him pretty fast. Little by little the car revealed itself the closer it drew to him. Before Fat Daddy knew it, the approaching vehicle was stopping diagonally on the side of him. And a very familiar scowling face emerged from out of the backseat, two guns up.

"Remember me you fat mothafucka?" Tyrell snarled harshly, before letting the lethal ends of his handguns talk to him.

Blowl, blowl, boc, boc, blowl!

Boc, boc, blowl, blowl, boc!

Bullets whizzed through the windshield of Fat Daddy's Chevrolet Monte Carlo, peppering his face and lap with broken glass. Fat Daddy's face scrunched up as hot ones struck his chest and shoulder. Hurriedly, he threw his whip in reverse and looked over his shoulder, mashing the gas pedal. The tires of the hood classic screeched as it sped away backwards, continuously taking shots, from not only Tyrell's lethal weapons, but those of Shavon and Latrell as well.

Blowl, Blowl, Bloc, Bloc, Blowl!

Bloc, Bloc, Blowl, Blowl, Boc!

Bloc, Bloc, Bloc, Bloc, Bloc!

Broken glass and shards of metal poured down on the pavement like droplets of rain, littering the streets. The bullets kept on coming, flying through Fat Daddy's car, ripping through his dashboard, knocking the stuffing out of his passenger seat and shattering the back window glass of his vehicle. Fat Daddy's Monte Carlo grew smaller and smaller to Tyrell, Shavon and

Latrell as he backed up. Tyrell had hopped out of his car and continued firing at the retreating vehicle. But once he realized that his target had gotten too far for him to pose much of a threat, he ran back to the car and jumped in, slamming the door shut behind him.

"Hurry up 'fore this mothafucka gets away!" Tyrell urged Latrell, who promptly swung his vehicle around and went after Fat Daddy. His whip ripped up the street, leaving debris and brittle leaves in the wind.

Meanwhile, a wincing Fat Daddy touched his wounds and looked at his bloody palm. His eyes went back and forth from the windshield to bleeding areas of his body. He glanced up in the rearview mirror and saw the headlights of Latrell's car quickly closing up the distance behind him. Using his bloodstained hand, he went to pull his blower from underneath the driver seat, while trying to keep his eyes on the windshield. He fucked around and looked down too long until he managed to grab hold of his gun. As he was coming up, he was blinded by the oncoming headlights of a MAC truck, which was honking its horn madly. Fat Daddy's eyes nearly popped out of their sockets and he gasped. He grabbed hold of the steering wheel with both hands and sharply swung his Chevy to the right. The swift action flipped the vehicle and sent it over the divider, tumbling down the sloped trail that led into the woods. There was a loud sound of crunching metal and glass exploding and raining down. Fat Daddy's Chevrolet Monte Carlo slammed into a sturdy tree violently, causing a few leaves to drift below.

"Uuuuhh!" Fat Daddy groaned as he hung upside down inside of his car, his eyelids narrowed into slits. Blood oozed out of the gash in his forehead and dripped upon the broken glass below him. Gasoline trickled from the gas-tank of his vehicle, and fed the fire that was quickly spreading throughout it. Fat Daddy's nose twitched as he smelled the overwhelming scent of the flammable liquid, and felt the warmth of the fire. His eyelids peeled open and he suddenly came alive, looking about with a throbbing headache. Looking around, Fat Daddy saw that the fire was spreading throughout his car and heading toward the gas-tank. "Oh, shit!" he said aloud, recognizing the real danger that he was in. Panicking, he tried to unbuckle the seatbelt, but found it jammed. His heart thudded as he acknowledged that his life was in jeopardy. Fat Daddy looked around frantically, and found a shard of glass, amidst several others. He frowned up and bit down on his bottom lip, as he strained to reach the shard. Blood ran down his wrist as he grasped the shard. Hurriedly, he sawed at the seatbelt until it gave, and he crashed down onto the ceiling of his wrecked vehicle.

Fat Daddy knew he was too rotund to fit through the driver's window, so he'd have to go through the windshield. Using all of his might, he kicked at the broken windshield until it gave out, crashing onto the ground. Fat Daddy crawled through the broken glass as fast as he could, slicing his palms up on it. Gritting, he pulled a piece of glass from out of his hand and tossed it aside. His attention was quickly adverted when he heard a car's tires screeching to a stop behind him. Fat Daddy made his way through the front of his whip and took a peek over his wrecked vehicle. He saw the car Tyrell was busting at him out of, idling at the divider. He then saw him hop out with a gun in each hand. A female hopped out of the car on the opposite side and made to join him, but what he said next halted her footsteps.

"Fall back, Ladybug, I got this!" Tyrell told the woman over his shoulder, before he hopped the divider and made his way down the slope.

Seeing that Tyrell was on his way down, Fat Daddy knew that he was living on borrowed time. And that the best way for him to defend himself would be with his gun. Fat Daddy ducked his head back inside of the vehicle and searched for his blower, amidst the broken glass. Once he spotted it, he reached for it, but the sound of bullets whizzing through the air and slamming into the side of his vehicle startled him. On top of that, the fire was cooking the door of the gas-tank, causing its paint to blister and bubble on it. Fat Daddy knew that his ride was seconds away from exploding, so he had to get the fuck from out of there before it was too late.

"Grrrrrrr!" Fat Daddy winced as he pulled himself up to his feet on the side of the car. When he looked over his shoulder, he saw Tyrell still coming down the slope. Right after, the fire surrounding his car roared, and he turned his face away from it. Fat Daddy took off, running as fast as he could, huffing and puffing, out of breath. He took a couple puffs of his inhaler, and that's when his Monte Carlo exploded. The force from the blast sent Fat Daddy up in the air. He crashed back down to the ground and scrambled back upon his feet, slowly. When he looked back, Tyrell was running after him, occasionally stopping to take a shot at him. Fat Daddy had just moved from a tree when one of Tyrell's bullets slammed into it and sent a spray of debris in the air.

"*Haa, haa, haa, haa, haa, haa, haa!*" A winded Fat Daddy limped along as fast as he could, occasionally stopping to take a puff of his inhaler. He got a few feet before he stopped at another tree, leaning up against it to take a breather. He doubled over with his hand on his knee, huffing and puffing. "*Haa, haa, haa, haa, haa, haa, haa!*" Hearing hurried footsteps and gunfire at his back, Fat Daddy took off, running again. He kept on running and looking over his shoulder, every now and again.

Blowl!

A bullet ripped through Fat Daddy's calf and came out of his kneecap. Fat Daddy howled in pain and flopped to the ground, landing hard on the side of his face. Groaning, he pushed himself up from the surface and tried to get up on his feet. Just as he managed to get up on his good leg, Tyrell ran up and tripped it right from under him. Fat Daddy fell back to the ground, helpless and hurting. He gritted his teeth as he slowly turned over on his back. His heart thudded hard when he saw Tyrell standing over him, with both of his guns in his hands.

"Come on, man! You ain't gotta do this!" Fat Daddy pleaded, lifting his meaty hand into the air. He was trying to shield his face from Tyrell, who'd just pointed his gun at him. Big mistake! Tyrell pulled the trigger of his blower and its barrel ignited. Fat Daddy's hand erupted in a crimson mass, and his chubby, severed fingers went flying everywhere. "Aaaaaahhh!" He looked at what was left of his hand in shock, and tears ran from the corners of his eyes. He looked back up and saw Tyrell's scowling face. And for a split second he would have sworn on a stack of Bibles that he saw him transform into the Devil. "Please, man, please! I'm sorry! I apologize! Don't kill me! I don't wanna die!" A fresh set of tears stung Fat Daddy's eyes and flowed down his cheeks, dripping off his chin.

Tyrell eased one of his handguns inside of his waistline. He placed his finger to his lips and leaned down toward Fat Daddy, shushing him. "Sshhhhhh!" A weeping Fat Daddy swallowed the lump of fear in his throat and sniffled, trying his best to calm himself down. Tyrell pressed his gun underneath Fat Daddy's chin, which tilted his head back. Fat Daddy's nose twitched and his bottom lip trembled; more tears flowed down his cheeks. He knew that this was the end. Tyrell pulled the trigger of his gun. A bullet ripped through the top of Fat Daddy's skull. His blood and brain fragments flew from out of his head and rained down upon the ground, dotting it up.

Tyrell stood upright and wiped the specs of blood from his face. He took his time to observe his handiwork, and the horn honked behind him. He tucked the gun on his waistline, and ran back up the slope, hopping the divider and jumping into the backseat. As soon as he slammed the door shut, Latrell pulled off in a hurry.

Chapter 14

When Baby Boy had gotten a call from Diabolic saying he'd recovered the shipment, he didn't waste any time hopping into his Mercedes-Benz AMG GT and peeling out. He headed straight for the spot that Diabolic and his goons were posted up. Although he was pleased to have gotten his weight back, he wasn't about to uphold the deal he'd made with Latrell. Fuck that! Since Diabolic said he had Latrell and Shavon at the spot with him, Baby Boy was going to confirm every brick was there and accounted for. Then, he was going to have his goons execute Latrell, Shavon and Mank. He wasn't about to jeopardize his life by letting his enemies keep theirs. Nah, he was going to clean house, and make sure there wasn't any one left to come after him and his empire.

Baby Boy pulled his Benz outside his spot and killed the engine. He blew smoke from his nose and mouth as he mashed out his cigar inside the ashtray, extinguishing its ember. He grabbed his .45 automatic handgun and stepped out of his car, tucking it at the small of his back. After slamming the driver's door shut, he made his way upon the curb, buttoning up his suit's jacket. He made his way upon the porch of the house and knocked on the door. He cleared his throat, with his fist to his mouth, taking in his surroundings. A moment later, he heard the deadbolt coming undone, as well as several other locks. The front door was snatched open, and he was yanked violently inside of the house.

"What the fuck?" Baby Boy hollered out as he was forced up against the wall. The nigga that pulled him in ordered him to spread his legs and place his hands on the wall. Baby Boy put his hands against the wall, but he wasn't spreading his legs fast enough. So homeboy kicked his legs apart, roughly. He then switched hands with his gun and patted him down quickly with one hand. When he came across a .45 automatic in the small of his back, he looked at it and then whacked Baby Boy across the back of his dome with it. "Aaah!" Baby Boy hollered out as he fell to the carpeted floor, on his hands and knees. "Ah, man, what the fuck is your problem?" he asked as he crawled across the living room floor on his hands and knees.

"You're my problem, bitch!" Diabolic spat angrily, slowly walking up behind him. He stopped where he was and pointed Baby Boy's own gun at his back, pulling the trigger. A loud gunshot rang out, and fire ripped through Baby Boy's left buttock, causing him to holler out in agony.

"Aaaaaaaah!" A wide eyed Baby Boy threw his head back, screaming. He grabbed his wounded buttock, and blood seeped between his fingers. He looked at his hand, and it was masked with blood. "Yo', fam, what the fuck is this about, huh? What the fuck is up?" Baby Boy asked, he looked over his shoulder, and Diabolic kicked him in his ass. He hit the kitchen floor hard on the side of his face grimacing.

"Shut the fuck up, nigga! I'm doing the mothafucking talking here! Or, have you forgotten?" Diabolic kicked Baby Boy in his side, making him howl in pain. He then rolled over, holding his side, looking up at the man that had assaulted him. His eyes were full of tears, so it was like he was looking through a cloudy diamond. He couldn't quite see the face of the person standing before him. But when they did talk, he did think the person's voice sounded familiar.

Tears poured out the side of Baby Boy's eyes when he squeezed his eyelids shut. When he peeled them back open he could see clearer than he did before. Baby Boy's eyes stretched open in shock as his mouth hung open. He couldn't believe it was his big brother, Diabolic, standing over him with two guns. He watched as he stuck one of the handguns in the front of his jeans, and pulled a pair of handcuffs from around his back, tossing them on the floor before him.

"Yo', bro, what the fuck is this? What the fuck is this about?" Baby Boy asked as he lay on his side, holding his buttock, bleeding all over the kitchen floor.

"Handcuff yo' self to the pipe under the kitchen sink, nigga!" Diabolic said with a scowling face, tears constantly spilling down his cheeks. His nostrils were flaring, and his jaws were locked so tight that the muscles pulsated in his face. His eyes were red-webbed and glassy, not to mention swollen, so Baby Boy could tell he'd been crying. If he didn't know any better, he would have sworn someone had died, but that couldn't have been the case. Because whether it had been friend or family, Baby Boy would have known that they'd lost a loved one.

Unless! Oh, my God, he knows. But how? How the fuck did he find out? Baby Boy's eyes grew bigger when he realized that his brother had discovered his dark secret. *Wait a minute, there's no way he could have found out. I can't expose my hand yet. Not until I know what the deal is.*

"Bro, talk to me, lemme know what's going on. I'm clueless here, fam," Baby Boy told him, scrunching his face and clenching his teeth, to combat the burning sensation he was feeling in his ass after being shot.

Baby Boy's question pissed Diabolic off even more. He balled his face up tighter and bit down hard on his bottom lip, looking away and clutching his gun tightly. His head snapped back around to Baby Boy and he could see the contempt in his eyes.

"Look, nigga, I'm not finna tell you but one last time, cuff yo' self to the mothafucking pipe!" Diabolic made emphasis by pointing his gun at him threateningly.

"Bro, listen to me. We're family. I'm sure that we can –" Baby Boy's eyes shot open, and he screamed so loud that every tooth in his mouth was visible for Diabolic to see. He could even see that little pink thing at the back of his throat shaking from the vibration of the shrill. Diabolic had shot him in his kneecap, which was one of the most painful areas on the human body to be shot. "Aaaaah, fuck, man, what the fuck is wrong witchu? Grrrrrr!" His face balled up as he clutched his kneecap, slicking his hand wet with blood.

"Do like I said, or the other one going in yo' dome!" Diabolic swore and pointed the gun at Baby Boy's forehead. He tapped his weapon's trigger with his index finger, which triggered its infra-red beam. A red dot instantly appeared on Baby Boy's forehead.

The tears in Diabolic's eyes continued to flow. They dropped off his chin and splashed on the floor below.

"Grrrrrr!" Baby Boy gritted his teeth in agony to fight back the pain in his legs. Slowly, he grabbed the handcuffs and clamped the metal bracelet around his wrist. He then opened the cabinet below the kitchen sink, and smacked all of the cleaning products aside so he could see the plumbing underneath. Once he came upon a pipe, he handcuffed himself to it and looked up at Diabolic. He wanted to ask him why he was doing this to him, but his fear of being shot again wouldn't allow him. So he just lay there, bleeding profusely and hoping to get an explanation out of him.

"Alright—I'ma ask you something—And I want you to tell me the truth," Diabolic said after he sniffled and wiped the dripping teardrops from his eyes, with the back of his fist. He then lowered his hand at his side and stared Baby Boy directly in his eyes. "Did you putta contract out on our father?"

Baby Boy didn't even flinch when Diabolic asked the question, but his heart thudded madly. He was hoping ordering the hit on his father wasn't the reason behind him lying there bleeding. But unfortunately it had been. The only thing he couldn't figure out was who in the fuck told on him. Still, he wasn't going to fold just yet. Nah, he had to be sure that his brother was positive that he'd dropped the bag on their old man. Because if there was any way that he could wiggle his way out of this situation, then he was going to damn sure try.

"Bro, I don't know what niggaz or bitches are putting in your head out here, but I didn't sanction a hit on pops. I could never do that, man. I loved him to death." Baby Boy swore, while looking his brother square in the eyes. He lied so smoothly that he was believable.

Diabolic sniffled again before continuing to talk, "Put that—put that on our mother's grave that you didn't put the hit out on 'em, man. Put that shit on ma."

There was a few seconds of silence between the two siblings. Baby Boy continued to hold his brother's gaze. When he spoke this time, he made sure to speak slow and clear. "I. Did. Not.

Order. A. Hit. On. Our. Father—I put that on our mother's grave. That's the honest-to-God truth, so help me . . ."

Diabolic squeezed his eyelids shut, and more teardrops fell from the brims of his eyes. He bowed his head and shook it pitifully. He couldn't believe how his brother could look him in the eye, and lie like that. The little grimy mothafucka was bold enough to put it on their mother's grave.

Diabolic mad-dogged his brother, and lowered the red dot to his stomach. "You lil' lying mothafucka!" He pulled the trigger of his gun, and a bullet whistled through the air, tearing through Baby Boy's stomach muscles and lower intestine.

"Gaaaaaaah!" Baby Boy shrieked, and then clenched his teeth, vein bulging at his temple. He grabbed the area of his stomach where the bullet had entered, applying pressure to stop the bleeding. The blood stain on his button-down was quickly expanding. It sort of looked like he'd spilled red wine on his shirt.

"You're a piece of shit, you know that?" Diabolic pulled King Rich's locket from out of his pocket and held it up for Baby Boy to see. "I know you remember this, don't chu?" Baby Boy looked up at the locket in awe. He thought he'd never see it again. He recalled the nigga he'd hired to kill his pops had yanked it from around his neck after carrying out the hit. "From the look in your eyes I can tell that chu do. The nigga that chu fronted the bread to, *to* murder our father, snatched it from off his neck. That same man is here now." Keeping his eyes on Baby Boy, Diabolic turned his head slightly over his shoulder and whistled. A moment later, Latrell and Huge emerged from out of the master bedroom, walking into the kitchen with someone wearing a black pillowcase over their head. The person they had in their possession seemed to have a hard time walking. In fact, he was limping. When Baby Boy glanced at the leg he was reducing the pressure on, he could see that it was wrapped in a bloody bandaged. It was then he figured the man must have been either stabbed or shot in his foot.

Latrell? What the fuck is he doing here? Baby Boy looked back and forth between his brother and Latrell. He wondered what his role was in everything. And what he'd done to make his brother switch up on him.

"Huge," Diabolic called after the enormous goon.

"'Sup?" Huge asked, ready to carry out any orders given to him.

"Go down in the basement and sit on lil' man until we finish conducting business up here." While giving those instructions to Huge, Diabolic kept his angry eyes on Baby Boy.

"You got it. I needa collect the lil' nigga's dishes anyway." Huge walked around Latrell and proceeded to the basement door. Once Diabolic heard the basement door click shut, he started back up talking again.

"Why don't chu do the honors and introduce our special guest to my baby brother?" Diabolic told Latrell. A scowling Latrell turned to the man he held closely to him, and grabbed the back of the black pillowcase, which covered his head. With one strong yank, he snatched the pillowcase and revealed a battered and bruised Worth. The contract killa looked like he'd been to hell and back. It all made sense to Baby Boy now. They'd somehow found out that he was the trigger man behind King Rich's murder, and tortured him until he told them who'd hired him to do the job.

Fuck! I knew I shoulda hired somebody to off his ass, too! Baby Boy couldn't help thinking. Unfortunately for him, Latrell had hit up Diabolic and told him all about the *mastermind* behind his father's murder. He couldn't believe it at first, but when he brought him the receipts. He didn't have any choice but to accept the blatant truth. Diabolic knew in his heart what Baby Boy did was a violation punishable by death. But he had to hear what he had to say for himself before he rocked his ass to sleep.

Baby Boy looked away, and took a deep breath. When he looked back to Diabolic, his face was twisted in a mask of hatred, and the corner of his top lip was twitching. He was as hot as fish grease. Throwing caution to the wind, Baby Boy spoke angrily this time: "You know what? Fuck it! I did it! Yeah, you heard me right! I fucking did it! I had the old man whacked 'cause I wanted to sit at the head of the table. I was tired of living in his fucking shadow, not to mention, he was talking about letting you be the heir to his fucking throne. Talk about adding insult to fucking injury! Whatta smack to the face! I couldn't have that. No way, no fucking way!" Spit flew from his lips as he yelled, vein throbbing at his temple. While Baby Boy was popping his shit, Diabolic was mad- dogging him, with rage flashing in his pupils, and his jaws clenching and unclenching. "Well, there you have it, big bro; a full fucking confession. You wanna know something else? That paperwork I gave you on the lil' homie, Trevante, was utter bullshit! I had Breedlove doctor that shit up. I tried to cash the lil' nappy headed nigga out to kill you, but he wouldn't budge. He was loyal. I couldn't risk him telling you, so I hadda convince you to whack 'em." He stared at Diabolic whose eyes welled up with tears and ran down his cheeks. He was angry and hurt, but Baby Boy didn't give a fuck. The crafty son of a bitch was smirking. "I orchestrated this whole elaborate scheme and played you for a fucking fiddle, pretty clever, huh?" Baby Boy threw his head back, laughing maniacally and slapping his hand against the floor for emphasis. His laughter was very loud and exaggerated, and it pissed Diabolic off.

Abruptly, Diabolic's hand swung upward, and he pointed his gun at Baby Boy's chest. He pulled the trigger of his blower back to back to back.

Blocka, Blocka, Blocka, Blocka, Blocka, Blocka, Blocka, Blocka, Blocka, Blocka!

The muzzle flashed in Diabolic's scowling face, with each pull of his trigger. He emptied the entire clip on Baby Boy's ass. He then ejected the magazine and loaded another, cocking his gun again. He pointed it down at an already deceased Baby Boy and unloaded on his bitch-ass again.

Blocka, Blocka, Blocka, Blocka, Blocka, Blocka, Blocka, Blocka, Blocka, Blocka!

Diabolic pulled out Baby Boy's .45 automatic handgun. He sat it, and his own gun, upon the kitchen counter. Latrell and Worth frowned up as they watched him unzip his jeans and pull out his thick, flaccid dick. Diabolic aimed his meat at Baby Boy's twisted, bloody body and said, "You lowdown, dirty, treacherous, backstabbing, short pile of shit!" Diabolic relieved himself on Baby Boy's lifeless body. His yellow piss splashed on the horrified expression on Baby Boy's face, as well as his bloodstained suit. Diabolic shook the piss dripping from his pee-hole on the floor. He then put his meat back inside his jeans and zipped them up. Next, he turned around and picked up both of the handguns. He tucked the .45 automatic into the front of his jeans, while he held on to his own gun. When he looked up at Latrell and Worth, they were looking at him like he lost his mind. "What?" he asked like it wasn't a big deal he'd not only murdered his own brother in cold blood, but took the time to desecrate his corpse.

"Nothing. We still gotta deal, right?" Latrell asked.

"If my hunnit bricks are in the trunk of your car like you claimed, then yes," Diabolic assured him. Latrell had brokered a deal with him. He'd give him the hit-man—Worth—who took out his father, and the one hundred birds in exchange for Mank's freedom.

"Alright, let's go get chu those bricks, then." Latrell led Worth toward the backdoor, with Diabolic following closely behind them.

***

Hearing someone descending the basement's staircase, Mank sat upright from where he was lying on an old, raggedy mattress. The blood on his face had dried and caked up. The swelling and bruises of his face had begun to heal over the period of his captivity. His jeans and socks were dirty, and he smelled awful. He hadn't bathed since he'd been taken hostage. Mank pulled something from the small of his back, and held it out of Huge's sight. The big man approached him, but stopped in his tracks, smelling something rank. His faced balled up from the putrid smell, and he smacked his hand over his nose and mouth. He and Mank exchanged glances, before he walked over to the big beige dirty bucket he'd left for him to use as a toilet. Still holding his hand over his nose and mouth, he peeked over into the bucket, and saw that it was halfway filled with mushy brown shit and piss.

"Goddamn, boy, this shit funky as a mothafucka!" Huge declared as he picked up a square wooden board he'd found in the corner of the basement, placing it on top of the bucket. "I'll come back to dump yo' bucket once I put these dishes away." He kneeled down, picking up Mank's empty cup and plate. His brows furrowed, seeing Mank's plate had been licked clean. He looked at Mank with a surprised expression on his face, holding the dishes.

"Youngsta, you licked this plate clean. That T-bone musta been good."

"As a mothafucka," Mank claimed with a weak smile.

"I'm glad you liked it. I prepared it myself." Huge grinned. Before he'd gotten involved in the streets, Huge had his mind made up to become a chef and open up his very own restaurant. Those plans were derailed when his father skipped town, leaving him to be the man of the house, and take care of his mother and six siblings. Since then, he made it his business to cook whenever he got the chance to share his gift with his friends and family.

Huge was about to stand upright until something crossed his mind. He looked down at the empty plate, and creases formed on his forehead. He looked back up at Mank and said, "Where's the bone from your steak?"

With a snarl, Mank sliced Huge across the throat with the bone from the steak he'd been sharpening on the floor for hours. Huge's eyes doubled in size, his mouth hung open in shock, and blood poured out of the deep slash in his neck. He dropped the dishes and stood upright. He gagged and coughed up blood, grabbing at his slippery neck. Huge took two steps backward, before falling back on the cement floor. He held his bleeding neck, as blood continued to pour out of it like a spilled can of paint, quickly expanding over the surface. Mank watched in satisfaction as the big man continued to hold himself and repeatedly kicked his right leg. He was fighting to stay alive, but his life's blood was slowly leaving his body. Mank observed him take his last breath and kick his right leg for the final time. Once Huge had gone still,

Mank cautiously approached him, kicking his sneaker to make sure he was dead. After he confirmed his death, Mank rifled through his pockets. He came up with two sticks of gum, lint, and a couple of wrinkled dollar bills in the first one. It wasn't until he got to the second pocket that he came up with the small silver key that held his freedom.

Mank smiled triumphantly as he held the key up to the light, and kissed it. He unlocked the shackle around his ankle, removed it, and tossed the key aside. Next, he pulled the gun from the front of Huge's jeans. He cocked it, and put a hollow-tip in its chamber. Hearing talking above his head, somewhere outside of the house, Mank crept over to the staircase. He placed his back against the wall and moved alongside it, blower held up at his shoulder. The young nigga proceeded up the steps, cautiously.

***

Diabolic, Latrell and Worth walked into the backyard. There were two masked up goons, each with an AK-47, flanking Latrell's whip. They held menacing expressions behind their masks, and their trigger-fingers were itching to kill on Diabolic's orders. Latrell left Worth standing where he was as he pulled out his car keys and started toward the trunk of his car. It wasn't until Diabolic stopped him that he froze in his tracks.

"Hold up, nigga! I know you don't think I'ma let chu open that trunk and pulla strap on me, do you?" Diabolic snatched the keys from Latrell's hand and pointed the small black box at the trunk, pressing the button. The trunk made a—*Thunk!*—sound, and cracked open. Diabolic lifted open the trunk and found Shavon and Tyrell lying inside with their handguns pointed at him. His eyes nearly leaped out of his head, and his mouth dropped open. He was shocked beyond belief. He'd cleared his gun halfway from his waistline, but it was already too late. Shavon and Tyrell were already opening fire on his ass.

Blowl, Blowl, Blowl, Blowl, Blowl! Bloc, Bloc, Bloc, Bloc, Bloc!

The bullets sounded like firecrackers as they went off, ripping through Diabolic's body and making him dance on his feet. He dropped his gun in the process, and fell to the floor. Right then, Worth's arms came from behind his back and caused his duster to fall to the ground. He swung twin black Berettas with silencers on them from behind his back, pulling their triggers. A bullet each ripped through the centers of Diabolic's goons' ski-masks, knocking bloody brain matter from the back of their skulls, before they could shoot down Shavon and Tyrell. The goons collapsed in a heap on the ground, blood pouring out of their heads. As soon as they did, Shavon and Tyrell hopped out of the trunk, and dumped on Diabolic some more. Talk about overkill!

They then lowered their smoking guns as they stood over Diabolic's dead body, looking over their handiwork. Shavon had tears in her eyes as she harped up mucus and spat on the bullet-riddled corpse of her son's killa.

"That's for our son, you bitch-ass nigga!" Shavon said, which made Latrell take notice of the identical tattoos on their forearms. It was an image of their son JaQuawn on a bicycle. "Rest in Paradise Prince JaQuawn Dalton", alongside his birth date and passing, encircled the image.

At that moment, Latrell and Worth walked over to the holey, bloody mess that was Diabolic. They examined his bloody holed body before acknowledging one another.

"I take it this makes us square now?" Worth asked Latrell who had set the entire thing up. He'd given Worth the Berettas with one bullet in each of them to take out the goons. He'd only give him a shot in each of his guns, so he wouldn't get the notion to blast on him and everyone else. Latrell knew Diabolic would have his goons pat him down, but they'd overlook Worth, considering he was a hostage.

"Yeah. We're square." Latrell shook his hand.

"Okay. I'm gonna gon' and get outta here." Worth turned his back to walk away and Latrell gave Shavon a nod. Swiftly, she placed her handgun behind his ear and pulled the trigger. Specks of blood smacked Shavon in the face instantly. She watched as Worth collapsed to the ground, seemingly dead.

A frowned up Latrell spat on the ground while keeping his eyes on Worth, crossing himself in the sign of the holy crucifix and saying, "Rest in peace, King Rich."

Tyrell tucked his gun on his waistline and said, "Look, now that I've made good on my end of the deal, I'm gonna gon' and go." Tyrell had come up with this plan, which wasn't really too much different from the plan Shavon devised. In her initial plan, Diabolic got to live, and keep the work. But Tyrell, knowing that Diabolic was directly responsible for the murder of their son, came up with a plot, with Diabolic being whacked and him walking away with the bricks. Everything winded up working out.

"Gon' and go," Latrell told him.

"Yeah," said Shavon, "go ahead and leave. You've earned it."

"I don't have to worry about any of y'all tryna pop me in my back, like ya'll did homeboy here, right?" Tyrell nodded to Worth's body.

Shavon tucked her guns on her waistline and raised her hands, showing she wasn't a threat. "No one here is gonna pop you, you're free to go."

"I wouldn't take her word for shit, if I were you!" a voice rang out from the back of them. When they turned around, they found Mank behind them, with a gun pointed at Tyrell.

"Mank, where'd you—?" Shavon began but was interrupted by her younger brother.

"I was down in the basement. I took out that big son of a bitch down there and took his strap." Mank explained as he kept his hateful eyes on Tyrell, along with his blower. "I can't believe y'all was about to let this smoked-out-ass nigga walk when he has blood on his hands."

"Blood on his hands? Mank, what're you talking about?" Shavon frowned up, not clear of what her younger brother meant.

"Korey!" Mank shot back at her. "This mothafucka has my brother's blood on his hands. This shit is his fault. Had he not ran off with all of that work, then Korey wouldn't be laid up in the 'spital teetering between life and death."

"Mank, please don't do this—think about—" Shavon was cut short by Mank.

"Man, mothafuck alla that!" Mank cocked the slide on his gun and pointed it back at Tyrell, which made him ease his hands up in the air. Mank frowned hard and bit down on his bottom lip. He gripped his gun so hard that his knuckles cracked. His finger slowly began to pull back on the trigger.

A terrified Shavon looked back at Latrell and said, "What're we gonna do?"

"There's nothing we can do—it's all in his hands," Latrell said as he and Shavon looked back and forth between Mank's finger on the trigger and an unflinching Tyrell. Tyrell's eyes were locked on the young nigga's eyes, and his jaws were clenched, waiting for whatever that was about to go down.

Mank's finger pulled back further on the trigger, about to fire his gun, when someone's cell phone rang.

Shavon pulled her cell phone from out of her pocket and looked at its screen. Her eyes lit up when she saw that it was the hospital on the display. "Mank, hold on! This is the hospital right here, don't do anything, okay? Don't do anything until we know what this call is about." Shavon accepted the call and pressed the cell phone to her ear. "Hello?" Her eyes moved from left to right, listening to what she was being told. "Okay, thank you. Ma'am, I'm going to put chu on speaker so the rest of my family can hear the good news—so, can you say that again? Okay, thank you." Shavon pressed the *speaker* button on the cellular, and extended it to Mank.

"Hello, this is Nurse Demetria calling from General Hospital. I am delighted to tell you that Korey Tyson came from outta his coma today. He's still very weak, but he's alive and doing quite well."

With that having been said, Shavon took the cell phone off *speaker* and brought the cellular to her ear. She spoke to the nurse jovially. "Yes. Everyone is soooo happy, right now. Thank you.

Thank you so much. We'll be down there to see 'em, shortly." She disconnected the call and put her cell phone away. She then turned her attention back to Mank. "You see, baby boy? Korey is alive and well, you don't have to shoot Tyrell. You can let 'em go, you hear me?" Shavon extended her hand and slowly moved toward Mank. She grasped Mank's gun by its barrel and lowered it, gently. She then tucked it at the small of her back and embraced her brother, rubbing his back.

Tyrell lowered his hands and took a breath. He opened the back door of Latrell's car and lifted up the backseat cushioning, revealing the lumpy sheet containing all of the work. After lying the cushioning back down, he slammed the back door of the car and hoisted the sheet over his shoulder, looking like a ghetto ass Santa Claus. Tyrell looked to Latrell, who had a solemn look on his face. He then looked to Shavon, who was still hugged up with Mank. Mank was mad-dogging him. Tyrell saluted them, and walked out of the backyard, becoming one with the darkness.

Six Months Later

Tyrell kneeled down to Whitney's grave and laid down a bouquet of the most beautiful red roses. Staring down at the words chiseled in her blue marble grave stone, he said, "I love you, baby," kissed his fingers, and pressed them against the stone. He rose to his feet and gave his lover's grave one last look, before taking a deep breath and walking back to his luxurious vehicle, with the shiny metal Jaguar on its hood. Tyrell jumped inside of his whip and picked up his lighter from the ashtray. He removed his marred glass pipe, which still had crack in it, from the glove box. He stuck the crack pipe between his lips and turned the lighter upside down, igniting a bluish yellow flame. The fire cooked the off-white rocks inside the crack pipe until they melted and produced smoke, which he sucked into his lungs. A look of euphoria spread across his face as he shut his eyelids, and a smile curled the corner of his lips.

Although Tyrell had taken the bricks and rebuilt his empire, he was still heavily dependent on drugs. He made sure to hide his addiction from his workers, because he wasn't sure how they'd react knowing they were taking orders from a crackhead.

Tyrell took a few more puffs from his crack pipe before he put it and the lighter up. He shut the glove box and fired up his Jaguar. Once he glanced into the side view mirror and saw that there weren't any cars coming, he hit his turn signal and drove off. He drove from out of the cemetery, and merged into Los Angeles traffic. He cracked open the windows of his vehicle and allowed the fresh cool air inside, letting it ruffle his clothing. Next, he changed the channels of his stereo, until he found a song that he was satisfied with. A moment later, DaBaby's "Suge" was pumping from the speakers of his ride, causing his entire vehicle to rattle, especially the trunk.

Tyrell nodded to the infectious music pumping from his sound system, as he bent corners. He made his way down a one-way street, where he halted at a red stop light. Still nodding to the sound of the music, he looked into the side view mirror and saw a beat-up, old black van waiting at the light behind him. Thinking nothing of the vehicle, he continued on through the traffic light once it had turned green. Tyrell whipped through the streets, without a care in the world. It wasn't until he heard the eruption of his back tire that his forehead furrowed with lines, and he found himself with his first problem of the day.

"Fuck!" Tyrell fumed as he turned down the volume of his music. He made a right turn on a block, and ended up under a freeway path, hearing several cars racing up and down the frequently traveled route above his head. Tyrell pulled over alongside the curb on the right side of the street. He popped his trunk and hopped out, making his way to the rear of his whip. He grabbed the spare tire out of the compartment. Using one hand, he walked it over to the deflating tire. It was at that precise moment that he heard the screeching tires of a vehicle coming to a halt beside him. The sound was so loud that he whipped his head around instantly, a frown fixed on his face. His eyes nearly popped out of their sockets, and his mouth damn near hit the ground when he saw the van he'd spotted earlier in traffic. Its side door was snatched open, and two masked up niggaz clutching micro Dracos, with seventy-five round drum attachments, hopped out. One of them was wearing an oxygen mask over his nose and mouth, with a sky-blue crinkly hose attached to it that ran from it to a tank of oxygen, which was secured in a black canvas bag and strapped over his shoulder. The man wearing the oxygen mask used one hand to support himself on a cane, while the other hand clutched his Draco. He and the other masked man had murder in their eyes, and their jaws were locked, to display their clenched teeth. They stood side by side, holding their choppaz. Tyrell swallowed the lump of fear in his throat. His stomach twisted in knots as he looked from gunman to gunman, wondering why they hadn't cut him down.

Tyrell spat on the ground and looked back up into the eyes' of his would-be killaz, saying, "Well, what the fuck y'all niggaz waiting on?"

Right then, the masked up niggaz' Dracos spat flames, swift and deadly, chopping Tyrell's ass down. He fell up against the side of his Jaguar, and slid down to the pavement, leaving a bloody smear behind. Tyrell found himself with his right arm stretched across the side of his car, and with his right leg tucked underneath him, while his left one was outstretched. Fortunately for him, he was so high off of crack that he barely felt the bullets riddling his body. Tyrell looked up at the masked killaz, gasping and wheezing out of breath, blood spilling over his bottom lip, dripping off of his chin. The front of his shirt was bloody and filled with holes. He struggled to get up on his feet, all the while talking big shit.

"That's all you—that's all you bitch-ass niggaz got, huh? That's all—you got? You—you hear me? Huh? You didn't hear that it's gon' take more than that to keep ol' Tyrell down, huh? Huh, you fucking—you fucking cockroaches." Tyrell hollered out while swinging his fist, blood misting from his mouth as he spoke. "I'm the king of these streets, you hear me? Huh? The mothafucking king!"

Ratatatatatatatatatatatatat!
Ratatatatatatatatatatatatat!

The back window of Tyrell's Jaguar shattered, and glass rained down upon him, as a flurry of bullets struck him and the side of his whip. He lay down on the ground, with his leg still tucked underneath him. He stared up at the masked up killaz accusingly, as his hand absentmindedly grasped at the broken glass in the street. He tried to say something, but only managed to cough up blood. His vision doubled as the masked up niggaz stood over him. The one wearing the oxygen mask pulled it down around his neck. He then pulled his ski-mask above his brows, revealing exactly who he was. It was Korey. He had a thick nappy beard, and his hair was so matted that it locked up and started to grow locs, all of which were different sizes and lengths. Korey was considerably smaller since having been shot, and he looked frail and weak. Thanks to him being wounded, he'd lost one of his lungs, and had to be on oxygen, probably for the rest of his life.

"You—remember—me—right?" Korey talked with a wheezy, nasally voice. He had trouble breathing without the added oxygen being fed into his body. Tyrell didn't utter a word in response. He just lay there, staring up at the unsmiling niggaz. "Well, this—is—payback for me—getting shot—on the—account—of you," Korey said before pulling the ski-mask back down over his face, and placing the oxygen mask back over his nose and mouth. He, and the masked up nigga standing beside him, who was Mank, pointed their choppaz down at Tyrell. Tyrell told them, "Fuck you," in a raspy voice, and held up his middle finger at them. Right after, there was an eruption of bullets.

Ratatatatatatatatatatatatatatat!

Ratatatatatatatatatatatatatatat!

Police sirens wailed not too far from the murder scene, as a masked up Korey and Mank lowered their smoking Dracos. They then ran back to the van, where the getaway driver, Latrell, was waiting for them. As soon as they were secured inside the van, Latrell glanced at his watch, checking the time.

"We've got an hour to make it back to y'all sister before she wakes up and wonders where the fuck we've gon'," Latrell said. Shavon hadn't gone along for the ride. The fellas knew that she would try to convince them not to carry out the assassination, so Latrell slipped a sedative inside her bottled water, which put her fast asleep.

Mank pulled the door shut and hollered up front for Latrell to pull off, to which he hastily did.

THE END

Submission Guideline

Submit the first three chapters of your completed manuscript to ldpsubmissions@gmail.com, subject line: Your book's title. The manuscript must be in a .doc file and sent as an attachment. Document should be in Times New Roman, double spaced and in size 12 font. Also, provide your synopsis and full contact information. If sending multiple submissions, they must each be in a separate email.

Have a story but no way to send it electronically? You can still submit to LDP/Ca$h Presents. Send in the first three chapters, written or typed, of your completed manuscript to:

LDP: Submissions Dept
Po Box 944
Stockbridge, Ga 30281

DO NOT send original manuscript. Must be a duplicate.

Provide your synopsis and a cover letter containing your full contact information.

Thanks for considering LDP and Ca$h Presents.

Tranay Adams

Coming Soon from Lock Down Publications/Ca$h Presents

BOW DOWN TO MY GANGSTA
By **Ca$h**
TORN BETWEEN TWO
By **Coffee**
THE STREETS STAINED MY SOUL **II**
By **Marcellus Allen**
BLOOD OF A BOSS **VI**
SHADOWS OF THE GAME II
By **Askari**
LOYAL TO THE GAME **IV**
By **T.J. & Jelissa**
A DOPEBOY'S PRAYER **II**
By **Eddie "Wolf" Lee**
IF LOVING YOU IS WRONG… **III**
By **Jelissa**
TRUE SAVAGE **VII**
MIDNIGHT CARTEL III
DOPE BOY MAGIC IV
By **Chris Green**
BLAST FOR ME **III**
A SAVAGE DOPEBOY III
CUTTHROAT MAFIA II
By **Ghost**
A HUSTLER'S DECEIT III
KILL ZONE **II**
BAE BELONGS TO ME III
A DOPE BOY'S QUEEN II
By **Aryanna**

CHAINED TO THE STREETS III

By **J-Blunt**

COKE KINGS V

KING OF THE TRAP II

By **T.J. Edwards**

GORILLAZ IN THE BAY V

TEARS OF A GANGSTA II

De'Kari

THE STREETS ARE CALLING II

Duquie Wilson

KINGPIN KILLAZ IV

STREET KINGS III

PAID IN BLOOD III

CARTEL KILLAZ IV

DOPE GODS II

Hood Rich

SINS OF A HUSTLA II

ASAD

TRIGGADALE III

Elijah R. Freeman

KINGZ OF THE GAME V

Playa Ray

SLAUGHTER GANG IV

RUTHLESS HEART IV

By **Willie Slaughter**

THE HEART OF A SAVAGE III

By **Jibril Williams**

FUK SHYT II

By **Blakk Diamond**

THE REALEST KILLAS

Tranay Adams

LIFE OF A SAVAGE III

By **Romell Tukes**

QUIET MONEY II

By **Trai'Quan**

THE STREETS MADE ME II

By **Larry D. Wright**

THE ULTIMATE SACRIFICE VI

By **Anthony Fields**

THE LIFE OF A HOOD STAR

By **Ca$h & Rashia Wilson**

Available Now

RESTRAINING ORDER **I & II**

By **CA$H & Coffee**

LOVE KNOWS NO BOUNDARIES **I II & III**

By **Coffee**

RAISED AS A GOON I, II, III & IV

BRED BY THE SLUMS I, II, III

BLAST FOR ME I & II

ROTTEN TO THE CORE I II III

A BRONX TALE I, II, III

DUFFEL BAG CARTEL I II III IV

HEARTLESS GOON I II III IV

A SAVAGE DOPEBOY I II

HEARTLESS GOON I II III

DRUG LORDS I II III

CUTTHROAT MAFIA

Tranay Adams

By **Ghost**
LAY IT DOWN **I & II**
LAST OF A DYING BREED
BLOOD STAINS OF A SHOTTA I & II III
By **Jamaica**
LOYAL TO THE GAME I II III
LIFE OF SIN I, II III
By **TJ & Jelissa**
BLOODY COMMAS I & II
SKI MASK CARTEL I II & III
KING OF NEW YORK I II,III IV V
RISE TO POWER I II III
COKE KINGS I II III IV
BORN HEARTLESS I II III IV
KING OF THE TRAP
By **T.J. Edwards**
IF LOVING HIM IS WRONG…I & II
LOVE ME EVEN WHEN IT HURTS I II III
By **Jelissa**
WHEN THE STREETS CLAP BACK I & II III
THE HEART OF A SAVAGE I II
By **Jibril Williams**
A DISTINGUISHED THUG STOLE MY HEART I II & III
LOVE SHOULDN'T HURT I II III IV
RENEGADE BOYS I II III IV
PAID IN KARMA I II III
By **Meesha**
A GANGSTER'S CODE I &, II III
A GANGSTER'S SYN I II III
THE SAVAGE LIFE I II III

The Dopeman's Bodyguard 2

CHAINED TO THE STREETS I II

By J-Blunt

PUSH IT TO THE LIMIT

By **Bre' Hayes**

BLOOD OF A BOSS **I, II, III, IV, V**

SHADOWS OF THE GAME

By **Askari**

THE STREETS BLEED MURDER **I, II & III**

THE HEART OF A GANGSTA I II& III

By **Jerry Jackson**

CUM FOR ME I II III IV V

An **LDP Erotica Collaboration**

BRIDE OF A HUSTLA **I II & II**

THE FETTI GIRLS **I, II& III**

CORRUPTED BY A GANGSTA I, II III, IV

BLINDED BY HIS LOVE

THE PRICE YOU PAY FOR LOVE

DOPE GIRL MAGIC I II

By **Destiny Skai**

WHEN A GOOD GIRL GOES BAD

By **Adrienne**

THE COST OF LOYALTY I II III

By Kweli

A GANGSTER'S REVENGE **I II III & IV**

THE BOSS MAN'S DAUGHTERS I II III IV V

A SAVAGE LOVE **I & II**

BAE BELONGS TO ME I II

A HUSTLER'S DECEIT I, II, III

WHAT BAD BITCHES DO I, II, III

SOUL OF A MONSTER I II III

Tranay Adams

KILL ZONE

A DOPE BOY'S QUEEN

By **Aryanna**

A KINGPIN'S AMBITON

A KINGPIN'S AMBITION **II**

I MURDER FOR THE DOUGH

By **Ambitious**

TRUE SAVAGE I II III IV V VI

DOPE BOY MAGIC I, II, III

MIDNIGHT CARTEL I II

By **Chris Green**

A DOPEBOY'S PRAYER

By **Eddie "Wolf" Lee**

THE KING CARTEL **I, II & III**

By **Frank Gresham**

THESE NIGGAS AIN'T LOYAL **I, II & III**

By **Nikki Tee**

GANGSTA SHYT **I II &III**

By **CATO**

THE ULTIMATE BETRAYAL

By **Phoenix**

BOSS'N UP **I , II & III**

By **Royal Nicole**

I LOVE YOU TO DEATH

By Destiny J

I RIDE FOR MY HITTA

I STILL RIDE FOR MY HITTA

By **Misty Holt**

LOVE & CHASIN' PAPER

By **Qay Crockett**

The Dopeman's Bodyguard 2

TO DIE IN VAIN

SINS OF A HUSTLA

By **ASAD**

BROOKLYN HUSTLAZ

By **Boogsy Morina**

BROOKLYN ON LOCK I & II

By **Sonovia**

GANGSTA CITY

By **Teddy Duke**

A DRUG KING AND HIS DIAMOND I & II III

A DOPEMAN'S RICHES

HER MAN, MINE'S TOO I, II

CASH MONEY HO'S

By Nicole Goosby

TRAPHOUSE KING **I II & III**

KINGPIN KILLAZ I II III

STREET KINGS I II

PAID IN BLOOD **I II**

CARTEL KILLAZ I II III

DOPE GODS

By **Hood Rich**

LIPSTICK KILLAH **I, II, III**

CRIME OF PASSION I II & III

By **Mimi**

STEADY MOBBN' **I, II, III**

THE STREETS STAINED MY SOUL

By **Marcellus Allen**

WHO SHOT YA **I, II, III**

SON OF A DOPE FIEND

Renta

Tranay Adams

GORILLAZ IN THE BAY **I II III IV**

TEARS OF A GANGSTA

DE'KARI

TRIGGADALE I II

Elijah R. Freeman

GOD BLESS THE TRAPPERS I, II, III

THESE SCANDALOUS STREETS I, II, III

FEAR MY GANGSTA I, II, III

THESE STREETS DON'T LOVE NOBODY I, II

BURY ME A G I, II, III, IV, V

A GANGSTA'S EMPIRE I, II, III, IV

THE DOPEMAN'S BODYGAURD I II

Tranay Adams

THE STREETS ARE CALLING

Duquie Wilson

MARRIED TO A BOSS... I II III

By Destiny Skai & Chris Green

KINGZ OF THE GAME I II III IV

Playa Ray

SLAUGHTER GANG I II III

RUTHLESS HEART I II III

By Willie Slaughter

FUK SHYT

By Blakk Diamond

DON'T F#CK WITH MY HEART I II

By Linnea

ADDICTED TO THE DRAMA I II III

By Jamila

YAYO I II

A SHOOTER'S AMBITION I II

196

The Dopeman's Bodyguard 2

By S. Allen

TRAP GOD

By Troublesome

FOREVER GANGSTA

GLOCKS ON SATIN SHEETS

By Adrian Dulan

TOE TAGZ I II III

By Ah'Million

KINGPIN DREAMS

By Paper Boi Rari

CONFESSIONS OF A GANGSTA

By Nicholas Lock

I'M NOTHING WITHOUT HIS LOVE

By Monet Dragun

CAUGHT UP IN THE LIFE I II

By Robert Baptiste

NEW TO THE GAME I II

By **Malik D. Rice**

Life of a Savage I II

By **Romell Tukes**

LOYALTY AIN'T PROMISED

By Keith Williams

Quiet Money

By **Trai'Quan**

THE STREETS MADE ME

By **Larry D. Wright**

THE ULTIMATE SACRIFICE I, II, III, IV, V

KHADIFI

By **Anthony Fields**

THE LIFE OF A HOOD STAR

Tranay Adams

By Ca$h & Rashia Wilson

BOOKS BY LDP'S CEO, CA$H

TRUST IN NO MAN

TRUST IN NO MAN 2

TRUST IN NO MAN 3

BONDED BY BLOOD

SHORTY GOT A THUG

THUGS CRY

THUGS CRY 2

THUGS CRY 3

TRUST NO BITCH

TRUST NO BITCH 2

TRUST NO BITCH 3

TIL MY CASKET DROPS

RESTRAINING ORDER

RESTRAINING ORDER 2

IN LOVE WITH A CONVICT

LIFE OF A HOOD STAR

Coming Soon

BONDED BY BLOOD 2

BOW DOWN TO MY GANGSTA

Tranay Adams

CPSIA information can be obtained
at www.ICGtesting.com
Printed in the USA
LVHW050626161020
668921LV00011B/1391